# ENGLAND EXPECTS, YET AGAIN

### RODERICK WILLIAMSON

CHANDLER
BOOK DESIGN

First Published in Great Britain in 2009
by Yold Ltd.

A CIP Catalogue of this book is available from
the British Library

ISBN 978-0-9561283-0-0

All characters are purely fictional.

Cover image: ©istockphoto.com/ David Whitworth

Cover design and typeset in Garamond 11pt
by Chandler Book Design,
www.chandlerbookdesign.co.uk

Printed and bound in Great Britain by the
MPG Books Group, Bodmin and King's Lynn

TO PHILEROSAPE

# I

"Bon appétit, Gruinnard."

The send key was pressed.

Nearly seventy two hours later, within the Cabinet Office of a muggy central London the BBC television news presenter, on the wall mounted screen, was abruptly switched off mid-sentence. The short silence in the room after the ending of the broadcast tingled with an air of brittle irritability.

"It does not feel right. No, not right at all," grumbled Alex Haye, who at a relatively youthful forty-five years of age had three months earlier surprisingly won the general election at the first attempt standing on a platform of honest and fair government. The British electorate had wanted change and it was a sea change that the left the established professional political classes beached like desiccated driftwood. Every so often in Britain the tectonic plates of the political world shifted, and shifted decisively. It seemed that the British population had had more than a bellyful of spinning uber-cynical PR merchants, covering the usual corruptions, self aggrandisements, caving in to vested interests, incompetence and brazen bare-faced lying. Haye however was now, currently tasting his first serious mouthful of vintage hypocrisy and he was sure, very sure that it was a sour taste and also one that he

1

did not wish to acquire. He also was feeling the considerably oppressive weight of the 2012 Olympics in London pressing down on him, while he continued to smile out to the world as he and the cabinet wrestled with the burgeoning costs and the ever-deepening pile of risk assessments. If only he had a few more compartments in his head to file away all the 'what ifs'. Haye had inherited the hosting of the greatest athletics spectacle in the world, and he had discussed among his closest colleagues that it was an expensive party to throw in London and was haunted by the fear that the ongoing costs would help fashion a millstone around the neck of his new government and destroy their future election-winning capability for decades to come, if not forever. A number of cities were still wrestling with summer and winter Olympic debts incurred many years ago, while at the time they had their few weeks of glory in the eye of the world's media. At an earlier cabinet meeting he had joked with his ministers about thanking the Greeks for starting this overgrown school sports day; one wag had responded that if the event didn't run smoothly then we would all be winning the sack race. It was typical cabinet gallows humour that was not recorded for posterity in the official minutes.

"Let me remind ourselves. The citizens of this country elected us to speak the truth, and to speak the truth even if it leads to short term damage for the government. I am determined to carry that mandate, irrespective of whether we score some cheap poll popularity. Which looking at the latest polls it seems we are plumbing new depths of voter support," as he said this he began to roll-up the sleeves of his less than crisp Charles Tyrwhitt white shirt and loosening his tie, sub-consciously perhaps indicating that he was preparing to get stuck in. He knew it was not exactly a decisive Churchillian moment but he felt it was time to show some gutsy leadership.

He continued, "we have inherited the hosting of the Olympics and with security costs alone heading north of nine hundred million pounds, and with perhaps up to half a million extra visitors to London. We cannot allow some new security threat to surface and get the media winding-up the excitable British public into premature panic stations. Those busybodies like nothing better than a good scare story. The press will delight in merrily painting some Doomsday scenario or other."

His deputy, the even younger Emma Darbyshire and another political novice, slowly ran her left hand through her dark brown hair which had just begun to accommodate a few un-dyed silver strands. She had a kind, guileless face which also had a rare beauty, which was not usually seen in wizened, prematurely aged or porcine parliamentary circles.

"Alex, just remember Healey's first law of holes. When you are in a hole stop digging. We've made a mistake, probably through political naivety, let's learn from this and really try to be honest to the public we serve. And as they say back in Lincolnshire, give it the straight John Bull."

The third person in the room let a small wry smile betray his thoughts. Sir Peter Cross, as Cabinet Secretary had served the previous four governments and with his impeccable civil service career built upon the solid base-rock of a Repton and Oxford education, knew instinctively that his duty was to keep politicians from damaging the nation by some misguided principles or manifesto promise. He sometimes loftily gave off the air that he was nothing more than a playground supervisor looking after some unruly urchin charges. The dazzling whiteness of his tailored white shirt and gold club crested cuff-links fitted in with the smoothness of his verbal contributions.

"With all respect, our first step is to ensure that there is no undue fear felt by our citizens and none created with the rest of the world that does business with Great Britain PLC. Britain has, and will no doubt in the future be ready to see off any threats to its security," Sir Peter checked to see his two young office holders would be receptive in continuing to follow his advice. Although he was the unelected head of the paid service he knew by experience that the two elected government leaders would defer to him as long his arguments were persuasive and buttressed by precedent and political acumen. He was certain of one thing, that he despised them when they climbed upon their self-righteous soapbox to preach their so-called wisdom unto the multitudes. However, he was too wily an operator to ever let his annoyance surface to the extent that his consummate professionalism could be challenged.

Sir Peter continued and glanced over to the deputy PM, "however, this is far more serious than the recent unfortunate media furore over your husband." Sir Peter, in his exquisitely grey pinstripe Saville Row made to measure suit, could use words to wound without raising the volume or tone of his cultured, well-lunched voice.

Emma Darbyshire did not react to Sir Peter, her dark brown eyes held his without flinching. Since the new government had been formed their had been a simmering tension between the deputy PM and the elite representative of the civil service; Emma Darbyshire had made an unspoken resolution to try and rise above the fray but had already felt that Sir Peter Cross was trying to drive a thick wedge between Alex and herself. Although the barb he uttered today, had caused a sharp stab of hurt to her feelings. She would not give him the satisfaction of seeing her wounded by his words. Sir Peter had referred to the story that had broken out like a nasty rash in the media during the previous month. It was where Emma's husband had been widely and gleefully exposed in a particularly distasteful press scoop. Although it had been only initially splashed in the News of The World, all the other papers joined in at the scandal trough and devoted extensive column inches to the expanding basket of dirty washing. It clearly linked him to financial corruption of the insider-trading share variety, abusing his position as husband of the Deputy Prime Minister to seal a few dodgy deals with even dodgier foreign governments, and a brace of undeclared mistresses, one of whom was expecting his child. The feeding frenzy had swept the gamut of the media with the radio and television political commentators pontificating on the potential ramifications; although she had tried to keep the failing marriage alive it was already in intensive care before the revelations broke. Emma Darbyshire, oblivious to her husband's chicanery, had to deal with the bitter personal blow compounded by tangible political damage to the government. The media chorus had made great play of her naivety and guilt by association regarding the finances and the alleged "open" marriage. Although her solicitor had advised libel action on some of the more fantastical elements of the articles, she decided to ignore the lies, as she knew there was too much sickening truth in their stories concerning her husband. She had however instructed her solicitor to ensure the unhappy union was terminated at the earliest possible moment. Her own private and persistent sorrow of failing to start a family was partially mitigated in that she was glad no child of hers would have to be dragged through the press mud; a very sticky and foully pungent media mud. Emma Darbyshire now hoped the ferocious journalist attack dogs would move on and find something else to sink their teeth into, preferably Sir Peter and his ilk, which always seemed to inhabit a charmed safe haven in the inner sanctum of British government. New governments are elected; they come and go at the voter's behest, but the padded comfort-zones of the upper echelons of the British Civil Service march untarnished onto the honours list and their gloriously-superannuated days of rest in the Home Counties and the land of gentleman's and golf clubs. No looking over their finely tailored shoulder at the harsh taskmasters of the electorate and the insatiable twenty four hours a day news machine whose voracious appetite needed constant feeding, with truth, lies or speculation, (and preferably a mix of all three.)

"Sir Peter, Emma as you well know, has my full and ongoing support, which I am sure is echoed by the rest of the electorate who voted us here. Not only that but I count her as a close friend beyond the world of politics. Also the post of deputy Prime Minister is not a token, vanity post. This is a new style of government. John in Number11 will look after the nation's purse. I am also confident that he will not be conspiring to manoeuvre himself into my job, the country's had enough of that Machiavellian nonsense," the Prime Minister's voice carried a distinct gruff tetchiness. "Right, now can we try and find a way out of this? And think a little less about kow-towing to multi-national media barons, who frankly do not give a thought about the best interests of this country. We've been elected for five years if we can hang on to our slim majority. Let's see if we can last the course and try and get our manifesto through. What did they say in the Clinton years? 'It's the economy, stupid!"

Sir Peter nodded and slowly began to justify the damage control actions, "I fully appreciate that you do not sit easily with the strategy of providing the story that the explosion on Gruinnard occurred due to an old Second World War military ordinance cache accidentally igniting. The media will probably rehash a few old articles about it being a closed island used for anthrax weapons experiments during the Second World War. I will get the Ministry of Defence to let them have some juicy titbits on Gruinnard's history and then their attention will have moved onto some celebrity scandal.

The vast majority of the population of our nation has, and is this most regrettable, the attention span of nervy gnats. If you have the misfortune of watching anything on television it will confirm the level to which our cultural life has sunk. Most depressing, but a dependable fact, I can assure you. When we have time we probably ought to be giving some attention on improving the content in this area. A change of Director General, perhaps. It may provide valuable political dividends later."

Nobody had the energy or initiative to argue with Sir Peter on his line of argument or to get into a debate on the failings of the BBC and the commercial television networks.

"Haven't our intelligence services come up with anything yet?" enquired Emma, trying getting back to the issue in hand. She was seeking to steer the conversation away from Sir Peter's machinations and media red herrings.

"I asked our Head of Intelligence Valerie Garfoot to provide a confidential briefing tomorrow at eleven am and she will update us on any information that has been gleaned. I strongly advise at this point that we do not give any details to the rest of the cabinet or indeed any of the other friendly security services until at such time we have a clearer picture," replied Sir Peter. He looked confidently to his superiors to concur.

Alex Haye responded. "Agreed. Well for now anyway. And just one thing more Sir Peter, I do not want to be put in a position of lying to the British public again."

Sir Peter nodded graciously.

Emma Darbyshire watched Sir Peter and felt an involuntary shiver of enmity. She realised that the civil servant did not bring out the best in her own character; she felt a spasm of guilt regarding her thoughts towards him.

The Prime Minister got up signalling the end the meeting,

putting on his jacket to head for the Commons and to face another onslaught from an Opposition scenting weakness, perhaps a terminal weakness, within the young, inexperienced leadership. He grabbed one quick sip of his nearly cold tea before leaving at a pace.

Sir Peter watched respectfully, tidying his papers into his briefcase as the meeting closed. The three principals left the room, with the only thing resolved that Sir Peter's mendacious spin would remain and the PM had drawn a line on any future sleight of hand in government public relations. The security issue itself was still a complete mystery. Emma thought to herself that this was the end of their political innocence. Her mind also fast-forwarded in speculation to the next general election and their one-off government would be sent to the interesting footnotes of British parliamentary history. Their period in office ending as the equivalent of a one-hit pop wonder, way back in the pop glory days of vinyl records.

Trafalgar Square was a thrumming, humming hive of activity, although perhaps as not as busy as the frenetic efforts being seen in Stratford in east London, as final preparations were being completed for the 2012 Olympics. The city resembled a great, teeming ant hill, with worker ants scurrying here, there and everywhere. The mayor of London knew that the landmarks of his great city would be visited by the anticipated human influx, and it would also be featured on hundreds of television, film and newspaper backdrops for the global media moshpit. It was a marketing opportunity par excellence, for the city and for him. The grand old dame of London had to be looking her very best to ensure that it remained as a top three global destination for business and tourism. The mayor knew she would scrub up rather nicely. The pressure was being screwed down upon the street scene contractors, who were employed on tight, but highly remunerative, contracts to deliver a clean tourist-friendly ambience. The cleaning contractor for Trafalgar Square was a national waste management outfit called Cory Limited. Inside their purely functional portacabin office perched on the edge of the Square, the site manager was calling through to his boss in the Dagenham office to the east of the city, "Frank, I need to know where that other statue has been stored or else I'm going to be one down when we hand it back. And I ain't taking the flak for this cock-up, not after the last bit of argy-bargy"

"Look Phil I'll sort it out. It's not the sort of thing to get nicked. No, mind you what am I saying, they'd nick the fences off the Palace. It's getting worse than Merseyside these days. Have you seen the Evening Standard, some vandal has necked the six ravens at the Tower, you know the ones with their wings clipped. It's a bit cruel of the country to clip their wings, if you ask me. One o'them myths if the ravens leave the tower the kingdom falls. But never mind the kingdom falling we've lost a monument and it's at least fifteen flaming foot long! Phil, it was put in special storage; it's a national treasure. Just like you Phil, no my friend, you just concentrate on making sure we've met the cleaning spec or else your team can chuffing kiss their performance bonuses goodbye!"

"Whoa, steady on pal. We're getting that money. And don't threaten me Frank. That's threatening talk that is. Just remember the men have sweated cobs and if the money ain't paid Cory will be drowning in grievances from the GMB! We'll raise it with the Mayor."

"Strewth Phil, can you hear me shaking in my Airwairs. Funniest thing I've heard today. Let me find the statue of old what'sisname and try and you make sure your men are grafting, really grafting, so you can eat your dinner off that Square. Instead of knocking off the ravens why they haven't necked all of them pigeons, it beats me? Dense-brain do-gooders still feeding the vermin; flaming health hazards those flying rats. Hang on the other phone's ringing, make sure you call me tomorrow."

# 2

"Oi, wake up you disgusting piece of scum."

The four youths ranged themselves out into a semi-circle around the figure lying under a stained and frayed turquoise nylon sleeping bag. It was nine pm and the damp March air chilled the less than salubrious alley way lying just off the busy thoroughfare of Notting Hill Gate. The figure in the sleeping bag stirred clumsily and warily. An unshaven face appeared from under a greasy looking beige baseball cap with red lettering which advertised Toni's Tapas World of White City.

Another youth growled down at the figure on the ground, "Polish rubbish, are you? Are you?"

When there was no response he followed up with a threatening, "didn't you hear me you dirty tramp?"

The first antagonist began to rock on the balls of his feet, perhaps trying to whip up the hate levels that bubbled inside his head. The other youths glanced across at their leader and began to smile in a leering way as they could feel that some fun was going to be had. The man on the ground felt the tension of fear in his own body ratchet up as the air positively began to crackle with menace from the four youths arrayed around their quarry. Someone had to pay for the youths' right to take their frustrations out, so they could feel some petty triumph in their mean and dull existence. Their Saturday diversion of trying to attack some northern soccer fans had only resulted in an exchange of verbal insults, foul taunts and provocative gesticulations, frustrated by the timely intervention of the long-suffering Transport Police ensuring that mayhem at the London transport interchanges was yet again prevented.

Another of them, with his Bench sweatshirt hood up, began to pick up on his pack leader's theme, "clear off home to your garbage rat-eating country," punctuating his bile with a ball of phlegm successfully aimed at the heavily-outnumbered figure.

The alleyway, behind the row of shops selling second-hand goods and greasy food, hummed not only with the capital's traffic noise but with the tension of impending violence. A gentle rain glistened in London's extensive and never-ending light pollution. It penetrated even this grimy alleyway that otherwise served as a parking place for the hulking waste containers used to house the perpetual excremental stream of the capital's business waste.

One of the youths pried open a red waste container and pulled out an empty green wine bottle and tapped it menacingly into the palm of his hand. It had a meaty and foreboding thud. The sound of glass on flesh.

The figure under the sleeping bag had not spoken in return and warily moved into a semi-crouching position. His eyes were frozen wide like a rabbit in the vicinity of a predator, several predators. The sleeping bag which had been his comfort zone slipped to the ground, a black thought crossed his mind that it may well end up as his own funeral shroud. Fight or flight discounted he took his last option, negotiation. He licked his dry cracked lips as the fear turned his mouth into a desert and he held his shaking hands forward as if to push away the threat facing him.

"I, I err don't want any trouble," his voice sounded pitiable and clearly betrayed his Dorset accent. He straightened himself up into a standing position and felt that he still might have a chance to escape a beating since they hadn't yet tried to attack him. A concurrent thought added to his queasiness, that perhaps they were enjoying it as a game of cat and mouse and the attack. His breath shortened as the fear invaded his physical senses. He was preparing to shape himself into a ball and protect his head and his private parts if they tried to use him as a football.

The youths could see that he was a rough sleeper in his forties and with these odds not capable of fighting back when they decided to sound the aggro starting bell.

"He's not East European rubbish come here to steal our jobs and infect our women. He's a thicko yokel," brayed one of the gang.

"This is London, you hear! You divvy village idiot. We are going make you want to crawl back to your field so you don't dirty our streets," growled the thicker-set youth, who seemed to set the pace for the others. He reached inside his jacket and pulled out a yellow lighter fuel can. The other three thugs nervously flicked their eyes at each other and at the sight of the can of lighter fuel and they all felt a boundary was being stepped over, although none of them was prepared to lose face and call a halt to the implied escalation of hostilities. The boundary crossing only added to their mounting blood lust. They knew their only risk was soiling their trainers when they delivered a kicking to their target.

An expletive-decorated call of "burn the tramp!" was met with grunts of approval.

The terrified object of their hatred desperately glanced behind him to see if a new escape route behind him had miraculously appeared, the locked high doors confirmed the dead-end layout of the alley.

The initiator moved a step closer to their intended prey and squirted a fine rainbow-crescent jet of lighter fuel onto the crumpled sleeping bag, within seconds it was followed by a lit match. Blue flames instantaneously leapt up as the lighter fuel combusted, the smell of the alley mixed with the smell of petrol and burning nylon. Another squirt of fuel made the yellow flames leap up fiercely again. The intended victim darted his eyes between his tormentors, who were hideously illuminated by the eruption of fire. They laughed at the flames, which died as quickly as they had risen. The dancing tongues of fire had ceased and left an acrid smell of burning man-made fibres in their nostrils. The human target stamped down on the smoking sleeping bag. The pall of burnt nylon combined with the fear running riot in his senses, made him begin to dry retch.

"You're next retard! Or do you wanna have a go? Got any balls, bumpkin?" laughed one of the thuggish semi-circle. The group all moved a step closer to the cornered quarry. Each relishing the victim's palpable fear, they enjoyed the power and the electric tension before the first fist and boot went in.

"Stand clear! Or face action at close quarters," came an unhurried voice from behind the gang. The sound seemed to echo and resonate off the walls. The voice's firmness made the youths freeze momentarily; they turned around slowly and apprehensively. Once the owner of the voice came into view, the youth's concern evaporated into surly sneers.

"It's not old bill. It's a one-armed bleeding bandit," their relief exhaled into guffaws and snorts of derision.

"Come on then, cripple," their joint taunt to the stranger reverberated around the alley.

"I never thought tonight we'd end up in a ruck with the handicapped." Their hateful leers now turned to the surprise interventionist at the opening to the alley, about ten or twelve feet away.

"Right have a go hero! You are going to get your head kicked in for your troubles. You don't mess with this crew." One of them pulled out a vicious-looking telescopic cosh to guarantee victory in hand to hand street brawling.

Before they had moved three steps the stranger moved swiftly to close the distance between them. Within seconds he was right in between them. The lighter fuel was knocked out of the youth's hand and was followed up immediately by a cracking left hook to the jaw. The stunned youth reeled to the floor, pulling over the wheelie bin as he grasped out for support. The other youths were now the other side of the upended bin. In an instant the stranger had leapt onto the bin and was again right into their midst. The sheer speed of the stranger's initiative had caught them unprepared. The stranger dodged one clumsy punch and the arcing swing of the cosh, whilst he barged the other one of them against the wall. The bottle now smashing on the floor, and then he landed another heavy left hook into the face of the other youth. The gang were instinctively on the balls of their feet as they dashed away from this unexpected assault to regroup back at the alley entrance. As two of them held their mouths, one felt the blood beginning to flow from the blow received. The four of them now could clearly see that the odds were massively in their favour and their gutter street fighting pride was not going to allow them to walk away. The group's Dutch courage and sense of hurt pride ignited their desire for vengeance.

"Let's do 'em," one seethed.

"There are only two of them and one of the muppets is disabled. Steam 'em!"

"Disabled but you didn't feel his bleeding fist," rued one who had caught the stranger's left fist.

Just at the moment as they gathered to charge down the alley to overwhelm the two men, a passing Police car slowed down to check what these youths were doing. The blue flashing lights of the car percolated into the alley. Their streetwise-tuned senses instinctively told them to scarper and not give the authorities any opportunity to extend their petty criminal records. The incriminating cosh was dropped and they split up, dashing off into the West London night, the police sensing they had some rogues in sight decided to pursue one pair whilst calling for re-enforcements to locate the others.

The stranger moved the smoking mess of burnt sleeping away to the side of the alley, stamped the smouldering remains and brushed away the remnants of the broken wine bottle with his other foot.

The stranger fixed the man in the eye, "your name?"

"It's Tom, and thanks. You really saved my skin; I thought I was definitely in for it. You certainly gave those thugs a surprise. Especially with, you know, being...." Tom gestured towards the stranger's empty right sleeve.

The stranger smiled, "I call it my fin." He moved the top of the right sleeve by a movement of whatever stump was still left under there.

"Well it was not too unfavourable odds. Four louts against the two us. Although arguably it was eight arms against three," he laughed.

Tom also had a small nervous laugh, which was also a release from the build of fearful tension inside him.

His timely protector continued, "I could not tread these perilous paths in safety, if I did not keep a saving sense of humour. It has reminded me somewhat of the boarding at Cape St Vincent. Climbing over these bins was an echo of boarding across two ships rammed together. Invigorating and in a good cause, your own safety sir."

The fanciful flight of his language took Tom by surprise, "yeah, well those thugs were no laughing matter. What can I say but, thanks again, thanks a million."

"I trust my timely intervention was not unwelcome with those ne'er do wells. I am not normally a man who demeans himself with street brawling and I believe the action taken would be deemed proportionate by a local magistrate in the light of the circumstances. The years pass and we still have these thuggish, undisciplined oafs roaming the streets. Perhaps we should return to the press gang to bring some respect and direction to their pitiable lives. Anyway Tom desperate affairs require desperate measures. And my name, my name is Horace. Although I'm usually called..," before he could finish Tom interrupted.

"Yer don't hear that very often, Horace. Well howsabout Ace?"

The unlikeliest knight in shining armour smiled at his new shortened nickname.

"Ace? Ace, yes I will go with that," he sounded pleased with the name's ring.

"So Ace it is then. And thanks again. Anyway let's move on before they think about coming back, I don't fancy seeing their faces again. And I owe you a drink or three."

A few miles away tucked away in the affluent side of Holland Park, in an upmarket house whose location and tasteful fittings would make estate agents salivate themselves, into a feeding frenzy, a woman was dialling a number in Lithuania. It was a telephone number she knew by heart and she treasured the link it gave to the man whom answered her calls.

As she waited for the connection, the middle-aged woman pried opened the curtains to view the night sky of the city.

The stars glittered in the nearly cloudless sky and she saw the moon was nearly full.

The call was answered.

"Leo, how are you my love. It is all planned. The news is looking good."

She smiled as she listened into the receiver.

"I know. I have no regrets but I must still be careful. There is too much at stake. Yes, I am feeling quite well, as long as I keep up my medicine. Until then, my love, please keep safe my darling. Yes for always, always."

She slowly replaced the receiver and continued to look out of the window to see the London evening sky, seemingly lost in thought. The night sky showed a vapour trail of another continental spanning jet heading across to the Heathrow hub, and the everlasting kingdom of lost luggage.

# 3

In the far from full first class section of the TGV train as it pulled out of the sweeping Paris suburbs, heading south, a sleek laptop was opened. The inbox highlighted incoming mail from 'le petit caporal.' The email was opened.

> *"Cherie,*
> *Please remove the B & B from the checklist*
> *and let's keep a 'warm' welcome in the hillside.*
> *A whiff of grapeshot always worked.*
>
> *A new group bulletin is to be despatched within*
> *48hours.*
> *Au revoir.*
>
> *N.*

The email was promptly deleted as the female reader sat back to view the passing French countryside scenery as it unfolded in a smooth green blur.

The racing green coloured Jaguar deftly manoeuvred around

Trafalgar Square, which was currently boarded up in a state of cleaning and refurbishment ahead of the summer's 2012 Olympic games, several of the monuments being covered up for renovation work. The city's landmarks were going to put on their very best face. The Jaguar smoothly pulled up and deposited a smart business-suited woman in her early fifties outside the government offices; she briskly walked up the steps, past the uniformed police officer standing guard outside. The policeman nodded respectfully and continued to monitor the quiet street. All appeared peacefully well in the city which was enjoying the best part of the weather.

Valerie Garfoot smiled and nodded in greeting as she entered the high-ceilinged room, which was dominated by a huge circular mahogany table, polished to a mirror-like shining gleam. This very table had been privy to many crises and scares from Britain's past, from hot war to cold war, terrorism to foot and mouth and it was probably waiting to be the furniture for the ministerial response to the next flu pandemic. Garfoot's own professional mannered poise did not betray the dark thoughts which were beginning to dominate her increasingly-sleepless nights. Another day, another briefing she told herself. She then sat down to join the small group comprising of the Prime Minister, his Deputy and Sir Peter, who were the inner group of the new government seeking to resolve the new nebulous threat to the country's security. Valerie Garfoot had already concluded that the new government's approach of a small nucleus to discuss such security issues was a prudential way to move forward. She removed and polished her rimless glasses and as head of Britain's internal and external security wings, began her briefing on the situation, namely the unexplained mammoth explosion on Gruinnard.

Following her short summary, which she had not tried to pad out with empty speculation, Valerie Garfoot asked the small group if there were any questions.

The first question was not what she had anticipated.

"Valerie, are you well? You're looking awfully pale?" enquired Emma, showing her concern.

"Yes, yes I am reasonably well, but thank you very much for your concern. I can't deny though I have some tiring responsibilities."

Alex Haye lightly tapped the table with his fist, his eyes red-rimmed from lack of good sleep and mental strain, "Valerie, really is that absolutely all we know? It's not very helpful. Surely we've got some idea? I don't like being in the dark."

"From an inspection of the island the explosion was a very large blast. If it had occurred within one of our mainland centres of population we would be facing literally thousands of casualties. All we know I'm afraid is that it wasn't an airborne bomb or missile, it appears someone has taken the trouble to sail there and taken time to unload a large consignment of rock blasting material and set it off. It was way beyond the sort of explosions we experienced in Northern Ireland during the Troubles. It has left a huge crater. However whoever perpetrated this act did not leave any evidence which could serve as a trail. It appears to have been clearly planned and organised with military precision. But it must be said a very, very bizarre choice of target. Although in terms of safety to our citizens we at least have had no harm done to anyone. As I alluded in the briefing I can only suggest someone is sending us a message, the meaning of which I am completely at a loss to say."

"Don't we have any sort of monitoring of that diseased and desolate piece of rock?" asked the Prime Minister testily.

Garfoot, sipping from her glass of mineral water, then shook her head, "none I'm afraid. There are warnings posted as you approach Gruinnard. I must re-iterate a very strange choice of a target. Someone either gets a big kick out of explosions or is sending a signal. A very big, loud signal; and as we can see they have certainly got attention at the very top."

Emma Darbyshire looked distinctly uncomfortable, as she tried to focus on matters of national security while thinking ahead to her later meeting with her solicitor to ensure the smoking ruins of her miserable marriage were finally extinguished. She wondered if anyone realised that she was lacking concentration on the subject in hand. The self-inflicted sharp pinch on her hand was her mechanism to keep focussed on the matter in hand.

Emma, trying to get to the nub of the issue, then asked the obvious question. "No terrorist groups, extremists or cranks trying to claim responsibility? Surely that's what follows when these groups are seeking attention or blackmail. Even if they didn't do it themselves, some group likes to get the publicity by claiming the action."

Garfoot straightened her leather notebook with both hands as she replied, "yes you're right, but no, it appears the world at large has accepted the story about the accidental ignition of left-over ordnance from World War Two. So far we do not have the worried concerns of the general public to worry about. Full marks to you Sir Peter on the media control."

Emma Darbyshire detected Sir Peter's slightly smug smile and perhaps he was chalking up another victory for the upper-echelons of the civil service over the democratically-elected leaders of this country. She decided to let some of the air out of the Cabinet Secretary's smug sails, "so, what happens when the truth comes out? Once we start covering up, where will it stop? And furthermore we still do not have a single clue about who created this explosion. Perhaps we should be asking the Cabinet Secretary to undertake a root and branch review of our intelligent services." She knew that the threat of a huge workload might even ruffle the immaculately attired feathers of the Cabinet Secretary and give at the same time a jolt to Valerie Garfoot.

Sir Peter felt the undercurrent from the Deputy Prime Minister and as he smiled he consoled himself with the thought that she was just like many of the previous young and principled politicians who always came round to his gentle guiding about the reality of running the business of UK plc. Who did she really think she was, a piddling Deputy PM; a jumped-up backbencher, in a party and government that was still wet behind the ears. Being hectored by a female ex-secondary school teacher; risible, he concluded. Sir Peter, without betraying his thoughts which were shrouded within his professional mask, he laughed internally at her empty threat.

"Ah yes, the truth, if and when that ever comes out rest assured that the public will have moved on. I do not have to remind you of the size of the public's attention span. And if something comes out then we can have some long-running enquiry that will extinguish anyone's interest in the matter. Otherwise it will make an interesting story in thirty years time when the cabinet papers are released. I agree that we appear not to have clue at the moment about the perpetrators, but I trust that Valerie will ensure no pebble left on that god-forsaken Scottish island will be left unturned. Please Valerie do, do make absolutely sure we don't have any of your intelligence protégé's going down with some hideous sixty year old poison. We do need to keep down our death in service pension payments. Always remember the dear long-suffering tax payers. My other advice Prime Minister is we wait, and if there is a serious player behind it they will show their face sooner or later."

"Thank you Sir Peter, I am sure Emma and I have a lot

to learn about statecraft, but I still feel very uneasy about a potential unseen enemy and I feel extremely uncomfortable in peddling lies or spin, however convenient they may be. Valerie, I want some informal liaison with your security counterparts in Europe and the States to see if anyone has any light to shed on the matter. Right in three hours I have got to see two thousand schoolchildren in Birmingham who are very excited about the Olympic Games. I do not want to go down in history for having some security problems wrecking our showcase to the world. I do not want a Munich Olympics, overshadowed by terrorists. Unless there is any further development I am leaving this issue Valerie in your more than capable hands. But please rest assured I want to know who is behind this and if they pose a threat to us. Any information on this matter must be shared with me personally as and when it appears."

As the meeting broke up, Emma Darbyshire felt Alex had belittled her by his comments about them having a lot to learn. She was sure that Sir Peter was enjoying the little games of control and one-upmanship, divide and rule. In her mind she knew that the relationship between her and the cabinet secretary would never reach the temperature of lukewarm. Upon leaving the building her government chauffeur wove the ministerial car into the thickening and noisy London traffic as they headed for Kings Cross and a hopefully fast train back to a constituency surgery with her electorate back in Lincoln. She mused that what she probably needed was to get involved in the bread and butter issues of her constituents. Whilst she had often been amazed at her rapid rise from being selected as a parliamentary candidate to becoming part of the leadership of the party and then actually winning the election, and now sitting within the apex of British political power. Not at all bad for an ex-secondary Religious Education school teacher, she reminded herself.

Although Emma Darbyshire knew that political life could end at the shortest of notice and its power and fame were, in her view, exaggerated she continued to measure herself by the life of her constituents in Lincoln and it was where she hoped that she was making a real, tangible difference in people's day to day existence. It was this honest and entirely guileless motive that had drawn her into the grubby political bear pit world in the first place, rather than the usual egotistical thrusting for power and elevation. Please dear God keep my feet on the ground was a silent prayer as she travelled in her tax-payer funded executive wheels.

Emma Darbyshire decided she would keep going for the constituents and the rest of the nation who had elected this government even though she felt she was drowning in the rough waters of her much-publicised failed marriage. Her country and constituents needed her, and she owed it to herself to make the best of the talents she had. Light and bushels.

The young twenty-something white-uniformed masseur with her shiny black hair tied into a ponytail was just spreading the last piece of thermal mud onto the back of the short, paunchy Italian politician, who was taking a rejuvenating break at the upmarket spa resort of Abano Terme, thirty miles or so away from the beautiful city of Venice. Abano Terme was where the well to do and those in the know sought the cure from the spa waters and to benefit from a celebrated and unrivalled Italian cuisine; slow, delicious food served to entertain the most jaded of palettes. The five star rated Hotel President, with its attractive faded glamour, was used to providing sufficient anonymity for the higher echelons of the Byzantine world of Italian politics. It was a safe, secure and relatively anonymous sanctuary. Although for all its qualities of a retreat and a place to seriously de-stress, it was not quite a complete escape from the omnipresent links of mobile telecommunications, which were burrowed like an irritating tic buried deep into the hides of modern human lives in the twenty first century.

The Italian politician's pleasing reverie about his planned tryst with his shapely mistress later that afternoon and his mud application were interrupted as his sleek silver mobile phone rang. With a weary bear-like growl, he stretched over to read the screen. He saw the two words, 'new bulletin.'

Without looking at the masseur, who had retreated a deferential distance when the phone had rung, he fiercely barked, "shower, I need to shower it off. Now, now!"

Tom rubbed his bleary eyes and flicked away a small piece of crust from the corner of his right eye, as the morning crept tentatively into the doorway of a similar, although a somewhat safer alleyway than previous nights. It was where Tom had headed for after his narrow escape; it was a temporary lair, a place to crash and lick his psychological wounds and thank his lucky stars he wasn't licking his fleshy wounds.  He felt his new and unusual companion's eyes surveying him; he didn't particularly appreciate the interest. Now he was awake he couldn't dismiss the strange episode of the previous night. Tom was very surprised to see his street saviour still with him.

"Stone me! You're still here. Ace for a moment I thought the booze had made me dream about last night. Hell of a close shave it was. I was just a gnat's ..."

"Think nothing of it. When duty calls, men of honour act," came the calm and firm response. Ace was standing facing Tom, who wondered if Ace had bedded down in the alley or had just stood up awake all night.

After a short silence with Tom feeling a strange emotional resonance with the words of duty, honour and act, Horace continued, "why are you living like this, you seem like someone who has abandoned their self-respect? In short, you've given up and given in. To me you appear reasonably sound in wind and limb, although you would be wise to turn away from the charms of the grog. You should be doing better than living like a low life alley cat. I think it is time to change course my friend."

He didn't realise his new mate would mutate into some kind of social worker and life coach; he thought if Ace carried on like this he would better off on his own; he really didn't want any sermons, he could get that at the Sally Army hostels. He also didn't need to listen to therapy from a stranger, who was probably as screwed up as himself. But he unexpectedly felt new feelings bubbling up inside his head and he felt a strange and sudden need to open up to Ace and speak from the heart, something he hadn't done in truth for several years. This morning it felt like a boil had been lanced inside his soul, he could sense the infected matter begin to seep away. Tom felt a sliver of internal cleansing; for him in many a year, a novel feeling.

Tom's gaze dropped a little and he felt a shiver of shame. Although he was generally very reticent about opening up himself to another person, however close or even challenging himself as to his sorry state. Perhaps he was in what they called in the world of counsellors and therapists – 'denial.' But today and talking to Ace he felt unusually relaxed and open enough to confess, "I've lost more than that, believe me mate. I haven't always been living rough as a dosser. I served eight years in the Royal Navy and I'm proud of that if nothing else in this life. Felt I was serving the country. When

I left the service I couldn't settle in any jobs and the drinking got worse. Unfortunately there is too much drinking in all of the services, and when I left what levels of self control I had over the booze just evaporated. I ended up losing my marriage and getting to see my children. The drink sometimes helps me to forget my failings and their faces. I know I let them down. They are well shot of me. Moved up from Portsmouth, drifted around and eventually ended up here nearly getting set on fire for kicks. If the drink doesn't do for me insides, then some mental hooligan, or spaced-out druggy will put an end to my misery. And you know what I often think that wouldn't be too bad a thing, what's it worth hanging on for? No one will miss or mourn me. Anyway Ace, before I begin to search for some warming liquid breakfast, what's your story? With that jacket and get-up you looked like you've just got dressed out of a skip from one of the theatrical suppliers down Charing Cross."

"Tom, thanks for your honesty I know it is hard to share our real feelings. But you've recognised your failings and I know you can move forward. The good Lord gave us all one great quality and that is hope. Hope. Let that word roll around your mind for a minute. Ah my clothes, no they are not from some theatre production as you suggest. However I do confess that it has been many a year since I have seen my own personal tailor. I also know that time and fashion has moved on. Although I am certain in one important matter, which hasn't changed and that is that when danger threatens our country, a call will go up and there will be those who respond to the challenge. Yes, a call always goes up."

Tom's eyes widened as he tried to understand the conversational flow. His first thoughts seemed to conclude that Ace had some problems in his head. Over the last few years he had come across a good many people with mental problems who had acted in a scary disturbed manner. The man Horace, before him certainly looked crazy enough, dressed up in a period top jacket and it looked even worse in that he had clearly lost his right arm, to what who knows. Motor bike accident, diabetes, at this present moment he didn't feel like enquiring. Though when Ace spoke it wasn't like those poor souls on the edge of being sectioned by the social workers under the Mental Health Act.

Ace continued in his clear and steady voice, "I need your assistance on a matter of the utmost importance. As of today I am not exactly certain of what is required but I ask you to trust me. Sometimes the navigational aids are not always clear. But we need to set sail to face these challenges head on. Are you ready to sign on?"

It began to chime ominously in Tom's mind about someone he came across in a homeless shelter in Bristol; and that bloke had kept coming out with these conspiracies all over the place. The newspaper was giving him secret messages and it all matched the letters he had from the Council and the television channels were all under the control of the secret Mormon church which still practised polygamy; he was one Special Brew of a vagrant. Bi-polar, yes that was what they said he suffered from and it looks like his one-armed saviour, who spoke rather too refined and authoritative for the rough sleeping community, was probably on his way from or back to the local secure asylum. Tom concluded Ace had pitched up straight from the local nuthouse and a certain caution would be required. He might turn on him, could be unpredictably violent, who knows what might set him off? He already seen Ace's violent armoury in close up, no holds barred action. Ace's surprising physical intervention did not fit in with his initial conclusion and ninety-nine percent of dossers would have run rather than put themselves in danger for someone they didn't know. No, that certainly didn't add up in Tom's head.

Tom stretched his arms up and yawned widely keeping his eyes on Horace, "Ace, tell me straight are you running away from some institution? Have you got medication? If you need to see a doctor or go someplace, I'll help you get there. Least I can do."

There was no immediate answer.

Tom felt that his appraisal was spot on the mark, and Ace's mind really was not anchored in reality.

Then Horace spoke very calmly and as he did, Tom could sense the deep authority in his voice, it was solid and seasoned like a hearty English oak used on an old sailing boat.

"No, no I can assure you I still have my mental faculties although I agree it may have been questioned in the past. Also I am not under the physician at present. Though I've had many a need of the medical trade including a surgeon to whom I owed my life, bless his name. But as you can see I have clearly lost my right arm. Unfortunately it is not the only the handicap that I suffer because I have also lost the sight in my right eye and the strength of my other eye has faded somewhat, plus I have a troubling hernia and I endure recurrent bouts of weakness after I contracted malaria. That was from many years ago when I was a lot younger from out in the Far East. Maybe sometime Tom I will share with you the stories behind my infirmities at a more convenient point. Perhaps you are surprised that someone in my condition could have seen off those base ruffians last night, well I am used to winning against the odds. Mind you Tom I am thankful for the arrival of the constabulary at the end of the alleyway which certainly helped us from facing a further attack. Now Tom, I have requested your assistance; I cannot go into too much detail at present. And to be brutally honest I am not exactly sure of all the details myself. When you enter a battle situation there are many, many variables and unknowns. But my friend I am very certain that the task will not be easy, indeed there may be some degree of danger. If you cannot make that choice I understand fully, because I know it all sounds rather strange. But the choice is yours and if you decline, then I will be forced to seek that help elsewhere. Tom when I look at you I can still see the sailor who can face the waves of adversity. It is no longer the days of the press gang; it is an open invitation Tom, my new friend. "

The voice had a calming and persuasive effect on Tom's raging doubts about Ace's mental condition.

Tom frowned deeply as his mind wrestled with confusion, and then in a manner that was quite out of character, he felt himself, lock into focus. As he considered this bizarre request, he also simultaneously wondered at that moment why he didn't feel the fierce need to taste some high alcohol proof lager. Although he could still remember the comforting warm taste in his throat and the dulling numbness it would shortly bring. There'll be plenty of time ahead to try and slake the unquenchable thirst, he reasoned.

# 4

Across the vast city of London, from the bottom of the social order to the peak of privilege, in the very different surroundings of the executive suite at the famous Ritz hotel, two small groups began to serve themselves from the luxurious breakfast buffet that had been provided for their exclusive benefit. The presidential-styled suite was completely sealed off from interruptions by a brace of security guards parked outside the doors.

Whilst sipping his Earl Grey tea, Jeremy Wheater, principal owner and executive head of the huge entertainment, technology and travel business called Pandora, signalled that it was time to continue their business negotiations. Wheater exuded an air of absolute confidence and was used to dominating any room where business deals were cut, and he was renowned in the media for his open-necked shirts and casual attire, which was his trademark way back in his younger, buccaneering days with his record labels and nightclubs. Wheater was a regular in the business pages and equally the gossip columns, using his profile to gain more coverage for his Pandora empire. He played up to the media, who returned the favours by giving him ample space in which his well publicised stunts and many business forays were widely documented. The two groups faced each other across the table. Facing the group from Pandora were the representatives from Xanti, the Chinese multinational with powerful direct and organic links to the People's Liberation Army of China. They were renowned, inside and outside China, as an organisation that always got their way one way or another, militarily, politically or commercially.

Jeremy Wheater kicked off the proceedings picking up from where they had finished off at the last meeting, "firstly, can I say you are the toughest and probably meanest negotiators I have ever come across. So credit where credit is due and as they say in the music biz, respect! And I can tell you gentleman some stories from Brazil and South Africa that would shrivel the testes of a bull elephant. Another time perhaps, anyway I am thinking of calling Xanti the yellow peril! Not exactly politically correct I know; but you sure as hell delivered. Pandora is now flying into every medium to large Chinese city plus the twenty or so African countries that are now effectively under Chinese control. My aviation competitors are wilting in the heat of the action. It feels good gentlemen, very, very good."

"With respect with regard to the African continent perhaps the word influence sounds more accurate than control," the lead Chinese negotiator replied in perfect English, without the trace of an accent or indeed passion. To his left their translator quietly interpreted for the steely-eyed and bull-necked Chinese figure just behind the lead negotiator, who always attended the meetings but never spoke. Wheater assumed he was their army connection, and Wheater had enough savvy not to investigate this avenue any further and aggravate his profitable partners.

"Honourable Mr Wheater, please rest assured that Xanti will always fulfil its words and it has the support of the most important elements within our country's leadership. This is a major year for us 2012; it is the Chinese year of the dragon. As I have told you on a number of occasions the Chinese people are an ancient people with a very long-term view. In fact it is view that stretches beyond our lifetimes and the lifetimes of our grandchildren. We prize loyalty and discretion very highly. I must ask is your security about our dealings still absolutely intact? Our whole relationship depends on there being no breaches of our plans and agreements."

Wheater replied, "now firstly, there is only one lifetime that I am interested in and that is the one that I am living in now. I am not a believer in life after death. Secondly, Paul here, is my trusted right hand man. He travels with me everywhere. If I go on my yacht, he will be there. I assure you only my picked female acquaintances get closer. Ha! Nothing has been committed to paper, computer or discussed with any third parties. The press have just accepted that our aviation business is just killing the opposition. Not literally I hasten to add. There is no trail or any kind of evidence whatsoever that leads back to anyone. We and you are business people who are talking about issues of mutual interest. Maybe we are doing a bit more than talking," Wheater and his shadow known as Paul grinned in tandem as he said this.

The interpreter continued to keep the silent one briefed. Jeremy Wheater was slightly unnerved that the silent Chinese never gave any facial indication about how he was feeling about the conversations being translated to him. It was an empty unreadable gaze which gave no inkling away. The British entrepreneur concluded it was either the most inscrutable negotiating technique or he was a near brain-dead goon at the top of the People's Liberation Army food chain.

The Xanti spokesman picked up the baton, "the very next stage we require is the transfer of all your telephone and computer business to be transferred to our proxy company Bastille Limited registered in the Grand Cayman Islands.

It suits our needs for protection from prying eyes and international tax efficiency."

"Steady on friend, not so fast and with all manner of respect, may I inform you that this part of Pandora is currently worth nine hundred million sterling, and maybe worth double that in another three years at current growth rates," responded Wheater, using his voice to emphasis his assertions. He had honed his negotiating technique over two decades of deal making and breaking, plus all manner of plate spinning and souped-up souk style haggling.

The Chinese lead negotiator seemed unfazed, smiled and took another sip of his green tea. "I would not dispute your assessment on the valuation. Our enterprise has impeccable connections within the Chinese government and its banking system and we will deposit one and half billion in sterling into any named account as well as transferring a forty nine percent holding of all the print, radio and television companies that we hold globally. This holding in itself is worth at least three times your technology portfolio. Mr Wheater feel free to have your financial team confirm the veracity of what I am saying, I invite you to undertake all necessary due diligence."

"That may come later as we move forward, but I know you are people who do not need to play any sleight of hand. It looks like we have a deal so far," replied Wheater, whose casual dress sense and youthful risk-taking approach had often seduced other parties during negotiations; it had also camouflaged his own ferocious steel-trap of a mind. His calm attitude did not betray the inward rejoicing over his inward mental calculations on the outlined fruits of this deal.

There a slight pause before the measured reply, "now of course we need your full support on our strategic, political and economic aspirations. For your information we are working with an extremely important strategic

European partner who, at his own request, remains anonymous at the moment but who will be shortly striding onto the international stage in the very near future. These requirements are entirely non-negotiable and no part of the deal will go ahead without a prior binding agreement. I also do not have to remind you that your airline and travel business can just as easily be rolled back at the same speed we have allowed its growth. Perhaps it can be summed up with those that are not for us; we will regard them as being against us."

Wheater's face did not flinch at the clear unambiguous threat, which he knew was not without a very firm foundation.

"Firstly,....."


Over a hundred miles north of London stands the beautiful historic City of Lincoln, famed for its magnificent jewels of the Cathedral and Castle scenically set upon on a hill, and the tourist-quaint Bailgate shopping area. Lincoln famed for its history and its engineering heritage is the urban and cultural centre for the green and agricultural landscapes of the mainly rural Lincolnshire. Emma Darbyshire, who had previously eschewed the offer of a 24 hour police bodyguard as a wasteful extravagance upon the taxpayer and as an unnecessary barrier between her and the people she devoted her life to representing, swiftly made her way on foot from the yellow bricked Victorian Railway Station. She was covering the short distance through the pedestrianised High Street to the unappealing sixties style concrete office block of the City Hall for her regular and generally mundane constituency surgery. She often thought that the City of Lincoln deserved a better place for his democratic centre than this building which was clearly no longer fit for purpose. On arrival she gave a cheery hello to the reception staff and as usual thanked the long-serving caretaker for setting the chairs and signage out for her. Her young twenty year old assistant Harriet, of the flowing hair and cutting wit, met her in the room, which was given over to her by the Council for her constituency duties.

"Hi Emma, welcome back to the real world. Cup of chamomile?"

Emma Darbyshire never turned down the wonderfully recuperative powers of an herbal infusion.

"Harriet just what would I do without you?"

"Sink without trace probably; no, definitely sink without a single trace. But don't worry about me, as I'll be able to find more meaningful employment, as PA to Johnny Depp perhaps. Not to worry, as I will be able to flog a copy of your political obituary that I have already penned and got tucked away. It'll probably earn me a new computer set-up from the one of the nationals. As I always say, be prepared to cash in your chips when the game is over."

"Well thank you, my mercenary friend."

Emma laughed at the intended jokes and matched Harriet's smile and was feeling a lot better already, temporarily forgetting the depressing affairs of the nation state and her own saddened heart over the ruins of her personal life. It was time to conduct the real business that she was elected for; she remembered the quote that all politics is local.

"Harriet, wheel the first one in and let's see if we can make a difference for one of our electorate."

"I'll serve up the first in the queue."

# 5

The fanatically pedantic and publicity-shy Indian billionaire steel and industrial magnate Sunil Dev was alone in his palatial gleaming chrome and tulip wood office, which was about the size of two combined school classrooms. The office was surrounded by a wall of screens which constantly flickered with an unceasing torrent of financial information on all of the world's share markets, currency movements and the up to date information on his global empire. His clothes did not betray his reserves of wealth, which were a simple oat-coloured cotton tunic with thin maroon leather sandals. Sunil Dev was immensely proud of two facts, the first was that he was one of the richest men on the planet and most certainly the wealthiest Indian and secondly he could trace his lineage back to the brave Indian independence fighter Tipoo Sahib. It was Tipoo Sahib, who Napoleon had sought as an ally on a proposed march on India to destroy a major trading artery of the British Empire, but Tipoo Sahib was eventually defeated by the British soldier Arthur Wellesey, eventually immortalised in the annals of British military history as the Duke of Wellington. Dev casually flicked at one of the three personal computers arrayed around him on his desk. A small light flickered in his cold, flinty stare as he saw an email message stating a new bulletin had been delivered.

Dev pressed a button on his desk that notified his team of sleek uniformed personal assistants, based in an adjoining office guarding access to Dev, on that no account was he to be disturbed. His instructions were always carried out to the final letter; he brooked neither incompetence nor dissent. Dev then proceeded to open the email, he remembered back to when he was initially recruited to the cause of the new emperor of the occident and orient. It was when he attended the international conference at Davos where certain selected individuals were secretly sounded out for their interest in working for the project to bring in the new world order. Once interest was reciprocated it took over two years of contacts and bulletins before Dev had a reasonable clear picture of how the flaccid, empty shell of the European Union would be welded to the power of Chinese muscle and endeavour to create a new dynamism. Other players, such as himself, would enable a smoothing of the ways internationally to ensure all relevant governments fell into line, thus allowing the sanctioned multi-national business empires to operate more efficiently and wipe out those other enterprises propped up by pathetic narrow national self-interest and wasteful subsidy. He was already aware that significant Saudi princes and pivotal players in Iraq and Iran were already starting to pledge their oil resources behind the project. Dev was happy that at last there was a man of impeccable heritage who could cut through the Gordian Knot of United Nations feebleness. A man with vision, a man of action and one who would share the spoils with those who rallied to his noble cause. Dev stroked the thinning grey hairs behind his right ear as he thought through his future strategies and business battle plans.

He was deeply enthused that this man, the new Napoleon, had surfaced within his own lifetime and at a point when he could contribute to the project's success and where he would personally reap his share of the glittering global benefits. To the victor the spoils, he reminded himself; it was something he reminded himself of daily. Without men of appetite nothing would ever be achieved. Also it would be a prime opportunity to settle scores with some other members of the global business elite, who had crossed him in the battle for ownership of businesses around the world. Dev had matured his decades-long grudges like fine vintage wine and would extract maximum pleasure when he could extract delicious revenge when the time was ripe.

Dev had for the last fifteen years been selectively picking the bones of what was left of the British manufacturing base and was salivating at the prospects of finally plucking the last few profitable morsels, left on its decaying frame. Then he could in effect reverse history and have a low wage English workforce sweating to make the profits for his brand of Indian elite, whilst paying suitable homage to the new leader. Dev saw himself as an Indian tiger in his business dealings; he sincerely believed he was that beast, wild, ruthless and worthy of respect and admiration; and more than that he wanted the old colonising empire of Britain to publicly bow the knee to his exposition of superior Indian entrepreneurship. The hunting season was about to begin in earnest.

Tom was still chuckling to himself about the shell-shocked look on the antique dealer's face when he showed him the tarnished-looking medal and ribbon that Ace had given him to raise some living expenses. It was the type of look where the dealer tries to look none too excited in a calculated ruse to depress the seller's price expectations, but on this occasion he can't quite hold back the excitement, which positively bulged out his eyes as looked upon the treasure trove. Tom thought that a lot of these dealers waited like vultures for the wary, unknowing and the just plain gullible. He wondered what the astronomical Portobello Road mark- up would be set at and maybe it was going to end up in a virtual EBay market space. However, when the dealer's gaze caught Ace looking directly at him through the shop window, it appeared to have such an instant, galvanising affect that he immediately handed over a thick wad of lovely twenty pound notes. Tom thought the professional dealer had somehow involuntarily handed over a far higher cash sum that was intended: perhaps Ace's formidable stare had spooked him, spooked him good and proper. Whatever made the hardened skinflint open up his tight wad was fine by Tom, he felt good being on a roll; second victory to Ace, two out of two wasn't bad going, maybe third time unlucky. This unexpected bounty then funded some decent second hand fresh clobber, which just about fitted, sourced from the local Oxfam shop for both of them. It also paid for storage for Ace's fancy dress in a locker at the nearby train station. Tom's old clothes were jettisoned with great pleasure to the waste bin. It left quite a bit of cash over, enough to keep several packs of hungry wolves from the door. Or should that be, alleyway.

"Ace, you were pretty trusting to give me that medal. Most of the rough sleepers I know would have scarpered with either the medal or most definitely the cash and spent it own their choice of poison. And by most, I mean every single last one of them. There is some honour among rough sleepers, but a windfall of cash usually cures them of it."

"I do not doubt your logic or train of thought. But all the same, I believe I am a reasonably good judge of character. Although Tom I readily accept that I am not infallible, our Good Lord knows that, but sometimes a risk is there to be taken. In life we all experience some serious ups and downs, just look at me saddled with just a fin instead of an arm! Worse than my collection of injuries, and to my everlasting shame, like you I have a failed marriage to boot. One thing to remember, never, never ask me to go on holiday to that accursed island of Tenerife, I have some very, very painful memories of the cold surgeon's knife off Santa Cruz." Ace exclaimed as he waved the sleeve of his missing right arm.

The last comment left Tom shaking his head in bemusement and wondering what mad tale Ace had concocted in his mind about the loss of his right arm.

Then much to Tom's surprise Ace declared that he wished, seemingly on a whim, to visit the Maritime Museum at Greenwich that very day. But it was only if Tom had no objection to the new plan. It had been a very long time since anyone had deferred to Tom; he felt his near-extinct self esteem surprisingly climb several notches.

Tom was surprised himself at how much he enjoyed the Naval Museum and its tribute to the domination of British sea power, a power which in its day was the envy of the world. Late into the afternoon Tom flagged and he holed up in the cafeteria nursing nothing more intoxicating than a strong cup of tea, leaving Ace to wander further into the exhibits. As he thought of Ace he was beginning to conclude that he must be a real Naval history buff, interested in the age of sail, signalling, armadas, broadsides and all that guff from before the age of steam and metal-hulled ships. He had pitched up with a Navy anorak, it took allsorts to live on the streets he reckoned and who was he to judge anyone their interests and eccentricities.

When Ace returned from his wanderings at the Naval Museum, he sat down quietly next to Tom, with a faraway look in his eye. Tom eventually broke the silence, "Ace I enjoyed that; really enjoyed it. Never been here before, which I suppose is a bit sad since I was actually in the service. I reckon you're really into the history stuff about the age of sailing and all that. Weigh anchor and splice the main brace!"

Ace appeared to ignore the brash humour of Tom's last remark.

"Fascinating, it was truly, fascinating. I could spend a long time on our proud Naval legacy. A few mistakes, here and there in the place, but the overall picture is correct. It brings back thoughts of a truly golden era. That was when Britannia ruled the waves. And even after the failure of Philip's fearsome armada and the providential wind has not our Navy saved us from at least two continental despots? There are two despicable devils that spring to mind, that were both determined to enslave the British Isles with their respective terrors cloaked in republicanism and National Socialism. Have you ever considered that the similarities of the two small corporals, both born outside of the countries that they both led to early glories and then onto their final destruction? It's interesting that the both of them eventually faltering upon the terrible and bloody fangs of the mighty Russian bear, before other nations managed to gather in force and crush their superhuman, nay infernal appetites. And remember England stood alone before both of these accursed monsters from hell. But Tom, forgive me when I refer to England it is an old habit, of course I mean Great Britain. There are many Scots, Welsh and Irish comrades that were very dear to me. We would not have been great without them, not by any means."

"Ah, Hitler and Napoleon, yes old Bony Parts, as he was known at school. Well even I can remember that bit of history. Not completely sozzled all of my brain cells away, maybe most of them though. But tell you what Ace I remember going on board HMS Victory down in Portsmouth. Now they were very, very brave sailors in those days. Firing broadsides at each other on the open sea. Must have had nerves of steel coil."

Ace's clapped his hand on Tom's shoulder much to his consternation and Ace's eyes flashed for the first time with what Tom could think of was a deep and burning passion.

"The Victory. Oh yes Tom, the Victory. What a vessel," Ace rolled out the word Victory in quite an unnerving fashion. "A splendid vessel! She was built in part from the heart of the best English oak. Is there a better wood to sail on? Tom, I hold some very bittersweet memories of that craft. She was built to sail and to fight the combined might of France and Spain. But Tom it has been a many a year since I felt that deck under me and the power of the wind driving ever forward a British man of war. Now perhaps we have spent long enough looking back. Let us chart a new course forward. There are things we must do; everything will, I'm sure, fall into place. It's the call you see. The call. Once the call has gone out we must find our place and meet the right people. Then the actions will follow. The Lord will guide us through the dark night, even the desperately blackest of nights; we just have to be open and receptive to the call." Ace's words had a resolute ring in Tom's ears as they both rose from the table.

"The call? I'm not sure what you're on about, mate," Tom shook his head.

"Ace, you've lost me good and proper this time. What exactly is the call; that you keep going on about?"

Ace appeared to ignore Tom's confusion over the 'call.'

"Tom after we find some proper warming nourishment. Hot nutritious food and mind there is no money for alcohol, is that clear? Good. Now I have some interesting entertainment planned for this very evening. I have just read a poster over there, informing us that at Charing Cross Road in central London there is a meeting of a historical society which features a talk on the 'Battle of the Nile.' If I was

45

being pedantic then perhaps more accurately it should be the 'Battle of Aboukir Bay,' where the victorious British fleet destroy Bonaparte's ships, which had carried the Corsican adventurer to the Egyptian sands, threatening our assets in the Indian subcontinent. It will be most interesting, most interesting. Perhaps I may be excused to make a point or two if the opportunity arises."

"Sounds like the battle of the buffs if you ask me."

Tom smiled and thought; Navy anorak he may be but one who has got us our next few meals sorted. Need to stick with him as least as long as the cash holds out. But he reasoned that for a historical nut, Ace didn't spout on for hours about all the Naval trivia he had amassed in his head; thank heavens, because if he did there would be a very early parting of the ways.

The following day after the historical society meeting, the events of which Tom still couldn't quite digest, they had forked out for a good nights sleep at a grubby and seedy back-packers hotel off Tottenham Court Road, although the accommodation to Tom in comparison to his recent al fresco sleeping quarters, it was positively the equivalent of a suite at the Hilton. The score or so individuals who had attended that night's meeting of the Nelson Society to listen to a talk on the Battle of the Nile had a most unsettling experience. Nestled unobtrusively at the back of the small hall, Ace and Tom had kept themselves to themselves. The both of them had not troubled the small bar serving a few drinks to the attendees, and Tom surprised himself again by not feeling the urge to have another taste of alcohol. He told Ace, only partly in jest, that he was a bad influence and to stop sobering him up; Ace smiled good-naturedly at the jibe. They were not exactly welcomed to the bosom of the greying middle-aged and elderly regulars, who were probably doing a good deed for their better half's by going out for the night with their half pint of beer or glass of port and Tom doubted if three quarters of them had ever got hitched in the first place. Armchair admirals with their comfortable pipe and slippers, one step removed from the train spotter mentality, he concluded. They religiously gathered on a quarterly basis to discuss the unmatched exploits of the country's greatest Naval, and perhaps all-service military, leader. During the obligatory question and answer section at the end of the presentation, there had been a couple of long-winded questions which were designed to show off the train-spotter knowledge of the questioner. After two or three of these, Ace had raised his left hand to make a contribution. Tom felt himself slink further down into his seat as he realised the assembled heads would turn towards him and Ace. Tom tried desperately to avoid any eye contact and turned his head down and began to stroke his nose in embarrassment. The evening's presenter had a slightly quizzical and concerned look about the raised left hand from one of the two newcomers who might just lower the tone of the evening. The presenter, with some hesitation, waved with a look of mild annoyance to Ace to ask his question. His look became more exaggerated and his jaw dropped slightly as Ace spoke freely and authoritatively for about fifteen minutes, seemingly filling in all the blanks from the presentation, correcting a number of other points and suggesting a number of areas which should be the subject of further enquiry. As Ace finished there was a strange silence as all of the attendees had swivelled themselves right round towards Ace and Tom. Tom thought that the audience's eyes appeared to be widening en masse in astonishment matched with a number of wild and hairy raised eyebrows. Ace then rose, with what Tom thought was possibly an impish grin, then nodded to Tom to get out of his seat and with a final farewell flourish of his left hand to the score of ageing

Nelson enthusiasts, they exited into the freshening London night air. Tom then proceeded to burst out laughing at the way Ace had blasted them with his incredibly detailed knowledge of the historical events.

"Ace, you just topped all the professional Nelsonites," laughed Tom.

"It's a subject I know only too well. Perhaps I wasn't being very fair."

After leaving the hotel, Tom thought his new friend must have had some leadership experience in the past, perhaps a history teacher or else he was raving Navy scholar, whose grip on reality was not quite secure. He grinned to himself, as he could see that his new acquaintance did not appear to be the sort who bemoaned his fortune. He'd lost his eye and his arm and the rest; Ace's attitude seemed to give Tom a feeling that he hadn't felt for quite some time. His example seemed to be to just overcome your disadvantages and not to cripple yourself with guilt and fear. Tom felt a sense of his own remorse just beginning to lift its deadening weight off his spirit and he began to feel he could do something positive again. Although he wasn't sure what he could do, but perhaps it was time for him to take a risk and see where Ace would lead him. Anyway he reasoned, so far Ace had saved me from a beating or worse and he has got me some new clothes and we've got some money for food. His Ace as 'loony on the loose' theory had taken a hefty knock after witnessing his performance in the Nelson meeting. He wondered that it was funny that the food requirement had usually followed the need for a strong drink of Tennent's super-strength lager or cheap rotgut cider. Tom felt a distinct lightness as he followed Ace down the street. Then out of the blue he heard Ace announce, "Norwich, yes, yes, we'll go to Norwich until I can think of a plan. Tom, did I mention that I'm a Norfolk man. From a small place you probably have never heard of. It is called Burnham Thorpe. But I was sent to school in Norwich. Yes, I have some mixed memories of Norwich Grammar School. Dreamt of making my name at sea; whilst sitting through many a lesson of drudgery. The sea though in many ways it was the making and perhaps the breaking of me."

"School days weren't my favourite time either. Ace, I've never been to Norwich before but I'm happy to go and see, but you realise Norwich isn't exactly walking distance. Mind you I suppose we could try and thumb a lift when we get to the right road out of London. And then again have you got any more of those medals that might make us some money for the train?".

"Tom, what meagre capital resources I have left, I think we'd better hang onto until things become a bit clearer. I accept your commission to thumb a lift to the fine city of Norwich and may the winds soon fill our sails," replied Horace with a dramatic flourish of his good left arm.

Tom grinned at the theatrical strangeness of Ace's mannerisms and thought he might burst into Gilbert and Sullivan next. He knew Ace was at the moment the only show in town and it was probably better than skulking around with the other wandering and desperate drinking dregs of the capital.

Tom led the way towards the nearest bus station to find the best bus to get them into a reasonable position of getting a lift in the direction of Norwich. He also calculated that his new companion had no idea or experience about hitch-hiking and the odds of the two of them getting anyone to stop and pick them up, was just this side of mighty slim. But then again, Ace hadn't said he didn't have any more of those lucrative old medals or access to other antique wealth, which could be turned instantly into living expenses. Tom reasoned he may as still hang in there at least until Ace's pockets were well and truly emptied and the well of good fortune had run bone dry. He didn't feel particularly like a leech or a sponge more of a companion for the road; the road most tramped.


Valerie Garfoot walked briskly past the main entrance for the iconic British Museum and could feel the great city of London girding her loins for the great public and media invasion that is the 2012 Olympic Games. She thought about her role as head of the intelligence services, not the first woman to achieve the position but still it was succeeding, and succeeding in spades in a man's world. It was a comforting thought that she had made another rather large hole in the glass ceiling of high ranking posts within the British establishment, which still remained by and large a man's prerogative. As she sat down on her usual wooden bench in Russell Square, she thought about her career in terms of the Olympics had it been a sprint, middle-distance slog, a marathon, or more likely the high jump, long jump and triple jump combined. She was genuinely glad that her face wasn't regularly splashed over the media and she could still enjoy the city without the restricting effects of a personal bodyguard, just a middle-aged woman executive in a smart Laura Ashley dark linen suit, enjoying the refreshing rays of an early British summer. Her only concession to her own personal security being the standard issue emergency alarm device in her handbag that could guarantee a posse of police around within minutes; anyway that was the theory when the office persuaded her to take it. No doubt it was another control mechanism on someone's risk assessment.

"Excuse me madam, do you mind if I sit here?" A short man about thirty years of age with the looks of oriental extraction smiled as he gestured to the empty place on the bench.

"Of course not Danny, and your manners are always appreciated," replied a sweetly smiling Garfoot.

Danny reciprocated the smile and sat next to her and opened his copy of the Guardian and made a good show of reading about the fortunes, or lack of fortune, of his beloved Charlton Athletic. However, in his view the sports pages were beginning to pig out on Olympic-related stories, rather than the more infinitely important football league.

They were alone on the bench and didn't look at each other, giving the impression to anyone who may be watching that they weren't together.

Danny spoke without moving his eyes from the newsprint, "my grade A source at the Chinese embassy has confirmed that there is one hell of a battle going on within the leadership of the People's Liberation army. But more than that he thinks one side is beginning to get the upper hand and wrest full control and in time all the public leaders will fall behind this new power bloc. He thinks the control of the state is hanging in the balance. One thing is for certain I wouldn't want to be in the shoes of the losing faction, hell no. The wrangling and manoeuvrings are still very much internal and it is not percolating out to any other intelligence agencies."

Valerie Garfoot preferred to hear the latest intelligence about the Chinese first hand from their best frontline agent in the UK, on Sino-UK intelligence matters. It was also more secure, as she was aware that both MI5 and MI6, and who knows the CIA as well, had been breached by agents in the pay of the looming and more or less menacing Far Eastern super power. She was currently pursuing a policy of leaving the yellow moles in place to see if UK counter-intelligence could identify the whole network. It wasn't the ones they had under surveillance that she was worried about. She had suspicions that the Chinese had another deeper entrenched network that was an even more deeply embedded nest of vipers which would remain when the more obvious agents were picked up and either given a long term residency at Her Majesty's pleasure or swapped for some poor soul, on the UK security service payroll, currently languishing in a high security prison near Shanghai or wherever.

"Danny, what is the new faction planning to do that might jeopardise Chelsea not winning the league?" Enquired the head of British intelligence, as she tried to use her limited football knowledge euphemistically, transposing the nation's interests to the vagaries of Premiership football.

"Ah, Valerie, please you know I am sensitive to foul language! Please don't use the 'C' word in my presence. Wash your mouth out. Well what I can glean from my source is that they want to ratchet things up significantly. For instance they want the Taiwan issue settling, no surprise there. They feel that their strategic moves across the globe now need to show some gains and this means that they feel they are overdue some serious respect from world players, particularly Uncle Sam. So far, so pretty predictable, however, now get this, my source has hinted that they are going to make some kind of play in the UK which will somehow detach us from our USA cheerleader role and the special relationship guff and then significantly influence the EU in China's favour. Now that's a newbie. And details? I have zero."

"Danny, this is extremely interesting and if accurate then of course, it is of major concern. And Danny it is not to mention vague; I need hard facts. Not hunches or vague possibilities, I want facts we can act on."

Valerie Garfoot wiggled her feet on the heels of her shoe as she tried to bring some comfort to her aching soles. One thing she had rued was her inherited genes of flat feet from her father's side of the family. As with most things in life, she knew, you could only play with the hand that you had been dealt with.

Danny continued, "Valerie my contact has indicated that he has some real red-hot information and I hope to reel that in next week and see just how much of a scorcher it really is. If it is burning hot then I'll be straight in touch, if it is just so so, then I'll update as per our museum meeting schedule."

"Thanks for the work so far Danny. Please continue to keep all this side of your work unrecorded and operate on our informal briefing method. I remind you that there is to be no discussion with other operatives or your desk supervisor. We both know the score and the high stakes at the moment. As soon as we, as our American friends say, have cleaned out the chicken coop then we can organise things onto a more formal footing"

"Sure thing, but I don't envy your weight of responsibilities. Saying that though, your salary would come in handy for the bookies," replied Danny, as he scanned the day's horse racing card within the sports section. "You think they've penetrated pretty deep then?"

"We've have got a couple of cast iron certainties, which are being monitored to see where they will lead. But I think the Chinese expect them to be picked up by counter-intelligence and they will have buried a deeper mole or cell within our happy intelligence family. I would not be at all surprised if they have also built up some significant operational capacity in some other government departments. They are also continuing to put a lot of effort into their IT hacker units to try and disrupt our communications."

Danny looked across and met her gaze, "maybe you have your spy-catchers watching me?"

Valerie let out a small smile, "Danny, I never rule anything in and anything out; you know I can't do this in our business. Cynicism and mistrust are my unfortunate watchwords. But anyone who swears loyalty to Charlton Athletic and is just about to throw away yet another ten pounds on a lame donkey running at Kempton is more close to lunacy rather than being close to our Beijing brethren."

"Perhaps you're right. I can thank my Chinese ancestors for the gambling gene. But as my father always told me, the house always wins, and I should have listened. Well chief until the next time. And Valerie and I wouldn't have your job for all today's betting stakes in China."

# 6

Alex Haye stretched and slowly yawned, as he was trying to concentrate on the less than interesting work on his laptop. There didn't seem anything to hold his attention so he flicked over to his email account, where there was nothing of note. He was just about to close down the programme when he saw the red highlighted urgent message arrive with its little hurrah in his inbox.

"What now?" he wondered.

The Prime Minister grimaced as he read the confidential email about a second huge unexplained explosion in the Brecon Beacons in Wales. Yet again, thankfully, there were no reports of any casualties and also no immediate claims of responsibility. Until he could get the latest security briefing he had a queasy feeling in his gut that this explosion was linked to earlier mystery blast on the island of Gruinnard. Where will the next explosion be he feared, maybe in the heart of a big city, maybe right in the centre of little old over-populated London? His mind tossed several possible reasons for the explosions around in his head; nothing really added up and he expected the confusion to return to wake him up at 3am in the morning, ruining the sound restful sleep he now only aspired to. Haye was feeling perfectly drained and he felt no hint of energy in his unresponsive limbs; he really was becoming Mr Lethargy Man. The aching, slow throbbing pain had started at the back of his ear, which was his usual sign that he was run down or his body was trying to fight off some mischievous virus. He made a mental note to take a few more vitamins and to bulk up on his fresh fruit and vegetables; he decided he needed to give his immune system at least a fighting chance. He had not been sleeping well either, which he knew must be part and parcel of a Prime Minister's brief, but he was having prolonged worry sessions in the wee small hours over the first mysterious explosion, now this second incident would provide yet more energy sapping nocturnal grist to his mill. Tonight Haye promised to demonstrate his practical support for the Scottish distilling industry by having a large malt whiskey or two as a Highland knockout nightcap. He continued to mentally grill himself over the incidents; what if there was nothing sinister behind both incidents he would be worrying himself into an early grave over nothing. If he carried on like this he would be suffering from some sort of nervous and physical collapse; he decided that he would also consult his personal doctor and see if there was any pharmaceutical solution to his mind not relaxing enough to sleep. Another two years of this and he reckoned his next election photo will be of a prematurely grey and balding Alex Haye, the Prime Minister's job must count as dog years in the ageing process. His near-hypochondriac ponderings on his personal health worries were cut short.

"Excuse me Alex, but I have a Mr Jeremy Wheater on the line and he says it's important," the PM's secretary informed her employer who was this afternoon, amongst other things, officially supposed to be having a moment to pore over the all the plans for his appearances over the Olympics to maximise the photo-opportunities and try and raise his party's stock with the electorate. Alex Haye was aware that media published polls and their own private polling were clearly signalling that the party was trailing well behind in third place and if a snap election was called now their brief bid to bring honesty and openness back to politics was about to end quickly and most disastrously.

Alex Haye looked up, realising that he hadn't achieved anything apart from letting his health worries give him a few more lines on his face. "Oh, thank you. Please put him through on the secure line and Janet, please absolutely no interruptions."

The Prime Minister wondered what the entrepreneur wanted? He knew that he never rang just to chew the cud. There was always an agenda.

Seconds later Jeremy Wheater was put through.

"Alex, old pal, greetings," the breezy and sometimes irritatingly confident tone that Alex Haye had become used to over the last five years filled the room as the PM switched the call onto speakerphone. He replaced the handset and turned to view the restricted view from his office window. Haye's furrowed countenance was at odds with the annoyingly jolly voice on the other end of the line.

"Jeremy, you know I nearly always have five minutes for my favourite businessman and generous party donor. You must be worth five minutes of my time, probably even more. Now please tell me what's so important that it needs to take precedence over the affairs of state."

"Ah yes, the affairs of state, it sounds so grand. I trust you keep reminding your little army of superannuated public sector workers that if it wasn't for entrepreneurs like me, they would have little to no tax revenues to squander. They probably sit there every day thinking up yet more schemes of how they can drain more tax out of the doers in this life. Now if you ever need a shot in the arm perhaps you should install me as the minister for business, I'm sure I could make your army of stuffed shirts begin to actually earn their salaries. I'm sure I would just need an hour a week to put a rocket up their gentle peaceful slumber. Now my friend, I don't need any favours. What can you possibly give me! Looking at the papers I thought it might be you who needs some favours. Just checking, but is this line secure?"

"Absolutely. No one, not even MI5 listens to my calls. I hope they would find something better to do with their valuable time," replied Haye dryly.

"Sorry to question it. Okay sitting quietly, then let me begin, Pandora, my beautiful, lovable cash cow, is about to experience exponential growth. We will shortly be within the top one hundred biggest global firms. And that, my friend, is going to benefit dear old Blighty."

The PM interjected, "benefiting Britain and no doubt yourself, Jeremy. Selflessness is not a quality I generally associate with you. But I am with you so far and congratulations, but I assume there is some obstacle to the global gold at the rainbow's end. And I suppose this is where I come in?"

"Alex my friend, we are both players and we both know that life is all about leverage. Sometimes you pull the lever and sometimes the lever is being pulled against you. Firstly, Pandora is getting into the cruise and container business in a big way, a very big way. In the next seventy two hours or so your Defence Minister will be aware of a large number of resignations from your leading officers within the navy. They are not exactly being press ganged but the financial offer they have received was impossible to resist. I don't mean it to sound like something from the Godfather. But it truly is an offer they could not refuse. I like to buy the best."

Alex Haye's brow began to deeply furrow and his eyes narrowed as the unexpected news sank in.

"Now please don't worry old chap its not all bad news! Pandora will invest £43 billion, yes billion, over the next

5 years on job creation in any areas directed by your civil shirkers. Instead of re-arranging the papers on their desk or filling their mileage claims, you can give them some real work to get on with. Also, listen closely to this, Pandora will clear all outstanding Olympic costs. Just think of the crowing you can do to other national leaders about a debt-free Olympics. And just ponder on all those expensive naval salaries and pensions you will be saving on for years to come. We will also commence the biggest shipbuilding programme since the last two world wars combined. That means real manufacturing jobs in hard pressed dockland areas, there'll be votes for you there. And on a personal note I will ensure that my donations to your party are quadrupled. These would be untraceable; the donations would be carefully funnelled through a number of discrete smallish donors. I think I can certainly help extend your little political project with the electorate's blessing. Giving you a war chest to fight the next election with, and you know with how things stand Alex you're going to need it. Think on this Alex at election time you will be able to go to the people to say that you have cleared the debts for that little sports shebang you are hosting."

"Jeremy, perhaps you can turn up for the sack race. I will tell you what, after this call I will ring Her Majesty and get you booked in for the quickie knighthood. You'll be right up there with Elton, Cliff and Mick," replied the PM sarcastically, "now let's cut the 'it's Christmas come early' stuff and tell me what you really want. I really haven't got all day to marvel at Pandora's performance."

"Sure, sure but I am not creeping to you for the old blade on the shoulder routine. Mind you Sir Jeremy Wheater has quite an appealing ring to it, don't you think? I don't rule it out for the future, hell it might be fun. No, my partners and I require to work together with the British Government on an innovative project. Simply this, the Government allows for a dual control of the Royal Navy and the merchant fleet will be nationalised, which then will also operate under a dual control, with Pandora funding the compensation payments. When you see the detail it will be a win win situation all round."

The PM interjected, "depending on which time zone you're in I could only assume you have been drinking too much or abusing some other substance. No, why not think a bit further how about Ryanair and Easyjet as partners with the Royal Air Force and Federal Express and TNT join up with the Royal Logistical Corps. Jeremy please, please start making sense because I am really busy," the PM's eyes closed in frustration.

"No, Alex I am perfectly sober and perfectly serious. The investment levels we and our partner are bringing are unprecedented. You owe it to the country, your party and your legacy as a Prime Minister to grasp this opportunity, mark my words my partner has other irons in the fire and is not averse to dumping England for a more receptive country. Perhaps that would be typical Britain, in terminal decline since 1901, a shrivelled and spent force. Just about surviving by having East European migrants providing the muscle while we shine each other's virtual shoes in a fool's paradise of a services-led economy. And just how much longer are we going to hold our head up on the world's stage with the economy stagnating, residents rushing to move abroad to get hold of some quality of life and our proud military virtually anorexic from lack of investment. But oh I forgot, Alex at least we are holding the Olympics, ra ra ra. I just hope for your sake we get a least a couple of gold's from Oliver Metcalfe in the middle distance races. Look my partners need a signal, either one way or the other by the end of next week. Neither Pandora nor our partners will be prepared to be messed around. Alex get back to me and don't let this opportunity pass. I plan to be on my yacht, just call me on my personal mobile."

"Jeremy, thanks for your upbeat analysis of the country. You seem to be remarkably coy about your new friends, just who the hell are they?"

"When you're ready to do business we can discuss that. As I said we need a signal, if you're serious about this or not. But Alex I must say if you reject this you won't be just losing the backbone of your leading naval officers, Pandora will be pulling completely out of England and our partner will move its considerable investments elsewhere and I will be making a long and loud song and dance in the media about how dear old England is going down the drain, thanks to your incompetent government. I'll have plenty of mud to throw and enough of it will stick, it always does. It's a ruthless game at this level. And once the money markets start to take fright you'll be in charge, for a short time anyway, of something akin to a banana republic. You'll be as popular as Robert Mugabe. And you'll go down as the leader who finally took what little remains of the great out of Great Britain. Now I need an answer in three days."

There was a short silence as the threat sunk in and Alex Haye tried to remain composed as he felt a hot choking volcanic anger well up inside of him.

The Prime Minister managed to contain his anger and continued in his dry unemotional tone, "well good luck with your expansion Jeremy. By the way I don't know if you can remember the parable of the rich man and his two barns?"

"No, I'm afraid I don't and I'll leave the Sunday school stuff for you, Prime Minister."

"Look Jeremy I have got to get on with running the country for a few weeks yet and you've got to get on to being as rich as Bill Gates or Warren Buffett. And in three weeks I will be welcoming the world to the start of the Olympics.

Goodbye. And by the way feel free to donate all our party funding to charity, where it can do some good. We don't need another penny from you."

He heard the call terminated at the other end without any of the customary politeness of a goodbye.

The PM switched the speakerphone off; his eyes seethed as the outrageous news and threats of Wheater's phone call coursed through his head. He pressed the connection to his secretary and proceeded to give her a start as he bellowed, "please get me Sir Peter, immediately."

The coach driver pulled over to stop at a pull in just ahead of the man thumbing a lift, as the electric door opened on the coach, a second man appeared at the coach door.

"Okay then where are you two heading?" the driver asked down to the man at the door opening.

"Well we're heading sort of Norwich way," Tom replied.

"Afraid that's a bit out of my route. I can take you north up the A1 and you can bale out at one of the service stations. Up to you."

Tom glanced across to his new partner and took his slight nod as acceptance and cheerily took up the offer and climbed aboard.

"Thanks mate I'm not sure we would have got any sort of lift today."

As the two hitchhikers got onto the seat across from the driver, they felt the vehicle steer back smoothly into the traffic and begin to head up towards the beginning sections of the A1 and the road north.

The driver was returning from dropping a tour party who were savouring the delights of the London Eye ,theatre land and a cheap rate block-booking on a hotel in the Docklands.

The driver rarely took the risk of picking up hitch-hikers but today he felt the need for some company. After fifteen minutes of the usual inconsequential banter, the driver wanted to satisfy his curiosity about his two guests.

"What's waiting for you in Norwich?"

"My friend Ace here used to go school there and since we haven't any other pressing engagements, so we thought why not. Maybe pick up some work," Tom felt a nice glow inside stating that they might be after some work. Heck he reasoned, thanks to old quiet features next to him, who appeared to be trying to sleep, he had nearly climbed up from bottom rung and was now talking about finding work.

"Well good luck to you. I'm heading back to Lincoln; my firm TransLinc has a depot just a few miles out of the city centre."

Ace opened his eyes at the coach driver's words.

"Served with a brave man from Lincoln once," his face seemed to mist over with the act of remembering.

Tom thought he'd better intercede.

"Ex-Navy man our Ace, just like myself," he explained to the driver.

Ace then continued.

"Not really sure I ever left the Navy, Tom. Anyway I feel that perhaps we should postpone our Norwich visit and see the City of Lincoln and maybe it will prove to be our way forward. So let us continue with our kind driver Steve."

"Okay Ace. Norwich, Lincoln I not sure I know the difference."

Steve the driver laughed, "well the football teams are a few leagues apart. But if you want work I know a local farmer who needs labour and you'll get a place to bed down and if you don't mind hard work and the company of east Europeans. I don't mean to be funny but you'll need two hands for picking the crops," the driver glanced over at his one-armed passenger.

Tom answered brightly, "his other arm will serve as two. No worries there, I've seen it in close action."

They continued to head northwards with the flat landscape to either side of the main road, Tom felt there was a certain bleak charm to the fields and small woods compared to his last few months in the built environs of the sprawling and fume-filled capital. At least the fresh air might do him good.

# 7

"Ah Prime Minister, can I introduce you to Mademoiselle Rives, she is the delightful representative of the French Intelligence service. Apparently she has come with some prime information and subsequent good news regarding those recent bomb incidents." Sir Peter smiled with one side of his mouth and gently rocked on the balls of his bespoke black leather brogues, as the PM's eyes caught the sight of the beautiful, dark-haired French agent. She was about five foot two inches tall and dressed stylishly in crisp black linen, which dramatically contrasted with the red of her lipstick.

"Prime Minister?" Sir Peter repeated as he tried to break the mesmerising spell upon Alex Haye.

To the Prime Minister the encounter was by far the most interesting part of his day so far; it immediately and most pleasantly, took his mind off his worries.

"Err enchantez," said Alex Haye, as he had to fall clumsily back upon his schoolboy French. "I'm always seeking to improve Anglo-French relations."

"An honour Prime Minister, an honour," she replied, as the PM quickly offered Mademoiselle Rives a seat. Her dark and dreamy French accent seemed to act like a fine intoxicating scent in Haye's nostrils. The chemistry in the air was combustible.

Sir Peter suggested they would probably need up to an hour to run through the information that M. Rives was about to present. Haye presumed the details were held within her laptop that she carried in an expensive-looking, deep brown leather tooled carrying case.

"Agreed, Sir Peter. Err yes at least an hour and hopefully longer if Mademoiselle Rives has time. No interruptions for an hour. I think I will see her alone Sir Peter to gauge the material. So yes, yes, absolutely no interruptions."

Sir Peter slipped his outside to the personal assistant's office to ensue an hour's uninterrupted briefing. He then moved over to refreshments table.

"Who would like a drink" Sir Peter enquired, "before I leave you two together to get down to business?"


Emma Darbyshire was skim-reading her copies of the serious national papers; although she had begun to wonder if all the press hadn't begun to limbo ever downwards towards the sensationalist celebrity gossip trough. She was waiting for her assistant to come round to her small terraced house in the more desirable uphill area of Lincoln, near to the Lawns complex. Her ex-marital home in New Malden, London would now be sold off as per the divorce. She hoped the sale would clear the outstanding mortgage and all the fees from her expensive legal team. Her assistant was about to join her to set off on a number of local engagements which were part of her duties in trying to make a real difference in the lives of her devoted Lincolnians. As she glanced at the paper her eye caught a story in the Independent between various mouthfuls of her gluten-free toast. The toast was part of a diet she had rigidly stuck to over the last twelve years to ensure her gluten intolerance did not make her feel too unwell day in and day out. The short news item informed her that a Chinese national from the embassy had been found murdered in the Chinatown area of London, apparently the murder weapon was a machete-type instrument. An embassy official said the victim had a known gambling problem and may have fallen foul of Triad-controlled illegal gambling dens. In response to the killing, the organised crime section of the Metropolitan Police were investigating the incident. The story connected at a tangent in Emma's head on where she should feel the government ought to lead on moral issues such as gambling and wondered if any further liberalisation was good idea. Her abstract ponderings were terminated as her mobile phone rang.

"Hello."

"Emma, it's Sir Peter. I need to have an urgent word with you."

Emma ensured that her voice did not betray her coldness towards the Cabinet Secretary.

"Well you've caught me so go ahead Sir Peter I've got just about five minutes before I start again on the constituency carousel."

"This is slightly awkward, and of course I am sorry to break it to you over the phone. Let me be straight. Emma, Alex has removed you as deputy with immediate effect. You are no longer from this moment the Deputy Prime Minister. I'm sorry that I have to deliver the news over the phone. The media will receive the details at noon today. It will state that the PM has accepted your resignation with regret but respects your request to spend more time in your constituency. Your replacement Kevin Scotton is already picking up the brief. Emma you know politics it's a rough old game, particularly at the very top. Alex wanted you to know that if a suitable cabinet vacancy crops up that you will be first in the frame."

The shock news hit her like a rough wave when swimming at the seaside, when it hits you full in the chest. She then felt a bilious whoosh roll across her stomach, for a second she thought the bolt from the blue would make her physically wretch. She twice swallowed hard and paused before she could gather herself to reply. If she had been doing a radio interview the pause would have sounded very ominously significant to the listener.

"I need to speak to Alex," her voice was streaked with emotion.

"You cannot."

"I need to speak to Alex," her voice rose as she persisted.

"You cannot speak to him. I'm afraid he is tied up with ensuring that the ship of state successfully navigates through the Olympics parade, protects its people from unexplained explosions and perhaps most importantly ensures he remains in Number Ten," Sir Peter's smooth delivery was becoming slightly ruffled as he wanted the erstwhile deputy leader to in modern management speak, to shut up, get over it and move on.

"No Sir Peter. I just cannot accept it. Especially, with absolutely not a single word from Alex."

"If you need to tell him that he has been a ruthless so and so, you'll probably have a chance in three months for a private meeting at the party conference. I understand you'll feel disappointed but the world of politics is one moment you're up and the next you're down. Now if you want to wash your dirty linen in front of the media and nail your colours to any other rebel malcontent members of your party that is your prerogative. But just think of what the infighting will do to the survival of this government, which is hanging by a mere thread as it is. Government survival takes precedence over your personal status and privileges of office Emma."

"Don't be so patronising," she felt herself getting hot in the face. "I can tell you that my career has never been about personal status or elevation. It has been my desire to make an actual difference for the public that we serve and I will continue to do that. And I will do that from the backbenches if necessary. And no doubt Sir Peter, you will see Alex before me, just tell him I'm sorry he is not man enough to do his own dirty business. Instead he has to send his little know it all civil service fixer. Is there any chance whatsoever that I can change his mind?"

"None Emma, there is no chance whatsoever. The government and the country have moved forward."

"Goodbye then," she replied as she abruptly switched the phone off and flung it onto her settee. The tears began to well up in her eyes.

The shock waves reverberated through her as her body shook with a few tears. She was alone with no one to share her humiliating dismissal from office. Then Emma's rational side of her mind raced with possible motives as to why and whether there was any real reason or personal incompetence of hers that had led her to her sacking. Why on earth hadn't she seen it coming? She realised there was nothing more she could do there and then; she had been successfully dumped out of the cabinet. Emma imagined the colourful language that Harriet would use when she shared with her the news. Whatever, she told herself, she must keep a clear, brave face for her constituency duties today. Save the tears and moping for the evening when she was alone.


Valerie Garfoot waited at her Russell Square park bench, enjoying the salubrious early summer air and waiting for an urgent update from Danny on the struggle inside the Chinese leadership. Out of the corner of her eye she saw a young man of possibly oriental extraction about eighty yards away heading her way. He seemed as if he was looking for someone, perhaps looking for her. Her nerves alerted her to the danger and she swiftly pressed the electronic control in her handbag and trusted that the system and police response would go to plan. She decided to sit calmly and wait. Valerie Garfoot could see that the young man, with striking black hair, was wearing a stylish black leather jacket. He had now spotted her and was moving at a pace towards her up the road, she dry swallowed with a slight tremble of fear.

Just then two young teenage boys ran across the road and blocked his path, they then began speaking to the young man and he was speaking back to them. The man was smiling at them but kept looking over at Garfoot, he then scribbled something on some paper proffered by the boys then left them and moved at fast stride towards her. She rose up from the bench and began to mentally run through her mandatory self-defence training which was last updated three years previously. It was personal defence training, which she hadn't used outside the training room and had assumed she never would need to. The young man with a serious frown on his face was now just ten yards from her as she turned to face him and meet his gaze. His eyes pored directly into her.

The piercing screech of the three unmarked Police cars as they braked sharply filled the air. Officers, including two carrying light sub-machine guns had inserted themselves in between Garfoot and the young man. They were now rapidly frisking the young man, who had been roughly spread-eagled against one of the Police cars as the officer quickly attempted to ascertain what, if any, concealed weapons this threat to the head of British Intelligence was carrying.

They found nothing on the weapons front. He was unarmed.

"Thank you for your prompt response," she said, in relief, to the senior Policeman. He appeared to be in charge of the units which had been despatched to her aid. He smiled and nodded graciously in return.

"It's not everyday that I get a chance to protect the Head of British Intelligence."

Valerie Garfoot said, "I need him taking down to Paddington Green because I need to ask him some questions in private. Please treat this matter as priority code one. I repeat no records or briefings to be made or passed on."

"Understood, however if it's his identity you need I can help you there."

"You can?"

"It's an easy one," replied the Policeman.

Valerie Garfoot had a surprised expression on her face, as the young man was handcuffed and put next to an officer in the rear of one of the police cars.

The Policeman held open the passenger door of his car and then got into the driver's seat and then continued, "well you obviously don't follow the football ma'am. Yes its Li Hongzhi, he turns out for West Ham United and his career is followed by millions back in China."

# 8

There was a double knock on the hotel room door on the third floor of the Flemings Hotel in the Mayfair district, which is just a short stride away from the pleasant grassy area of Green Park. Standing somewhat furtively in the corridor was Alex Haye, feeling distinctly self conscious in his black Wayfarer Ray Bans. He turned his back to someone passing in the corridor then he saw the room occupant use the fish eye security feature. Two seconds later the door slowly opened.

"Ah allo, Alex, what a most pleasant surprise, please do come in," she beckoned him in with her hand.

"Err good afternoon Camille, I was wondering."

"Oh yes, you were wondering, I understand Cherie."

"You do?"

She waved her hand dismissively to show that there was no need to explain his arrival at her hotel room in the early afternoon. He felt even more awkward to find out his visit was not a surprise.

Alex Haye slowly padded into the large deluxe size hotel room whilst glancing nervously over to the double bed with the sheets pulled back and then he turned back to face the unmistakably shapely and nubile figure of the French intelligence officer wrapped in a purple silk dressing gown decorated with a striking red dragon motif on the back.

He removed his sunglasses and stuffed them into his jacket pocket, "sorry about the disguise, but you know in my position I have to be careful. I don't think I would make a very good secret service agent."

"You are alone? There is no bodyguard downstairs maybe?"

"No, just plain me. Is that okay?"

"Belle. But I understand absolutely Cherie. Remember I know all about security. Yes, I know all about security. Ah but you look positively handsome, well for a politician anyway, ha. But with those sunglasses you look like err, yes a Blues Brother," she laughed mischievously.

"I know, it's the best I could come up with," he replied bashfully.

Her accent wafted over him and it seemed to act yet again as a heady olfactory intoxicant in Alex Haye's brain. The strong scent she was wearing strangely reminded him of his parents rose garden and it was reminiscent of the Zeferin Druin rose they had religiously tended over the years.

She sashayed over to a drinks table. As she turned her back to him, his eyes lasciviously dropped to see that she was wearing black heels and seamed black stockings. He swallowed as he felt the moisture dry up in his mouth.

"Now Alex I know it's a little early but I think we both need a drink to help us relax. Unwind a bit from the draining affairs of government. So tiring, you must be tres fatigue. You need to recharge."

She poured two tumblers half full with a glistening amber liquid.

"I don't normally drink at this hour, but to maintain good diplomatic relations I'll join you," he joked unsuccessfully.

"And it looks a bit like a treble," as he anxiously viewed the size of the drink.

"I thought the brandy might fortify you. Perhaps stiffen your sinews," she emphasised the word stiffen.

With a casual flick of her head she indicated for her visitor to take one of the balloon-backed chairs in the hotel bedroom. Alex Haye gingerly sat down, first crossing his legs and then uncrossing them.

"Now please Alex, take your jacket off and make yourself at home. The brandy will warm you up enough. We need to get to know each other now we are working together on this security problem."

"Yes, I'm relieved that you appear to have identified the culprits behind the explosions."

His Gallic hostess then with a slow tantalising poise bent down to pass him the glass As he took the glass she still held on it, and the action afforded him full view of her soft brown cleavage. Ensuring she had achieved the desired effect on his libido, she released his glass and walked over and sat in a chair opposite him.

"Thank you, most generous Camille."

"You are very, very welcome," she purred in answer.

Alex Haye took a long gulp of the fiery spirit. He coughed as the spirit burnt the back of his unprepared throat.

Camille Rives kept her eyes directly fixed on the Prime Minister while she placed her right index finger into the drink and then slowly circled the rim of the crystal tumbler with her now glistening finger. She then slowly sucked first the tip and then up to the knuckle of the finger. Alex Haye felt a dizzying excitement; a mixture of whatever was in the glass and a lust that had gripped his thoughts and his loins.

"Alex my Cherie. That is better and we are starting to relax. You know you must have the most stressful job in this country. It is important that you can have time for relaxing. And I tell you that you have such a handsome face. It has a lot of character. In France we kiss when we greet friends.

Do you know what French women are famous for? Would you like me to brief you on our cultural speciality of French kissing?" She laughed.

"Now that would be an interesting briefing to listen to," smiled Haye wanly.

"I could make it an interactive briefing with plenty of hands-on practical sessions."

The Prime Minister's head and other areas were now throbbing hard and the point of no return was passed and drifting way, way out of sight.

As she said this she placed her glass down and pulled open the tie of her purple silk gown. She was wearing a black silk corset and she smiled at the completely devastating effect she was having on her visitor. Rising to her feet she allowed the gown to fall silently onto the heavy pile carpet and with her hands on her hips turned slightly away from him.

He tried to clear his throat.

"Now do be a darling and just tighten the laces a little at the back. So it feels tight and firm."

Emma Darbyshire watched the late evening television news with her feet up on the sofa, her telephone was unplugged and her mobile switched off. She had suffered quite enough of calls from well-wishers, and those less than well-wishers and more importantly the media, who rather than commiserate just needed to fill their copy and try and get the angle on a top-level bust up in government.

The news edition showed pictures of the new deputy PM, the chubby-looking and florid-faced Kevin Scotton, who was touring some of the Olympic facilities and meeting some of the athletes from around the world. Those competitors, who in a few days time would be challenging for personal and national glory in Olympic combat. She felt no corrosive envy about Scotton having his less than attractive features being bathed in international limelight; no, she felt bitter about being spurned by Alex, when she still had an awful lot to give to the political life of this country. Not only that, but he had used a bureaucratic third party to do his dirty work. And Sir Peter was a proxy, which Alex knew full well that she had very little personal respect for. As far as she was concerned the Prime Minister was a typically cowardly male when it came to personal relationships, who couldn't or wouldn't meet her face to face to tell her the real reasons for his decision. He was not the man, or indeed friend, that she thought he had been. C'est la vie. Perhaps the toxic political power had really gone to his head and he was willing to sacrifice anyone, or even any principle to cling onto his own personal power base. Emma knew that her political vision was based on honesty, fairness and not trying to hold the reins of power at any cost. Maybe, she reasoned, she had paid the price for naivety and she should have been a bit more, 'tread on or be trod on.'

The newsreader then intoned that Alex Haye the Prime Minister had been confined to bed for a few days to shake off a chest infection but was looking forward to the opening of the 2012 Olympics.

The television was turned off with the remote control and apart from part of a chapter of John Steinbeck, a small glass of port accompanied by a wedge of Lincolnshire Poacher cheese, she planned a hot bath and an early night. The thought passed through her mind that perhaps she should broach with the constituency chairman about standing down at the next election. Let someone else have the opportunity or headache, depending on how you looked at it. She wondered if she had done all she could do on the national stage and it was time to return to a job in the real world, away from the parliamentary fantasy world and maybe pick up the pieces of her shattered personal life. There was another of those twinges of regret that she had been feeling over the last five years about not having a child; the dreaded ticking of her biological clock, which was amply aired in the agony columns for the middle class and female readers who were heading towards middle age childless. She decided to speak to Harriet first, and she was sure Harriet would give her the clear pros and cons of such a course of action. Her assistant was her always clear headed, and a no nonsense guide; just what she would have done without her assistant she dreaded to contemplate.

Tom looked around the unfamiliar Lincoln city centre streets and hoped his street-sense would help find an answer to their immediate need for shelter. Both he and Ace had marvelled from the approach to Lincoln at the majestic sight of the world-famous Cathedral with its three towers dominating the ice blue skyline. Certainly better than a wet weekend in a Potteries town, mused Tom as they sought to gather their bearings. Tom felt that wherever this excursion was heading with his new companion he was sure that if only lasted the next day or a few weeks it was certainly better than seeking the empty warm feeling of alcohol. Not only that he realised that he was no longer feeling like a leftover stale dog's breakfast, certainly the short-term break from the booze and the upgrade in food quality, which Ace insisted on, was making him feel a good fifteen years younger.

They found a spare bench on the High Street opposite the War Memorial, just beyond the temporary stalls for the local farmers market, and Tom waited for Ace to decide the next step. The warmth of the sun made Tom close his eyes and he could feel a rare small smile form on his lips. He felt unusually that day that there was a future, something ahead that be of worth rather than the day to day scrabble for booze and shelter. It had been a long time since he had even felt like a genuine happiness. He was still more than hazy about his new travelling friend. Ace was certainly not your average fiftish-years of age bloke. For one thing his skin didn't look wrecked like most vagrants he knew. Mind you he thought he had come across a wide range of people , from skag-head scoundrels to sanity-free zones to the salt-of –the-earth down on their luck types to the rarer sightings of your actual gold-plated saints. So far Ace was definitely hitting the blessed saint league, although he still had the nagging thought that he might turn out to have graduated from the lithium school of manner control. Tom could not tease out much more information about his past apart from having some Naval experience, a definite Naval historical nut and his physical disabilities. However, his mental abilities in conversation appeared to Tom to be as sharp as a brand new Stanley knife blade.

"Ace, answer me this one. I haven't had a taste of the booze since we left London and not only that, my craving ain't exactly raving either. I haven't joined the AA. So how come I'm sobering up?"

"Tom, my friend. To be blunt, I do not know. But I know what destruction alcohol can bring on peoples lives. I've seen the grog tear the sense and good character right out of men, even the best of men. If you can enjoy a little taste fine, if not leave it well alone. What little I know of England today there is an unhealthy dependence on the alcohol crutch. Youngsters drinking too much, too soon. It will do dreadful damage to individual lives and the health of the nation. But I do remember once, having a bath in brandy, yes a brandy bath! Imagine that. Better than being consigned to the depths. Yes I made them promise that. They promised to

79

bring my body back to England. Maybe one day we'll talk about that strange experience. Tom please enjoy the sober life, welcome it like a true dear friend. What I believe is that you don't judge a person by the colour of their skin or their beliefs or their station in life, no, you judge them on their character and their actions. Without good health, well how can you do any good works! Our health is the most precious jewel we can own. If I've helped you in anyway, then that is all to the good. But mark my words, it is down to you. You have to want to change. My father, as a minister, would call it a metanoia, a Greek word for a complete change. Although with regard to the body, I know I hardly look the picture of health." Horace grinned as he covered his good eye with his left hand and feigned blindness.

Ace continued, "my friend, I do not know why we met and I am no believer in fate. Let us see where this adventure leads. Sometimes the pathway is not at all clear. Let our Lord lead us on to glory."

Tom shook his head and felt that Ace was beginning to lose it upstairs with his talk of 'consigned to the depths' and 'a brandy bath.'

But Tom had no other plans. In the world of vagrancy the luxury of planning ahead was generally foregone. He had become in a state of living from one drink to another, one place to kip to another. He stood up and his companion followed suit and they moved out into the bustle of the street.

"Ok Ace. Why not head up the hill and have a closer look at the Cathedral. Then we had better find some food and a place to sleep."

"Tom, I hand the command of the watch to you. Now steer our good ship forward."

Several thousand miles away in Spain the sun was beginning to delight the British Diaspora who had moved to or holidayed along the Costa del Sol playground. Although it had seemed that a lot of the British had moved onto further fields of tourist tackiness in Florida, Dubai and Phuket. The landscape along the coast had been despoiled by the concrete rabbit warrens and garish business fronts. A beautiful coastline ravaged in an unquenchable lust for euros. The surrounding hills in front of the Sierra Nevada pitted with the sprouting flats and apartments, looking like fungus spores draining the life out of the landscape. Just along from Marbella, which had become such a byword for property corruption, is the pretentious whore plying her trade to the next lecherous sucker which goes by the name of Puerto Banus. Along the quayside among the yachts denoting conspicuous and crass wealth and taste, the crew of a huge gleaming white yacht named Pandora were busy preparing to take their leave from the quayside. Inside the vessel, stretched out on a soft leather cream sofa, Jeremy Wheater listened on his mobile phone to the latest update on his global dealings, his eyes widened as his chief accountant for his global business purred the tumescent financial headlines. His personal global equity was growing in a turbo charged rush and he toyed with a thought of throwing a monumental fiftieth party for himself next year on a Caribbean island, a party that would attract the A-list of celebrities and the minor royals. The glossy magazine brigade will no doubt devote acres of pages to the bacchanal, and no doubt he could agree a healthy fee for exclusive picture rights. He took another sip of his favourite tipple, when visiting an Iberian port, of sharply chilled Cava with freshly squeezed orange.

The white-uniformed captain of his yacht politely knocked on the door.

"Come in," replied Wheater.

"Sorry to disturb you sir, but we are now ready to embark. All the paperwork is cleared. What course do you want me to set?" Enquired the Pandora's skipper deploying due deference, who remained standing in the doorway, looking across to his employer and generous paymaster.

"Simon, I have just had some good news on the old financial front. I am so glad I turned my eyes to the east. So today I would like to set sail for La Rochelle. I fancy celebrating on French oysters and lobster tonight. And later on there is also a small get together in France that I have to grace with my presence."

Just as Wheater finished speaking to his captain, a young Spanish woman, with dark tumbling curls and dressed in a tight-fitting chamois bodysuit, slunk past the skipper and made herself comfortable in Wheater's lounge. Her slow walk emphasised the curves of her hips.

Jeremy Wheater pressed a switch which softened the lighting and automatically drew the curtains around the cabin.

"Simon, I think I will take a short siesta. No disturbances please for two hours and sail her smoothly on," he spoke to the captain with his eyes fixed on his shapely siesta partner, who had sprawled herself across one of the sofas. She lay back into the deep cushions and raised one leg off the floor onto the sofa. Her generous lips slightly parting in a sensuous smile and slowly stroked by her index finger, she could feel Wheater's eyes drink in her shapely Mediterranean brown body.

The skipper nodded knowingly and left Wheater.

He reached over to another Cava bottle chilling in a silver ice bucket and with a napkin opened the bottle with the customary pop.

# 9

After collecting his solitary sports holdall from the spasmodically turning luggage carousel, Danny made his way out of the utilitarian building with the rest of the passengers off the flight. He scanned the small dusty-looking surface car park facing him as walked out of Limoges airport, which was situated in central France. It was a flat, featureless landscape and an airport that would hardly exist without the patronage of the cheap flights of the Irish buccaneers Ryanair. His small North Face holdall contained a change of clothes and essentials he had picked up from where he had stashed them in a locker at Liverpool Street Station; he had taken the necessary precaution of not going back to his flat. His security training had paid off by always carrying his passport, plus a couple of spare alias passports, so he could grab a cheap flight out of the UK. He had used one of his cover identities that were not even known back at the office; he had been glad of these now that enemy agents may be accessing all UK security databases tracking who goes where. As he reminded himself, trust no one and look after the big number one, oh Danny boy. Funded by the couple of grand he kept in the locker for emergency disappearing measures. One reason he never married or had any long-term partner was that he could not live with the thought that he might just go missing one day and never come back. Not only that but how could they put up with his incurable sport and gambling weaknesses. He reminded himself that he had been lucky to escape with his life from the attackers in London's Chinatown, his worst fears had been confirmed from the national press describing the slaying of his contact. Danny felt a stab of grief at the loss of a good man who was helping the right side and had paid the ultimate price. Inside his head he ranted that MI5 should be able to look after its own and those who assisted it but he knew they were penetrated at various levels and if he became expendable to the opposition then his demise would only be mourned for a short period and then he would be replaced by another fool wanting to help Britain survive in the twenty-first century, where a new superpower was thunderously on the march. If only the British public knew the life expectancy of its intelligence agents who were working at the very sharp bloodied cutting edge of British defence.

As he walked into the hire car office across the road from the airport to book a metallic-blue Renault Clio with missing hubcaps he wondered yet again why he was flying and driving towards the centre of the intrigue, the one that his recently deceased contact had briefed him about before the murderous attack upon them both. Danny kept hammering three words into his head. Security, security, security, followed by my security, my security, always my security first; it was his personal mantra.

The female car hire clerk with the too-heavy eye make-up had a jaded 'I'd rather be puffing on a cigarette' look, which he felt the French females had virtually perfected. He had no doubt she just had Danny marked down as yet another Anglais zooming in on a cheap flight to soak up some French weather, and enjoy the more rustic lifestyle. Or perhaps an Anglais, who was probably visiting their little second-home in the Dordogne, where long wine fuelled retirements were planned. As this part of France had become the bolthole for thousands of British teachers and social workers, spending their days bemoaning about life back in declining Britain and whatever the current euro exchange rates were. He was now being careful not to use his bank cards or mobile phone to give any pursuers a helping hand. Getting into the small car and making a brief acquaintance with the left hand drive layout, he decided that after he had he found a place to bed down, he better work out plans A to F with several coherent and credible exit strategies woven in. One persistent thought tugged at the back of his mind, was she, Valerie Garfoot, the head of British Intelligence and someone he had a friendly network with, was she working for the Chinese faction seeking global bragging rights? Was she using him to milk him for information on those who were battling to stop the new Chinese faction; much stranger things had happened. And if so then what did this mean for Britain and, more immediately, Danny thought, what did this mean for his personal survival. Perhaps he was considered small fry and Garfoot could reel him in at any point when his perceived usefulness had come to an end; maybe he was just bait, to help her to see who or what else was sniffing about. He started the small-engine car and pulled out of the half-full car park. His first plan was to look for the nearest bed and breakfast a la Francais; he needed sustenance, sleep and some time to think. In three days he would either learn some intelligence that could help his country or he would not be backing another Gold Cup winner or be disappointed once again down the Valley. Valerie Garfoot, he decided, must be handled very, very carefully.

Back in the historic City of Lincoln, the urban centre for the large rural East Midlands County of Lincolnshire, Tom, now displaying more vigour than he had felt in years, had managed to locate the Nomad shelter in the east end at the start of Monks Road. They had missed it at first and were sent back after enquiring at the St Barnabas hospice charity shop on the same stretch of road. The Nomad centre was a place where the homeless could get a square meal. It was governed by the standard trinity of rules, no alcohol, no drugs, no violence; Tom knew the score, at other hostels around the country. After enjoying some welcome and surprisingly tasty hot fare, Ace surprised the server by giving a generous donation for the food and drink provided. The friendly shelter manager came over in his wheelchair to be next to Tom and Ace and asked what they needed and what their immediate plans were? He was pleasantly surprised to hear Tom was making, in the admittedly early stages, a good fist of staying away from the booze and Ace, well he couldn't make him out at all. Never met his ilk before, which was surprising as the Nomad shelter manager thought he had reached the point where no one and no hard luck story surprised him anymore. Working with the homeless made you feel that way, you needed to keep refreshing your own well of empathy and love for your brothers and sisters who were living on and off the streets.

"The shelter's here if you need it. To be honest though, I think you pair should be above this safety net. But if we can help on getting you help from the Council or whatever, we are more than happy to help."

Ace responded to the warm generosity shown by the manager, "I am hoping that Tom regains his pride and some of the discipline that he learnt years ago in the Royal Navy. It was and is an organisation that breeds the right sort of character; now I am an old seadog myself, and more than a bit worse for wear as you can see," Tom smiled as Ace did his flapping motion with what was remaining of his right arm. He continued, "I have got one thing to do before I can rest in peace again."

"And what is that?" queried the supervisor, who was quite mesmerised by the way of Ace's manner of speaking.

"Ah I'm afraid it is yet to be revealed! Sometimes the opportunity for glory appears out of the blue when you are not expecting it. Not expecting it all. I like to keep my one good eye trained on the horizon. You never know when the enemy's fleet will sail into view."

"The enemy's fleet?" murmured the manager.

The Nomad manager now had a bewildered look and rocked his wheelchair slightly back and forth trying to digest what had been said. He just couldn't make the man out or follow the conversation's direction of travel.

Tom laughed, "that is as much sense as I get! Don't worry about it, anyway thanks for the food and now we've come to Lincoln Ace, just what are we going to do next?"

Ace did not respond but had a pensive furrow across his face, which surprisingly still retained a strong trace of a gentle boyishness considering he must have been in his late forties or early fifties.

Seeing that the pair where in search of some guidance, the manager thought he should put in his two penny worth. "Tell you what," piped up the manager, as he collected up some dirty dishes and cups into a pile for collection, "why don't you pop down the road to our own charity shop. I know they are looking for some help on collecting furniture and donations. It's on this side of the road and less than two minutes away. You're welcome back here anytime; I would certainly like to chat a bit longer. It's been a bit out of the ordinary meeting you both."

"Thanks again for the food and we're here for a few days

so we'll have another chance to talk. Now a shop you say, needing help."

Tom saw Ace give him a slight nod and knew this was the next avenue they would try. He was still surprised that the desire to numb his nerves through the salvation offered by the ring-pull can was virtually extinct or maybe it was just hibernating for a while. But when he and Ace part from each other's company no doubt the roaring thirst will return like a raging torrent, returning big time and unslakeable.

"Hey, Terry get out!" Tom's daydreams were violently ended by the shelter manager raising his voice to young man, wearing a greasy worn-out padded jacket, who had just entered the dining area. He could recognise even at this distance that he was high on something, probably amphetamine-fuelled; the young man's eyes had a wild dancing gleam and his head was moving from side to side.

"You're banned and if you don't leave I *will* call the police, we don't any trouble," the manager's voice became shrill and coloured with a tint of fear.

The young man belligerently stood his ground and was not showing the slightest interest in the manager's straightforward request.

"Terry, I mean it, leave now," the manager's voice had clearly now lost any sense of authority.

Tom could see a couple of other people in the eating area begin to move further away as if they sensed, like fearful animals, that a spirit of impending violence had just entered the area. He could feel the atmosphere suddenly darken with that queasy stomach-churning sense of fear. The other homeless continued to move towards the stairs away from the danger on two legs that had walked uninvited in off the street. Whoever Terry was he clearly had a dubious reputation for violent mayhem that preceded his wayward unwelcome footsteps.

The young man began to swagger towards the manager, with a cocky shoulder swinging strut; the alarmed manager had now spun round in his wheelchair to get towards the phone fixed across on the back wall. From within his disgusting jacket the unwanted visitor produced the meatier end of a broken pool cue, in his chemically-altered head he was now about to deliver some overdue retribution for being kicked out and no doubt a thousand and one other grudges he was harbouring against every kind of authority. The feeling of temporary power over the people in the room tantalised his chemically-heightened feral senses.

He now brandished the club higher as the young man was now bent on hitting the first thing or person who came into his range. He then found himself directly facing an older grey haired man with one arm, who was now standing immediately in front of him blocking his path and his destructive urges. They were eyeball to eyeball; Ace could smell the pungent fetid breath of the younger man.

Ace's features were calm and his body completely still, as he looked straight into the man's eyes.

"Want some hero?" the young man angled his head and leered right into Ace's unflinching face.

"Want some?" He screamed directly into Ace's unwavering face, which displayed neither fear nor any other emotion.

The lack of any kind of response to his threat pushed his internal attack buttons in a hot molten rush of anger that coursed uncontrollably through his veins. Tom had already sensed that the scene was escalating out of control and he began to edge towards the stand-off. He was going to help Ace who had already risked his own self to save Tom in a West London alleyway. One good turn deserves another; although he could feel the fear tightly grip his bowels.

Just as Tom edged forward he saw the murderous arc of the cue descend towards Ace's head. It then stopped dead in mid-air and he could see that Ace had the weapon gripped in a vice-like hold with his left hand. Ace, then in one twist spun him around and frogmarched the startled man out through the doors and onto the street, with the cue end finally falling and bouncing on the pavement. It was like a stiff ballroom dance; strictly come outside dancing. And in other circumstances Tom felt he would have laughed out loud; he followed the two into the street, shouting for the would-be assailant's benefit, "they are calling the police."

Ace let go of his arm and the shocked trouble-maker was quickly on his toes and running down Monks Road heading back into the anonymous safety of the City centre, no doubt until his next brutish brush with the law.

Tom's shout about the Police made no difference as Ace's timely and firm response had saved injury and damage to the people and property within the Nomad shelter.

# 10

After she had gotten over the initial shock to her system Valerie Garfoot quickly appraised the situation and decided that Hongzhi was to be interviewed alone by herself in a freshly-painted room, at Paddington Green. Although she noticed, as probably only a woman can, that even with the new decoration it never removed the oppressive smell that seemed to be impregnated within the very walls. It was a smell of bleach, dust and serious trouble of the long sentence variety. The Head of British Intelligence wondered abstractedly, would they ever think beyond the colour of magnolia in the Police palette for interior decoration. The Metropolitan Police officers with her briefly double-checked whether she wanted someone in there with her as back-up or perhaps did she need the interview taping?

She promptly declined both offers.

The officers were not in a position to query the head of British Intelligence on her, strictly unusual, option of a one to one and with no tape back-up. They duly left Garfoot to speak to the Chinese national. The Policeman had just settled themselves comfily in the ante-room enjoying a welcome cup of tea and expecting a good half an hour to recharge their shift-depleted batteries, when they were surprised when less than fifteen minutes, perhaps nearer ten minutes, later the door opened.

Valerie Garfoot, in a business-like pose, framed the doorway.

The surprised Policemen quickly stood up attempting to show that they were still alert and on duty as well as in the presence of a very senior civil servant. One who at the very least could have a word with the Commissioner and have them back as neighbourhood Bobbies pounding the London pavements, in somewhere less than desirable, like Deptford or the Isle of Dogs maybe.

"Gentlemen, I'm finished here. Now please ensure our Chinese soccer star is very politely put back onto the London streets. It appears you have picked up someone going about their normal and legal business on the streets of London. I just hope he hasn't taken this the wrong way, or he has an enterprising solicitor seeking compensation. I also hope for all our sakes that there will not be a fuss in the papers. I have apologised and I suggest you add yours, offer him a drink and take him where he needs to be. I understand he is happy to oblige if you require any autographs for your children. Now good afternoon gentlemen."

Thanks to a Police chauffeur within a mere twenty minutes she was back behind her spacious and clutter-free desk in her own office, which was blessed with a pleasing view of the Thames wending its way through the great city. Valerie Garfoot caught her face in the mirror on the wall and she saw that her face was looking strained with tension and coloured with a ghastly greyish yellow pallor, she pushed the thoughts about her personal appearance to one side as she had little time to waste. She picked up the phone, ensuring the confidential secure line was selected, but before she could dial the number there was a knock on her office door.

"Come in," she said as she put the telephone down, and

looked up to see who required her attention.

She felt an out of character annoyance at the interruption.

Looking up she saw the door open and in walked Keith Bigham, the head of counter-intelligence and a member of her management team triumvirate. He was accompanied by one of his new recruits, probably a couple of years out of Oxbridge thought Garfoot as she quickly appraised the slightly nervous and embarrassed looking young man, who seemed to have his hair gelled into a Tintinesque quiff. It was an officer she had not seen around the office before.

Looking directly at Bigham, who was fighting a losing battle with middle-aged spread, she could clearly see that he had an unusual sparkly light in his eye. Bigham looked down at his boss as she was sitting at her desk and partially cleared his throat, somewhat theatrically, before he decided to speak.

"Errm Valerie, this is slightly embarrassing but I am here to inform that you are now under arrest, you will have to come with us. It…"

Before he could continue Valerie, showing not the slightest surprise, waved her arm, "Keith, please do save the speech. I will just get my handbag."

Two hundred miles north away from the bustling capital, Emma Darbyshire, checked the application of her No.7 brand mascara in the car wing mirror, as her ever loyal and ever charged assistant Harriet drove her towards a pre-booked constituency duty visit at Ruckland Court, a local old people's residential home. It was the meat and potatoes of her constituency work.

The news of Emma's dismissal from the cabinet still simmered hotly within her assistant.

"Emma, you might want to let it rest but I don't. Alex Haye should not have dismissed you like you were some casual agency labour. Didn't even have the gonads to tell you to your face or even deign to speak to you on the phone. If I ever get two minutes face time with him, I'll give him both barrels. Bet his minders will not let me get within fifty metres of him at the next party conference. Coward," she spat out the last word.

"Didn't have the gonads! Language please and come on Harriet, surely they taught you that politics is a rough old business when you took your political science course?"

"Rough and tough. Yes that is fair enough, but I expect some decency and principles from our leader. If he behaves like that to you Emma, what sort of person is he to lead the country, and I thought he was your friend. The word is trust. Trust just like the BBC forgot about. If you behaved like that with me you'd find me gone like a shot and signing up for a job with another party."

"I'll bear that in mind, my dear old friend. And I agree with you about that very big word, trust."

Emma Darbyshire, the newly replaced ex-cabinet minister, laughed at her assistant's fire, as she herself was now appearing to accept the fact that she would be seeing out her Parliamentary term sidelined on the backbenches, rather than close to the helm of the government. In an attempt to change the course of the conversation and lighten the atmosphere that had developed, she switched on the car radio to catch the latest news headlines.

The radio announcer informed the nation that the colourful British entrepreneur Jeremy Wheater, of the Pandora business empire, was feared lost as his luxury yacht had sunk off the west coast of France. The French coastguard and military helicopters were searching the area. There was no news so far as to why the vessel sunk with the apparent tragic loss of all the passengers and crew, and an enquiry would be commenced within the next few days.

"Ever met that Wheater chappie?" enquired Harriet, as she turned up the sweeping curve of Lindum Hill, in sight of the Usher art gallery and the side of the limestone walls of the museum, known as the Collection.

"Yes I did briefly, just the once. I said hello at some launch or other. Apparently he was generous to the party; Alex I think knew him reasonably well. I preferred to keep my distance from those sorts. They always had an agenda, a selfish agenda. It's usually the case where money is concerned."

"Perhaps he did a Maxwell? Drowning in debts and subterfuge."

Emma Darbyshire didn't respond and listened to the radio as the news carried on. She heard that the Prime Minister was still unwell and his new deputy Kevin Scotton would be at the opening of the new Olympic facilities in Stratford, East London with British gold medal middle distance hope Oliver Metcalfe running a lap of the track with the twenty school children, who were winners from a national charity competition. The cabinet public relations spinners made sure that their press release emphasised that Alex Haye would be fit to attend the grand opening of the 2012 London Olympics in seven days time.

With the magnificent east tower of the Cathedral and the statue of Tennyson and his dog to their left, they pulled through the Roman archway as the car continued to head down the leafy and wide road of Nettleham Road in the northern part of the city.

"Now if I had a nasty bone in my beautifully shaped body, which is adored and worshipped by nearly every man west of Skegness. I would reckon that Alex probably has a sniffling cold that he thinks is virulent pneumonia. Another sad case of man flu," smiled Harriet.

She continued, "oh, but he will be back for the big media feast. Basking in the limelight, the rat, well quelle surprise! Anyway let's hope that our best hope Oliver Metcalfe shows the rest of the world a clean pair of heels in the Olympics. It'll be exciting to cheer someone on. IN FACT I actually know his sister. Big name drop or what?"

"Well I hope the Olympics go well, particularly on the security side. I am glad we got the costs of the whole thing under some kind of control. I just hope the rest of the country doesn't end up paying them for decades to come. I hope it's a legacy we can be proud of. At least its not a showcase for a despicable regime as the last one was in Beijing. Do you remember their thug-like security guarding the Olympic torch through London before the last Olympics?"

"I do Emma yes, and remember all your unseen background work in government which will be airbrushed out of the story. Unless it goes wrong of course and then your name will be no doubt at the fore again. Starring prominently in scapegoat spin city. That wimp of a PM will be grabbing the credit or delegating the blame! And you used to say he was a friend, ha."

"I'm sure I'm not the first person to be let down by a serving prime minister. But Harriet, what would I do without you? Your feisty nature has cheered me up. For the record just how many men do you know west of Skegness?"

"Not enough that can measure up to my exacting requirements I can tell you. I've cheered you up? Good. But in Lincoln we have the right to be mardy. Let's enjoy one big delicious slice of mardiness."

They both pulled their 'mardy' faces, which was a game they usually played when getting over some depressing news or event.

Harriet pressed the car CD player and the sound of her

favourite pop group from the eighties After The Fire belting out their stirring song, 'Listen to me.'

Harriet joined in with the first line, "I know you think I am crazy but you've got to listen, you got to listen to me."

Which, whilst the lyrics were admirably clear and direct, they were not quite the standard of Lord Alfred Tennyson whose statue nestled in the Cathedral grounds to the left of them which they had passed by on their journey.

After the song faded out Harriet continued in a more serious tone, "do you miss your husband?"

Emma paused and kept her gaze fixed straight ahead.

"Not an ounce. Not one microscopic piece of an ounce. Our marriage was a ghastly mistake, which became all too apparent after only a couple of years. I suppose we are all entitled to make some mistakes in our lives. I have now rather given up on the idea of marrying again. Too much risk and perhaps too much possible pain; I am taking it as a sign just to grow old gracefully."

"You're not convent bound yet. Drop the sorrowful spinster act. If you were in your sixties I might give you that one, but not in your flaming forties Emma. Come on. I know the male species can, more often than not, be as disappointing as hell, but I'm sure there is some true male gold in them there hills. I hope to mine a rich vein myself in the next few years."

"Okay then I suppose my only hope then is an introduction agency; a classy one. If you want to see if it can work for me, please investigate further. Harriet I'll leave it up to you to write my details up. But please don't fix me up with any losers. I'll give it one go and one go only, I haven't the desire or the stamina to check out the whole herd. Maybe you will strike lucky for me, see if you can find me a knight in more or less shining armour or at least one than will clean up nicely."

# 11

Danny poured himself another glass of the cheap, red wine which had a decidedly roughish feel on his taste buds. It was part of his rations that he had picked up earlier at the nearby and well-stocked Supermarche. He started to mentally run through his options. Danny always liked to weigh the options especially if he was placing a large bet. No bet larger than his sacred skin. Betting on his own life certainly helped him to focus on the issues without letting the wine unduly dull his own flesh and blood risk assessment. He had spent nearly the last twenty years learning how to work out the odds. Number one, he told himself, this aggressive faction were apparently and maybe still are very close to taking over the running of the adolescent Chinese superpower. They were powerful, determined, working to some plan and completely ruthless and if they got their hands on those big Far East levers then we could be in a 1939 Germany, Poland and Soviet Union situation all over again. It was no secret in the world of spooks that the United States knew only too well that their satellite defence system could all be picked off at will. Militarily Uncle Sam would be tottering like a battered boxer in a title fight with a blindfold on, as good as defenceless. So when it was no longer the biggest bully on the block, the US would quickly squeal for peace. All the other democracies would either be sucked in to major conflicts or run up the white flag; as this new leadership could deliberately foment and provoke ructions and targeted unrest across continents. Thus tying up the free world's resources and resolve, the west would end up suing for peace and accepting some dreadful compromises. It would make the situation in Iraq appear like a parish council election. The future looked a distinctly yellow hue, but this yellow Reich would obliterate the majority of history's hard-won human rights and the environmental degradation of the world's resources would be fast-forwarded. The Chinese have industrialised and wrecked their environment at breakneck speed, ruling the world would hasten the nightmare scenarios of unchecked climate change. Now, Danny concluded this was a battle worth fighting for. And as an ethnic-Chinese Briton, he wanted China to change for the better, for the sake of its long-suffering people. For the sake of the world's future and its environment and for peace and a decent level of human rights China had to change. This aggressive internal coup within China needed to be stood up to by all powers around the world. He didn't kid himself that he was going to save the world. He was no Marvel pulp comic superhero. But he was trained to collect and provide intelligence which helped protect the security of Britain, it was his job and he had a certain pride in that he thought he did it well. Why else would he have the informal network to the big boss Valerie Garfoot herself?

Number two, they had killed his contact at the embassy and he had been lucky to escape with his life. Are they still on his trail? Were they already using our own MI6 resources to resolve to search and destroy probably the only Charlton Athletic season ticket holder working for the UK intelligence services? He knew his top boss and informal network contact Valerie, would have said that Charlton Athletic and intelligence services was way deep into oxymoron territory. He partially wished that he hadn't had such a professional closeness to Valerie and her unwritten instructions to him to delve into this Chinese intrigue, which had certainly put him more personally at risk.

Pulling another hunk of the fresh white bread from the stick, he sliced a piece of President-branded cheese, sipped some more wine, which now tasted much more agreeable as he continued to mull over the facts to date. The food and drink hit his bloodstream and his body felt a welcome energy uplift; he told himself he could get used to this French style living.

There were he conceded a number of pieces missing from this intelligence jigsaw. His recently murdered contact from the Embassy had told him that he believed some of the answers may be found at a gathering, which was to take place this week, bizarrely near the small French village of Romagne in the region known as Poitou Charentes. The main players apparently wanted to confer away from prying eyes. Knowing and passing on this information cost the man his life and nearly had done for his very self. So here he was approximately an hour a so away from Romagne in the middle of the huge and sparsely populated French countryside. The frying pan and fire cliché skittered into his head.

He questioned himself again, was this wise old son? These were global big-time players and his life would be dispensed with like a used tissue if they got their hands on him.

His mental risk assessment was completed, all appropriate boxes were ticked and tomorrow after finding out the latest horse and football results at the nearest internet café, he would implement plan A, whilst keeping plans B to J close to hand. Very, very close to hand.

Alone in the cabinet room Kevin Scotton appeared a man at ease with himself, relishing his sudden catapulting into the limelight as the new deputy Prime Minister. The sudden promotion had not fazed him in the slightest; to the high office born. He had felt he was justly due for some more promotion and recognition, his latest position was overdue and rightly deserved. From being a junior Minister covering mundane and the admittedly less than sexy Health and Safety regulations, he had now been standing in for the indisposed primus inter pares Alex Haye. Now he was the figure head for all the national and global media scrummaging as the spotlight fell on London for the Olympics. He had even begun to entertain somewhat titillating thoughts that maybe he was the man, not only for the deputy's post but for the top spot. The biggest glittering prize in British politics may be just within the grasp of his sweating palms. Opportunity sometimes knocks at very short notice, he reminded himself. In his line of official duties Scotton had kept to the script and not tripped over the furniture, and even managed to get a few witty wisecracks in about Metcalfe's chances for a gold medal in the 800 and 1500 metres. Maybe it would not only be Metcalfe storming around the final bend to breast the winners tape ahead of the straining competition. Maybe good old Scotton might just get the backing from the party and the country to take the top job. Scotton reminded himself that he must put some effort into networking with the other MP's of his party to ensure sufficient support was there if it came to a leadership beauty contest. The other night he had even had a dream where he was in straining into first place in a Chariots of Fire type scenario. The Olympics and his personal ambitions being fused together during his sound, satisfied sleeping. Someone else's problems, can be someone else's opportunities. Alex must have been pretty ill to be missing out on some of these cream jobs. Kevin Scotton's pushy wife had always told him to be a bit more aggressive and not to settle for second-best as a piddling junior minister in some back of beyond department. It was time to grab hold with both hands the most coveted political position in Britain. She had been even unsatisfied with his surprise move into the number two spot; nobody remembered number two's, she reminded him. It was the Prime Minister whose name and legacy was etched into the public's minds and the history books.

"Ah Kevin."

Scotton was woken from his ruminations of naked ambition by the unexpected arrival of Sir Peter.

"Hello Sir Peter. Where's Alex?"

Sir Peter sat himself down opposite the florid-faced newly-appointed Deputy Prime Minister.

"According to his doctor he is nearly ready to resume full-time duties. And that includes dealing with our favourite feral press pack. By the way Kevin, he wished me to pass on his thanks for how well you're doing on representing the government on all the Olympic PR duties. Alex has been monitoring all the good coverage you've gained. Just before his return he has informed me he is going to slip away for a couple of secluded days in the country. Some grade A respite care. Alex wants to be one hundred per cent fighting fit when he returns to taking over the reins," Sir Peter could see Scotton was pleased to hear the encouraging words of commendation and equally displeased about Haye's return...

"Will he be back for the opening?"

Sir Peter briskly replied, "absolutely, definitely."

"Oh good, I'm pleased, yes that's good news," came the hollow-voiced response, which failed to mask his sour feelings of disappointment. Scotton had kept alive a faint but fertile hope that he himself would be handling the first opening reception at the Houses of Parliament.

Sir Peter searched Scotton's eyes and could see that the

answer had mildly upset the jumped up junior minister, who had very quickly got a taste for the political high chair.

"I know you have shortly got the meeting at the palace. Please ensure Her Majesty is given the news that Alex will back in time for the opening reception. However there is one very important thing I need to brief you on, but it is something that is not for the ears of the Queen or indeed anyone else. Our former Head of Intelligence, Valerie Garfoot, has been found to be working for a foreign power, which means we have had, most regrettably, a traitor at the very top of our security apparatus. She now holds a dagger to the heart of our country's security. Ironically she appears to be in the pay of our old adversary the Russian bear. I know it all sounds a bit John le Carre. If the public find out about this, the government will fall and we will no longer trusted, quite rightly, by anyone else in the free world's intelligent community if we can't keep our own jolly house in order. Unfortunately I have some further bad news to inform you of, her deputy failed to apprehend her. Smacks of bungling, amateuristic incompetence I know. As it is I am not entirely sure that Bigham the officer responsible will live that down. However we can't replace the number two at the moment when the number one is working for the opposition. Imagine the scene, two strapping fellows go to her office and she overwhelms them with some form of gas gun. She is now missing, current whereabouts unknown. All of our intelligence and police services are on top priority to detain her. However, Alex has signed the standing order CAW/2207, which just needs your counter signature."

Sir Peter placed the sheet of paper on the desk in front of the new Deputy Prime Minister.

Scotton's face registered genuine shock at the tale of treason at the heart of British security.

"Are you sure that there is no mistake?"

"Unfortunately, not. We have incontrovertible evidence. As the auditors like to always tell us a, we have a complete paper trail. We expect her telephone records to further confirm the other evidence. She had a secret bank account in the Cayman Islands overflowing with funds from a front company controlled by the Russian secret service. A bit before your time but it has unfortunate shades of the Philby-era and the Cambridge traitors I'm afraid. Plus if she was innocent why all the Jason Bourne Hollywood escape antics?"

"Sir Peter, please excuse my ignorance, what is this document, which you are asking me to sign?"

Scotton stared down at the paper, his voice sounded slightly fearful.

"Standing order CAW/2207?"

"Yes, what exactly does it mean?" Scotton shifted his weight uneasily in his seat.

"Kevin, it is I assure you very rarely used. I can only recall it being signed on two previous occasions, outside of a state of war. It means that our people and other friendly intelligence services are given authority to use lethal force. In this case it is to stop our traitorous ex-head of intelligence and anyone providing her support. Our people will be given automatic immunity from any criminal or civil prosecution. In the light of unfortunate events it is an unpleasant necessity, I'm afraid."

"I am not sure that I want innocent blood on my hands. Surely we need to arrest her and let her stand trial and face good old British justice."

Sir Peter's body language and tone hardened, "the whole protection and defence of this realm may be at risk from her and whatever foreign power she is in league with. The Attorney General is of the same mind as me, that this cancerous growth must be cut out at the earliest stage. Every hour she is alive she is threatening the values of our democracy. Please be assured that whatever actions our forces take they will be proportionate and contained; all operations undertaken will be out of the view of the public and media gaze. You must realise that high office demands the taking of hard decisions. Sometimes very hard decisions, I'm sure you are aware that you need to display a steely ruthlessness at this level. Personally this has hit me hard, as I believed she had been a loyal public servant, certainly not a friend but a trusted colleague nonetheless. This affair has left a very bitter taste in my mouth. The sooner this matter is permanently swept under the carpet, the better"

Sir Peter could see that Scotton had become frozen like the proverbial rabbit in the headlights.

He decided to soften the tone to get the order signed. "Of course if we can apprehend her, we most certainly will, because we will then have the opportunity to get some information out of her. We need to roll up the rest of her traitorous team."

Kevin Scotton reluctantly took out his fountain pen to add his name underneath the recognisable signature of the Prime Minister.

He felt sullied inside and it had ruined his pipe dream of ambition for the rest of the day. It comes with the territory of high office, Scotton tried to console himself and for a moment wished he was back having a discussion with his genial team of civil servants on the minutiae of Health and Safety legislation emanating from Brussels.

# 12

The Nomad second hand charity shop situated on Monks Road in the east end of Lincoln, was a regular and well-accepted feature of the area. The east end of the city of Lincoln like so many other east ends around the world, was a place for hardworking families and areas of high-turnover cheap lettings for student, transient and immigrant workers. The red-bricked Victorian terraced houses were tightly packed together to house what would no doubt be referred to as citizens in a deprived area. The Nomad charity drop in centre and night shelter also on Monks Road stood across the road from the buildings of the revitalised Lincoln College. The Nomad charity had for many years raised funds for the homeless of this city, it had been started by a young man named Alan Perkins, who had a vision to help those homeless flailing at the bottom of society's pecking order. He resolved to add a bit more mesh to the safety net to try and help some individuals from complete homeless degradation. It could count on a number of success stories of re-stabilising lives and getting people off the streets into jobs and their own accommodation. Arguably it was the last chance saloon although to stay within its shelter you need to be on sarsaparilla and not the booze or dope. The

Nomad charity shop, which helped fund the work, was a cheerful and garish clutter of second-hand donated clothes, books, records and other bric-a-brac discards of a throwaway consumer society. They even had a selection of fresh bread and tinned foods donated from shops, bakeries and churches, which they sold on if they couldn't use them in the shelter's kitchen. Tom, who was used to foraging on the charity shop circuit and had often depended on them for some dirt-cheap clothing, led Ace through the doorway and into the shop.

They were greeted by a jolly female face behind the counter.

"Oh welcome the conquering hero! The centre has just rung me to say you were on your way. Thank you for seeing off that trouble causer. He has been a terrible nuisance."

"He looked a sight worse than just a nuisance," replied Tom.

Ace nodded and smiled and performed a theatrical bow at the shop assistant's kind words.

"Yes perhaps that young man is beyond a nuisance," she replied.

"He did the same for me in London, saved my bacon, good and proper," chimed in Tom. "Anyways, we were wondering if there was any work you needed doing? The manager said there might be some lifting required." Tom asked hopefully.

The woman's kindly disposition did not give them the impression that she would disappoint. She was one of those people whose countenance was one of giving and going on giving as she helped to shine a light of hope in the east end community of the city.

"Well I must say you've timed that well. Our trustees always have some need for a couple of helpers. I'm afraid we can't pay any wages, but you will get food and lodge. Are you still interested?"

"Capital, absolutely capital," replied Ace. "And by the way although we've never met before, I'm sure that your many good works over the years, both seen and unseen will be rewarded."

The assistant blushed slightly at the surprise forthright commendation. It was a complete detour from the usual conversation in the charity shop.

"Well thank you. I only do my little bit. I am not seeking any personal glory for myself you understand," she laughed a short trill and her smile brought out a new level of beauty in her face.

"Glory? Madam, I know what it is to pursue glory. But the small good works that are hidden from view are as great as those who are wreathed in national acclaim during battles for national survival. As it is written the humble will be lifted up. Yes they will be lifted up." His voice rose like a stage actor.

She coloured another flush of red and hopped gently from side to side and looked at Tom imploringly to see if he could rescue her from Ace's embarrassing line of conversation.

"Err well that's interesting," she clapped her hands together. "Now let me get our Kirby, he's one of our supporters, I'm sure he'll know what needs doing. I'll just call him he's only down stairs in the storeroom."

She called down the stairwell, "Kirby. Kirby, two new helpers have arrived."

Seconds later they could hear the clatter of footsteps on the wooden stairs and the Reverend Kirby Quiltfloe emerged from the basement

"Ah, the cavalry has arrived! My name's Kirby, very pleased to meet you."

Tom could feel no presenting edge or snobbishness from the minister.

The balding minister was perhaps in his early forties with a close cropped beard. Wearing a navy blue sweatshirt emblazoned with a Lincoln Rugby Club logo, he offered his open right hand to the visitors.

Tom took the initiative to respond.

"I'm Tom, pleased to meet you," shaking the minister's hand. "And this is Horace, although I call him Ace."

There was a slight awkward moment, as Reverend Quiltfloe's outstretched right hand could not be shaken by Ace's empty right sleeve.

Ace broke the deadlock by using his left hand to grasp the outside of the minister's right hand and shook it firmly twice.


Later that same day across the city in Lincoln, Emma Darbyshire was just about to slip into a welcome warm bath and had just unwrapped herself an unused Christmas present soap from Lush, which she was hoping would relax her and wash away her mild depression and feeling of lethargy. The phone rang. She was annoyed at herself for failing to activate the answer facility on the phone after 9.30 pm. She thought for a second at leaving it then with a horse-like snort of frustration, she got dripping out the bath and partially dried herself and descended the staircase in her dressing gown to pick up the phone. Looking down at the wet drips on the stair carpet only seemed to irritate her further. She felt her face blacken as she reached the handset.

"Hello."

"Emma, its Valerie Garfoot."

It was not a call she could have predicted.

Emma wrapping the full length white fleecy dressing gown more tightly around herself as she moved to sit on the nearby sofa. The caller was very much a bolt from the BT blue.

"Oh Valerie, it's strange to be hearing from you. Is everything alright? You do know that I am out of the government and am now sitting demurely on the backbenches. Officially I have resigned my cabinet post. I am now out of the loop as they say."

"Yes, Emma, I do know you were sacked, to put it bluntly. However you might not know that I am no longer the Head of British intelligence. So it's snap."

Emma's voice had a puzzled tone, "no, no I didn't know that. I do not recall anything in the news. What on earth has happened?"

There was a slight pause at the other end of the line.

"It's not something that will appear in the news. I don't want you to be alarmed, Emma. But I am on the run. I suppose what you would call a fugitive. They believe I have been working for a foreign power. Ergo a traitor. Believe me Emma it isn't true. It is absolutely untrue. I know the consequences if some one in my position is accused. Knowing the forces at work in this situation it may not come to trial; they will seek a quicker, more final solution."

Emma's eyes widened at the disclosure.

"Valerie, what can I say? I mean should I be calling the Police? Why did you ring me?"

There was a shaky nervousness to Emma's voice; she irritably flicked at her bath robe. She felt more chilled by the news on the phone than her not fully dry body.

Valerie's Garfoot's tone remained cool and unhurried.

"You might say a gamble. I feel that you can help and you have some close connections at the head of the government. First, if I was a fugitive why would I risk contacting someone like yourself? Second, I have told you the truth. I would never betray this country, never, absolutely, never. I know we have only met on a few formal occasions but I feel I can trust you. You must know that I am taking a huge risk just by calling you."

Emma ran her hand over the nearby radiator and dry swallowed as she tried to assimilate the news she was hearing, she slipped on her burgundy moccasin slippers that were just in stretching distance and wondered just what was going on. She began to feel a numb coldness take hold of her from head to foot. Another shiver shook her.

"Valerie, I haven't known you very long, but I have no reason to doubt you and as you say, why ring me up? I know it wouldn't make any real sense to contact me. Why would you take such a risk? Valerie I believe you but if you're innocent then there must be a proper legal process in all of this. This is England 2012 for goodness sake; we don't live under a military dictatorship."

Garfoot replied in a slow, precise tone.

"I am sure there is still a place for justice in this country; that is if I can get enough protection to ensure that I am not killed by the service I should still be leading. However I am convinced that the powers that be will ensure I am disposed of before any trial come take place."

"Valerie where are you now? Sorry I don't mean to try and find out where you are for the Police or whoever. Are you safe?" Emma gripped the telephone cord tautly and then wrapped one of her fingers into the cord.

"Emma, I am as safe as anywhere. I'm in Chinatown."

"But you're in the heart of the west end of London. That's not very far away."

"I did not say which country the Chinatown was in," Valerie Garfoot's voice lightened for the first time during the conversation, as she was able to surprise her confidant.

"Ah I see. Well I must credit you with a bit of nous being our Head of Intelligence."

"Former Head," corrected Garfoot.

"Valerie, I don't know if I'm flattered by your trust in me

but what on earth do you think I can do? You know I've been sacked and I am now merely a constituency MP. I can't for the life of me see how I can help you."

"Three things, just three things."

"Okay go on. I can at listen to them."

"Firstly, I haven't rung you to help me try and save my own skin; because with respect you can't. What I am going to tell you involves the future security of this country and possibly the entire free world. I want to know if you are prepared to get involved to try and prevent this threat or at least mitigate the considerable damage they plan to commit. Because if you are not, and I can perfectly understand you if do not want to, say so now. Just think for a minute of the situation I am in. If you want to help I need you to tell me now so I can brief you further. If not, I beg of you not to discuss this with the security services, but that will be your decision. I am not ringing to threaten you. But if you decide to let the authorities know, please wait a couple of weeks and by then you will have seen the conspirators emerge on the world's stage."

"Heavens Valerie. It's all rather James Bond, spy stuff. It's not some kind of high-level wind up is it?"

Valerie Garfoot rode roughshod over the suggestion.

"Will you help or not? Emma this is of the absolute utmost importance." Her voice answered the previous question for her.

"Valerie, I get the message. It sounds as if you want the answer here and now. Well where am I now? I have just lost my government post. My marriage is now officially over. To which I thank the Lord, and my dirty washing, as you know, was plastered over every grubby tabloid. I will probably lose my seat at the next election. As you can see, I haven't got a hell of a lot left to lose. Well c'est la vie. If the help you require is legal and above board and is as important as you say, I will help. Things haven't been adding up lately and my instinct is telling me that you are not lying. Well as far as much that you have shared with me so far. I suppose if I ring up MI5 tomorrow I could find out if you were at your desk or not."

"If you need to test me Emma then feel free, you will probably be told I am away on leave. But thanks for your understanding and support so far. It means a lot that you're going to help, thank you very much Emma. Now I will try to ensure you are not put in harm's way to the best of my ability. However I am afraid the legal and above board benchmark may need a somewhat liberal interpretation in the light of events, we may need to stretch the normal rules as we go along. Secondly, you are to speak to others only as you need their help in this matter. You must not refer to my contact or whereabouts to anyone unless you really, really need to and you can trust them with your life."

"Well okay, that's agreed. I am pretty good on the discretion front. Oh I've just thought, do you think my phone is tapped?"

"Not likely, but not impossible. Some risks need to be taken. I only decided to ring you in the last twenty four hours and the service would not expect me to contact you. No they are watching all their Russian interfaces."

"Whatever the Russian interfaces are. Anyway I hope your guess is right about the eavesdropping. You must have a good working knowledge of how the dark arts are operated."

"I would like to think so but without access to the department's resources I feel in some ways quite powerless and I fear we are facing overwhelming odds. But I would not be ringing you if I didn't think we couldn't do anything, I have a few contacts that are helping me to work against the grain. Finally, you need to listen to the following information, as it is all I have at the moment. Emma, have you ever believed in conspiracy theories?"

"I suppose the shooting of President Kennedy and Martin Luther King, possibly those two. Princess Diana murdered, no can't quite believe that one. There wasn't a man on the moon but on a Hollywood film set? No don't believe that one or anything I suppose anything involving UFO's. I leave it to the ever churning wheels of the conspiracy industry."

"Well I believe we are currently facing an absolutely global monster of a conspiracy. Now once I have given you the information as far as I have pieced it together I will try and pull in some more support to try and help us derail this threat, or at least delay it and give the country some time to prepare its defences. Let me try and explain a bit about this conspiracy. I now have access to the enemy's, and I mean the enemy's, bulletins. Thanks to my lucky Chinese sports star. This is what they call them, bulletins; they inform and guide the global grouping which appears to have coalesced around a small dynamic leadership, who have a figurehead with a special historical lineage. The historical connection is being played for all its worth and that appears to be one of their selling points. They have managed to pull together a large number of influential people around the world who are eager to run the world economy and politics for their own benefit; very much a new world order. Our country has been the target for centuries of the ancestral leader of this movement. But please forgive the cliché; they are genuinely aiming at global domination. They want to be running the whole shooting match. Forget the EU, the States, the United Nations, and the G8. This is going to replace all the current power blocs. I think I'd better start with Alex Haye, your friend and our Prime Minister…"

# 13

The weather in western France remained warm but cloudy with a slight threat of rain, but altogether preferable to the dingy gloom of the grubby internet café. It seemed an anonymous-enough place for Danny to spend a few euros and check out the latest football and racing results. The melamine topped tables still had the remnants of various adolescent felt-tip graffiti efforts. Whatever country he was in he always expected to see some depiction of the male appendage in graffiti hotspots. The French teenagers were not an exception to this rule. He logged on and studied the news about Charlton Athletic dismissing their manager and the names of his possible successor according to the excitable journalistic speculation and fan-base gossip. Once done, he checked his two private email accounts. In his first account, which took messages from his employer, was one from the deputy head honcho Keith Bigham, Danny was surprised as this was the first time he had ever had a direct email contact from Bigham, whom he had never met on a one to one basis, and had only been at a couple of group meetings with him over the last three years. The email instructed him to make urgent contact with the office, as there was reason to believe that he was a target for assassination. The service would provide every resource available to protect him. No kidding, thought Danny. The message ended with a instruction to report any contact or knowledge of the whereabouts of Valerie Garfoot. No more detail on why the office wanted to know of any contact or where she might be. How the hell can they lose the Head of British Intelligence, he wondered? Careless, tres careless.

Danny, read the email again. He instinctively realised that he would not be contacting the office just yet. Not until the smoke clears a bit and then Danny thought he would assess whether the British security services could really guarantee his safety. The whereabouts of Valerie? Keith, old boy, you're beginning to spook the spook, Danny told himself. Perhaps the assassin, who nearly did for me, was also after chopping the head off our organisation. Decapititez-vous, si'l vous-plait.

He decided not to reply to Bigham at this stage, although they would now know that the email had been opened and read. Danny realised that if he didn't get in touch, as ordered, then they would be making two plus two equal five back at the ranch. In for a penny, in for a euro he told himself in mixed metaphor currency.

His fingers quickly accessed his other secure account, which was not he hoped, known by the ministry and safely out of the reach of its IT hacker division tentacles. Danny quickly despatched two spam emails; they get everywhere, he grumbled. The third one was titled 'Chelsea for the Cup.' What sort of joker was ribbing him with his pet hate, the Kings Road clowns?

"Danny, 2 tickets for the cup clash. Seats in the Muse End. Ring 07767 833008 to confirm. Andy. PS fancy a Chinese after the match?"

Dismissing the ticket offering as some kind of camouflage, it must be in code, he reasoned. The Muse End, it sounds like

Valerie using the Museum hint, our usual meeting place, and Chelsea, well she knew that would get my attention,

Danny set off to buy himself a new mobile that he could use to ring Valerie, with a new number he felt a bit safer. He reasoned that he could ditch the phone immediately if he began to have any doubts about who was on the other end of the line. Thanks to le internet things were becoming curiouser and curiouser.

As newly hired hands of the Nomad Trust, Tom and Ace found themselves clearing out some small furniture and old jumble sale detritus at the Ermine United Reformed Church on the large Ermine East Council housing estate in the north of Lincoln. The solid red brick houses on the estate had been built in the 1950's and still had plenty of green spaces to enjoy and it still felt like it was a community that had not completely disintegrated from unemployment, broken homes and the lack of respect for the basic decencies in life. They had been left by the church minister to fill the van up so they could transfer it to the shop at the end of day. Ace showed no disinclination to lift and carry items due to his one armed state, he used his chest to balance any slack when lifting. They had been shown where they could avail themselves of a cup of tea, in the spartan but functional church kitchen. After a couple of hours working together amiably, they were ready for a break and at their tea break Tom finally got Ace into reminiscing, the gist of which reminded Tom of his uneasy concerns about his friend's mental condition.

Sitting down after their spell of lifting the no longer wanted tables, chairs and cabinets, they were enjoying a welcome cup of hot tea, Ace continued, "looking back on my life I suppose I have made many, many mistakes and errors of judgement. Mind you the man who has not made a mistake has never done a thing in his life. But Tom if it be a sin to covet glory, then I am the most offending soul alive. In the defence of this realm Britons have had to defend these shores from the ambitions of at least two small jumped-up corporals who wanted to dominate the world. We saw them off and in God's name we shall do so again if threatened."

"You mean Hitler? Ace we've had this conversation before," said Tom.

"Aye, and also don't forget the contemptible Bonaparte, although as a general he had my respect and at least he did not perish at his own hand in a bunker. Bonaparte was often at the head of his troops in battle. Although he was ruthless enough to leave his grand army to perish on the retreat from Moscow and earlier he abandoned an army in Egypt."

Tom felt slightly out of depth at Ace's grasp of military history. Running his hand across the stubble on his chin, he tried to find a bit more about what made his partner tick.

"Have you done a lot of reading about military history?"

Ace smiled, "I would describe myself more of a player than a scholar. Remember this nation stood alone during the early 1940's. The battle for the North Atlantic was a desperate, desperate fight for this country, as invasion by Hitler's hordes was imminent. The Soviet Union had their Stalingrad; the United States had the Normandy landings and the Battle of the Bulge, while we had the battle of the Atlantic that lasted practically the whole length of the war. I could tell you intimately what it was what like on the convoys and being aboard the most excellent HMS Revenge. The British seamen, whose bravery throughout our maritime years of dominance has never been equalled, saw off the U-Boat threat. Suffice to say that thank God, the course of history was changed. Then again go back one hundred and fifty years to 1798 and the glorious victory over the French fleet at Aboukir Bay, more popularly known as the battle of the Nile. While Napoleon scuttled off to fight in Egypt and threaten our Indian trade routes. The British Navy destroyed the pride of his fleet. And Tom you must know the sea battle that stopped Napoleon's invasion plans for good."

"Easy that one. 1805 battle of Trafalgar. We lost our greatest naval hero that day."

"Maybe he was just one of the many heroes of the Royal Navy through the centuries and perhaps after all, he was just another British tar doing his duty..."

"Hello."

The word rang out and Ace's soapbox musings were interrupted by the arrival of two women walking into the hall, their shoes making an echoing clattering sound in the empty hall.

"Excuse me, is the Reverend Quiltfloe about?" Asked Harriet to the two seated men who were in conversation and evidently enjoying their tea break and chat.

Tom and Ace were smartly onto their feet.

Tom replied, "ah we expect him back in a couple of hours. We're volunteers giving a hand."

Emma Darbyshire moved closer, "I see you're helping out with the Nomad furniture?"

"Yes, the shop needed two workers so here we are. My name is Tom and this here is my mate Horace."

"Well I'm Harriet and this is Emma."

"Emma Darbyshire MP," added her assistant proudly.

At that moment Emma caught the strong gaze of Ace and felt a strange and unexpected frisson of excitement, which came from she knew not where. The feeling slightly rocked her on her on her feet; she dabbed at an unexpected few beads of sweat that had broken out on her forehead. Ace bowed gently in a courtly manner and offered is left hand to Emma. She surprised herself my offering her hand which Ace took and kissed. She thought giddily that she had somehow stepped into a Jane Austen-type costume drama.

Ace spoke breaking the partially embarrassed atmosphere, "delighted to make your acquaintance, Miss Darbyshire. Please excuse me but may I be so bold to escort you to dinner this evening?"

Harriet let out a little snort of derision at the stranger's brazen effrontery.

There was a short silence as Harriet waited for her employer's riposte.

"Err… well yes. I would like that. I would like that very much," replied Emma, whose face had taken on a new light.

Harriet bit her lip and turned and glared at her employer, uncomprehending. She wondered what on earth had compelled Emma to accept a dinner invitation from a Nomad worker, possibly a rough sleeper himself, who she had literally just met. The loss of her position and her divorce must have knocked her senses for six. Surely she wasn't desperate to canvass for votes in the semi-reformed vagrant constituency.

# 14

Danny dialled the mysterious mobile telephone number and listened to the number ringing. It was answered on the fourth ring.

"Hello, who is calling please?"

Danny thought it sounded like a Chinese male voice. He was not certain if that was good news or not, more likely bad news on balance but he decided to probe just a bit further. He had already decided to abort the call if he didn't feel comfortable with the person on the other end of the phone during the first exchanges of conversation.

"It's a friend," he offered without revealing himself.

There was a pause at the other end of the line.

"Well my friend, please tell me which newspaper you read."

Danny hesitated at the left field question and debated whether to cut the call and toss the phone into the nearest bin. He decided to play along for the moment at least.

"The Guardian usually," he offered cautiously.

He could hear some muffled sounds on the other end of the line.

Then he heard a familiar voice,

"Danny, it's good to hear you."

"Valerie! Are you okay? Just what is going on? Perhaps I should have said the Sporting Life."

"Sorry for the little test it's just that if someone had been reading your emails I thought a question like that might throw them. I am as well as can be expected. As you have probably learnt I am now a fugitive from my own intelligence set-up. And it's a strange feeling going from hunter to hunted."

"No, all I have is a request to report any contact that I have with your good self. A fugitive, come on what's the story?" Danny cut rapidly to the chase.

"I don't know the full ins and outs Danny, but I have been put in the frame, probably to get me out of the way. The real story is the Chinese team that you have been investigating. They must be stopped or at worst delayed. Now I need your continuing support, I am no longer officially your boss and by rights you should be reporting this call. Even if I am now on the run so to speak, my main cause remains the security of Britain. Rest assured of that, even though the state has turned full force against me."

"Valerie I don't want to hear any about any causes or principles, and you know old Dannyboy can never be a traitor to Britain. I will do whatever needs doing to keep our country free from oppression," replied Danny.

"Traitor. That's a very strong word and I can assure you that it will never apply to me. Don't worry Danny I am not heading into Kim Philby territory. I admit that there are some things I have had to keep from the service and I will share them with you I promise, but not yet. Things are complicated enough. Unfortunately time and many other factors are not on our side. I need you to help me; I need to build up a small team that will work against this attack upon us. Will you join me in my extra-curricular activities?"

Danny felt that he needed to step cautiously and in his relations with Valerie, it would be one step at a time. His ultra-sensitive inner security antennae were twitching with a fury.

"Valerie, I don't understand what has happened to your position. But I won't tell HQ about this call. What I do know is that there is a ferocious battle within the Chinese leadership, British intelligence has been well and truly breached and my contact at the embassy is slain, with me escaping by a hairs breadth. I wasn't going to hang around in the country to be the next one to get a Chinese machete or bullet. I have covered my trail and I am following up the only lead I currently have."

"Have you been in touch with the office about your plans and movements?"

"No, as I say I have covered my trail. We both know they are working from within our set up, now how long would I last? The thing is Valerie, whose side are you really on?" Danny decided to confront the issue head on and he let the question hang accusingly to test her reaction.

There was no delay in the reply.

"Danny, Danny, believe me I haven't changed. I have not treasonable bone in my body. I would never ever work for a foreign power. There are some things I cannot share, but I need you to trust me and help." Her voice had a pleading quality to it, certainly a tone he had never heard from her before.

He lightened his voice to respond, "trust and obey, for there is no other way. It's just like I'm back at school assembly."

"Danny, I know you will help because if not by now, you would have put the phone down at the very least and perhaps sent the search hounds on my trail. Now to keep you up to date I also had to make a very quick exit under another identity. I am currently in Vancouver. I am staying down in its Chinatown. I got a lead just before I left from Li Hongzhi, who has picked up the baton from your erstwhile contact. See now Danny, I trust you with my location."

"Perhaps in our current predicament, trust is all we have left. Anyway what did you say? You mean Li Hongzhi of the Hammers. Oh he has got a lovely left foot. You're making me homesick for the great game. Don't tell me that football is coming home and it will save our bacon."

He heard a small laugh from the west coast of Canada.

"Yes, football of all things. Possibly for the first time football has produced something of use to me. His cover is still intact and he is so high profile that I think he will manage to avoid any nasty stuff, at least in the short term. And I have now assembled a few more pieces of the big puzzle. Danny now tell me if I am wrong. You are in France and there is some kind of get together of the prime movers involved in moving their strategy forward."

"Bang on target so far Valerie. Surprised you can't smell the Roquefort cheese wafting down the phone line. The meeting is by all accounts tomorrow. I not sure what good I can do. In fact it has crossed my mind that this should be the very last place to be in terms of my self-preservation."

"Danny, we both work for the security of Britain. Even if at the moment we have both had to flee from our own organisation. I know you can do something to help find us some information that will give us leverage to hopefully block or at least understand their game-plan or least put a serious spanner in their works. Just try and get as close as you can without leaving yourself at undue risk."

Danny chuckled, "undue risk. I will remember those two words. Undue risk; so okay the brief is accepted. I'll get back to you when I've got something. What will you do?"

"I need to get back to London because this is where I believe the heart of any action will take place. According to Li Hongzhi something is planned for London, something big, which will act as a touch paper for other actions around the world, which is probably why they needed to remove me by hook or by crook. I am trying to build some resources which will give us capacity to strike if an opportunity arises. If not then the consequences may be personally fatal and the freedom of our country may be lost, with who knows what impact on the rest of the free world. I honestly don't know about our chances."

"Valerie, don't talk to me about chances and odds, as I don't want to consider the length of them. I'll report back tomorrow, do you want me to ring this number?" Danny asked.

"Ring yes, but there will be a different mobile number inserted in a new email. It will only take a message. If all goes well I would like you to covertly return to London as soon as it is practical and be available for whatever I can pull together. Look out for someone in Russell Square carrying the previous day's copy of the Guardian. They'll be waiting in the Square for the next few afternoons. We haven't many days left. Sorry for the amateur cloak and dagger stuff, but we need to be very careful. Hope it goes well, and thanks for your support on this. It means a lot to be personally. I know what you must be feeling like being out on a limb."

"When you've supported Charlton Athletic as long as I have, I know how to hope against all the odds, and usually insurmountable odds."

Under the seasonal blue skies in a bleak industrial estate of Dagenham in one of the larger site units a phone rang.

"It's a call for you Frank. The Mayor's office."

"Hello, Cory Services can I help?"

"Yes this is Peter Thompson from the Mayor's office.

I need to speak to someone in charge of the Trafalgar Square refurbishments."

There was a slight nervous pause, "Ah, yes that's me. Frank Lockwood. Is there a problem?"

"Firstly, my name is Peter Thompson I report directly to the Mayor. A problem, oh yes, yes, you can certainly say there is a problem," his voice rose in a crescendo as he spoke.

"We are about to have the start of the 2012 Olympic games here in a week's time. And your firm has still got the largest column in Trafalgar Square still festooned with your scaffolding and covers."

"Ah, yes, well I....."

"This is just not good enough. I repeat not good enough. Now I do not have the time or the inclination to listen to any excuses. It must be sorted out immediately. Or else there will be financial penalties and I will personally ensure you and your organisation gets the bad press it deserves. And of course it will be last contract you'll ever get from the Mayor's office, and your company's name will be mud in local government. This not a threat, it is a promise."

"No, err yes. Understood, absolutely Mr Thompson, we'll sort it. Don't you worry that column will be ready. I'll be onto it as soon as I put the phone down. "

Frank Lockwood put the phone down turned his eyes to the ceiling and let out a growl of frustration, held the sides of his head with his hands and motioned to bang his head on his desk.

# 15

Reverend Quiltfloe was interrupted from work on his next Sunday sermon as he picked up the ringing telephone in the manse.

"What is it now?" He whispered under his breath.

"Oh, hello Emma, how are you? Yes I'm fine myself, now how can I help?"

As he listened his eyes widened and he held his chin thoughtfully. When he replied his voice showed his surprise.

"Well, err yes I suppose I can do it. But it's highly irregular, yes most irregular. Emma I don't mean to be personal but do you know what you are doing?"

The Reverend Quiltfloe fumbled for a pen, as he listened to her response, and proceeded to jot details into the large A4 size diary he kept next to the phone.

"As a friend you know I will help and as a Christian minister of course I support the course of action as a blessing from God. But it's so sudden."

His brow furrowed as he listened to the answer from the other end of the line. After a few ums and ahs, he managed to interject.

"Now don't worry I will not let you down. Of course I

will keep it under my hat if that is your wish. Now you need to bring the following…."".

Further south in the muggy air of the capital, in an office overlooking the Thames Keith Bigham, the acting head of British intelligence, scanned the screen of his top of the range laptop as he tried to stay on top of the incoming information from stations around the globe. A phrase popped into his head back from his earliest training about the loneliness of leadership. He wished he had a bit more energy in his lethargic limbs and he felt a sore throat coming on. Tasting his now tepid tea, he pursed his lips. He was acutely aware that his political masters would not overlook his risible attempt to take his former boss Valerie Garfoot into custody. From the barely suppressed smirks of the other intelligence officers he knew that currently he was a complete laughing stock at headquarters. It was a painfully sensitive issue and he wondered when, if ever, his reputation would be restored. He re-assured his bruised professional ego that no one could have predicted that she of all people would have pulled some stunt with a gas gun. Valerie Garfoot is a woman in her fifties, he consoled himself, and no one would have expected fireworks in her own office. If only he could manage to locate her whereabouts and do the necessary business, he knew his stock would surely rise again within the circles of power. How could she have been selling her country out? Bigham felt distinctly uneasy with his remit and he wrestled half-heartedly with his conscience that she should really face trial and allow the British people to see the traitor face her just desserts and mould her life away in a high-security prison, rather than the cold finality of the orders he had received at the highest level, to have her killed on sight. The thought of being eliminated weighed heavy on his spirit.

His stubby index finger deleted another time-wasting email from his system and then spun his chair round to contemplate the London skyline. At times of frustration like this he mentally clicked into his soothing routine, where he computed in his head his pension entitlements, the value of his house and the level of his relatively meagre savings and challenged himself to consider a downshifted early retirement in Mumbles, Wales, with its lovely coastal walks and pleasant beaches. It was one of several pipe-dreams that he regularly entertained in his thoughts. Before he had managed to finish his pension calculation there was a light tap on the door.

"Come in," he barked.

A young woman with her hair in a pony-tail came into the office with a single sheet of A4 paper in her hand.

"Good news chief. We have traced Garfoot to western Canada. In downtown Vancouver to be precise."

Bigham's solemn face creased into a wide grin.

"Canada, well I never. The Mounties always get their man! Or woman in this case. Are we completely certain?"

"Canadian intelligence were given a tip from within their Chinese community. Do you want me to ask them to move in?"

"Have we got anyone in the area?" asked Bigham, the smile no longer on his face. Opportunity knocks, he thought to himself.

"Yes I believe we have two of our people in the area they have been working on surveillance of some Sikh extremists based in the city. Cucksey and Westerman, both very experienced with firearms," she replied.

"Right, I need their direct line, I need to give them some explicit instructions. Ensure that the Canadians cover all possible escape routes from the city; we need the place sealed. Tell them this is the absolute highest priority. I, I mean we, cannot afford another mistake."

She forced herself not to allow a smirk to show; it was an item of office gossip between a number of staff who had known that Bigham had been bested by Valerie Garfoot when he had tried to apprehend her. The tale had still continued to gain a level of mirth amongst the cynical band of intelligence officers. They liked to extract the maximum mileage from any mess up, especially one which involved the two bosses.

"Right, I'll get their number for you and impress it upon the Canadians the importance of the operation."

"I don't need to remind you that this is urgent," Bigham added unnecessarily turning his eyes back to his screen.

Keith Bigham felt a ticklish dryness in his mouth and he made his way to his water cooler and felt buoyed up by the news for the service and his own career; who knows he might no longer be only acting as Head of British Intelligence. The sip of water tasted remarkably refreshing.

In the less-polluted and less-populated country air of south west France Danny had managed to easily locate the venue for the proposed gathering. His late contact in London had given him the date and French town, and it was here that he needed to monitor events in case it offered any clues to what was being put together at his country's expense. He wondered if the information has been correct as this very small town seemed to be the dead-end to nowhere; he had only sighted one old woman carrying a stick of bread heading home for lunch. Just outside the village there was a small stadium with tiered seating on three sides, presumably used for local sporting events. He drove a bit further on and then wandered back to find the stadium completely shut and locked-up and like the rest of the place deserted. More like a large English village than a town he thought; a place for farm workers and the retired. Strange place to use he kept telling himself. After a couple of circuits around the site he vaulted himself over one of the fences and made his way to the centre of the grass pitch. There were no markings so it appeared to be in disuse for regular sporting events. Seen better grounds in the Ryman League than this Danny laughed to himself, whilst scanning for anything that could indicate corroboration with the information which had brought him here. The football posts had been removed and there was a simple, rudimentary stage and rows of folding wooden seats on the pitch facing the stage. Could be a village meeting or livestock show; however it was all Danny had to go on and he quickly placed his listening gear in a suitable spot in the staging. Looking around the empty stadium he felt slightly chilled and unnerved by the emptiness of the place.

Could be wasting my time completely he wondered to himself? It certainly felt wrong; there were no positive vibes that the meet could be held here.

Looking out from the stage he could see the local tower of the church with what appeared to be a balcony offering a first class but safely remote free view of the stage. The distance of two hundred or so metres would still allow him a good view through his binoculars.

Looks like an early morning start getting in position on the church tower, he told himself, as he made his way back to his hire car. He felt a sinking feeling about this intelligence and wondered if he had been given the wrong place or the protagonists had moved locations, because who in their right minds would consider using this one chevaux town, especially a group who were allegedly trying to grasp the reins of the Chinese dragon to breath its oriental firepower against the rest of the world. If nothing happened tomorrow, it was all bets off and he would have to inform Valerie that he had been wasting his time. With this avenue closed it would back to London to see what Valerie was planning. And he hoped she wasn't planning the demise of her former Russell Square date.

# 16

Kevin Scotton was beginning to feel thoroughly at ease with the surprisingly small numbers of correspondence and reports that he had been asked to look at. He kept reminding himself that he must really grasp this opportunity to demonstrate that at the very highest position of power in Britain he was a safe and respected pair of hands. He knew how quickly you could change in the media and public eye from the sublime to the ridiculous or indeed from a Stalin to a Mr Bean. Scotton felt a degree of restlessness and wondered whether he should he be out cutting a dash somewhere rather than holed up in a dreary back office in Whitehall. If only his parents had still been alive to see their son leading the country, performing on the world stage and, if Alex, doesn't pull round soon, he would be gracing all the front pages during all the Olympic bash. A new suit and a visit to his hairdresser must be booked in; Scotton's personal vanity was never far from the surface.

The red light on his desk phone lit up signifying an incoming call. He carefully picked up the receiver.

"Kevin, hello it is I." Scotton immediately recognised the mellifluous tones of the Cabinet Secretary.

"Ah Sir Peter. Any news of Alex?"

"Yes, he is thankfully on the mend and he says he just

needs another couple of days away and then he can come back and pick up the reins. I will be spending a short time with him as we are just in the process of tidying up the details on the new constitutional policy. I confirm he will be back for the Olympic reception for European leaders and other VIP's at the Commons on Friday."

"But Sir Peter if Alex isn't up to it, am I to be on standby? I can be ready to stand in at short notice," queried Scotton hopefully.

"Not necessary I assure you. Safe to say both Alex and I have been hearing excellent reports of your efforts whilst guiding the ship of state. I am sure you have noticed that some of the more insightful lobby correspondents are suggesting that you might be the man to build on the foundation laid by Alex. You've taken to the role as a duck to water. May I be as bold to suggest that you could well end up in Number Ten at this rate?"

Scotton allowed himself a small smug grin in the seclusion of the office.

"Well Sir Peter you know I am just serving the interests of the country. My personal ambitions will always be secondary."

"Quite, quite. Now Alex is concerned that we have heard no news about the Garfoot problem. If this issue gets out our allies will need re-assuring that she hasn't compromised western intelligence to the Russian bear. It would help if you put some pressure on Bigham to get an early result. If he doesn't, I suggest he is replaced at the double. Remember he failed to arrest the woman in her own office. If Garfoot is apprehended sooner rather than later, it would reflect well on you since it was resolved during your watch. Since the demise of Emma Darbyshire you really are in pole position in terms of succession planning."

"Sir Peter, message understood I'll get right on to it."

Scotton felt a surge of enthusiasm to give a right royal rocket to Bigham and to get this Garfoot matter finally and decisively settled. Bigham's cage needed a really good rattling, because this was damn well affecting his own career ambitions. He was now truly incentivised following Sir Peter's gentle career hints and blatant political carrot dangling.

Immediately after the call with Sir Peter, Scotton was put through to Bigham on a secure line. Both men were in a similar predicament as they were each currently acting up into posts that were the summit of their personal aspirations, both aware that their own number one dream job could be taken from them at any moment. They both were acutely aware that it was a case of trying to scramble up to the pinnacle of the greasy career pole. Opportunity had knocked, big time.

"Ah Bigham, it's Kevin Scotton here. I urgently need to know if we have closed off this dreadful Garfoot business," Scotton tried to use his strong, resolute tone.

Bigham, barely containing his excitement, replied, "excellent news to report. You could not have timed your call better. We have an active operation underway which should hopefully be over within the next two hours. Without divulging any operational and tactical details we appear to have our quarry firmly within our sights. Yes, literally within our sights."

After the call ended Kevin Scotton reflected on the news and leant back in his office chair and then sprung up heading for a celebratory malt from the drinks cabinet.

Over in the French countryside, and as they say in Olde England, just as the sun was rising, Danny was making his way after leaving his small hire car over to the attractive medieval church building. He was carrying slung over his shoulder his large black North Face rucksack that contained his food and drink for the day, also including his headphones to listen into the electronic bug he had attached onto the stage and his high-powered binoculars. The outer door of the church wasn't locked which allowed him easy access towards the inner door. Once inside he saw a ladder which enabled him to make his way up the small tower, and then through a small wooden door onto the parapet. The air was degrees cooler higher up and Danny slightly shivered at the drop in temperature, being higher up and exposed to the fresh breeze. I could freeze or burn up here he thought to himself, musing on the two extremes, as he enjoyed the view offered from his new position. First things first, he reminded himself, check the gear. The bug was okay as it was even picking up the early morning bird chorus. He trained his binoculars on the stage and some areas around the small stadium; the viewing point was near enough perfect. Danny managed to shuffle himself into a reasonably comfortable spot using his rucksack as a cushion; he then prepared to wait. Maybe catch up my sleep quota he thought, as he closed his eyes, no longer able to see the glorious French countryside with its field upon field of golden sunflowers. It was a wonderful sight and could have easily graced a Monet oil painting. He thought it could have been a heck of a lot worse, such as a grey and drizzly Friday night fixture away to Bolton Wanderers watching Charlton slithering in the mud; the glorious mud of England to yet another honourable but predictable defeat. He knew that if today was a no-show then at least he would soon be back across the Channel on the double.

Several thousand miles over the Atlantic in the west of Canada, Vancouver stands as the spectacular gateway city to the wide and beautiful Pacific Ocean. Just beyond the main city centre streets a black Toyota turned out of the brisk and free flowing traffic and pulled up in a parking slot against the sidewalk. Two athletic looking men, perhaps in their early to mid fifties, with close cropped hair exited their car; at the same time they professionally scanned the street both ways. They then walked over to a group of three men standing near to a closed office entrance.

"Hey are you the British? Westerman and Cucksey?"

"We are indeed matey. And you are the Canadians finest?"

The two men from the Toyota were in the service of British intelligence in North America. Quick nods of affirmation followed by smiles and hands being quickly shaken.

"Pleased to meet you. Thanks for all the work on this one. Our target in place?" asked Westerman, who had a plain black shoulder bag carrying something of weight, the shape bulging the bag's sides.

"Yes indeedy. Our man with the telescopic lens on the building over there, he can see her, she appears to be enjoying watching TV."

"Well thanks for all your help. We just need all your team to melt away for an hour and then let the local police discover what we leave"

"Maybe one day you'll let us into the full story. Anyhows, glad to be helping out the limey secret service. You owe us a few beers, Anyway we've double checked and she is in Apartment 634 entrance second left around the corner. You sure you know the target? We don't want any innocent Canadians caught up in your hunting expedition."

"No fears there," replied Cucksey. "We always do our homework."

"We've disabled the lock on the front, just push it and you're in the building. Just make sure you don't involve any innocent parties. No collateral damage please, this is Canadian soil. Be seeing you guys."

"Don't worry we won't embarrass your government. And when we get the beers in make sure you get some friendly Canadian girls to come and drink with us."

The Canadian officer issued an order on his radio to his team to disengage as the British had come to finalise business. The three of them waved their hands as they climbed into a SUV with darkened windows and pulled off into a gap in the traffic.

"Showtime!" announced Cucksey to Westerman, patting whatever he was carrying under his jacket. It had over a score of years since they had both seen service as teenagers in the Parachute Regiment as they had engaged Argentinean forces on the windswept bog of a place called the Falkland Islands or the Malvinas, depending on which hemisphere you lived in.

They briskly moved around the corner. Their practised gazes were viewing all surrounding buildings, alert as old scarred alley cats. They were both dressed casually wearing dark fleeces, jeans and sports trainers. Cucksey had a baseball cap that he pulled tightly forward, which would no doubt preserve his anonymity against any camera recording.

They were soon outside the heavy racing-green door of the apartment block and as informed they gently pushed it inwards, it moved freely due to the pre-preparation of their Commonwealth intelligence buddies. Once inside they quickly weighed up the options, Apartment 634 was on the sixth floor. One would take the elevator and one would take the stairs and both meet outside 634. They didn't want their target slipping from their clutches.

Westerman hoisted his shoulder bag which signalled

he was having the elevator as he had the weight to carry. Cucksey raised is eyes in mock disappointment and started up the stairs.

As the elevator doors opened a tiny elderly woman, possibly just under-five foot tall, in a ruby red overcoat, which had seen better days, stepped out pulling behind her a tartan covered shopping trolley.

"Good evening young man," she confidently greeted Westerman, who smoothly turned into the elevator as he replied, "evening Ma'am", keeping his back to her as the lift doors closed. He pressed for the sixth floor and let a low whistle out of his lips, whilst he leant back against the lift wall.

Westerman left the elevator on the sixth floor and waited half a minute and he nodded to Cucksey, who was just coming up the sixth floor stairwell. The corridor was empty and the whole place had the appearance of a middle-class apartment block which was due an expensive makeover to cheer up its pervading dowdiness; it was as tired looking as the old woman's tartan shopping trolley. No words were now needed between the two operatives as Cucksey moved along the corridor and pointed out the target's door of 634. He then gestured for Westerman to take the fire escape door. The plan they had worked out on the car ride prior to meeting the Canadian agents was to see if they could get the door covered while one of them took the fire escape, to seal their quarry in. If one of them could get a clear shot from the fire escape there would be no need to force the door. It was better to be neat and tidy and not to frighten any Canadian horses.

Westerman made his way out onto the fire escape and seeing the rears of the apartments were numbered, presumably for emergency services access, enabled him to quickly locate 634. Being high up on the sixth floor didn't faze him, as a spot of vertigo would be the least thing to unnerve him.

He kept his body low and kept glancing over the street to see if he was being observed by someone in another apartment. The British agent lowered his bag and removed the short stock high precision sniper rifle. In less than ten seconds he had screwed the silencer onto the front of his rifle; Phaser not on stun. The agent was utterly confident in his shooting accuracy, evidenced by his fifteen years of near-daily dedication to the target range. As usual he felt the surge of adrenaline which he felt before any action, but it didn't make him jittery or his movements clumsy; he welcomed the invigorating rush as an old friend.

As he gripped the matt black metal of lethal weaponry he stretched his fingers to keep them supple. Westerman edged to the large window bay for apartment 634. He felt his luck was in as the main window was up at the bottom leaving him room to get his head and weapon through if the target was clear to be hit. The babbling noise from the television drifted out into the summer air. Westerman crouched forward and leaned across to get just his right eye with a view of the room. It was a large open plan layout of a room; he could see the back of Garfoot's head about ten or twelve feet away as she watched the television from the sofa. There was no sign of anyone else in the apartment. Westerman felt no moral problem about the authorised slaying, and of a woman to boot Even though neither of them had ever killed anyone outside a recognised battle zone; orders are orders. His previous training in the Parachute regiment and subsequent transfer to the Special Air Services, prior to his current employment with MI6, had made a potential state tool of frightening precision and ruthlessness. All he knew were his orders and that Garfoot threatened the security of British intelligence assets, she was also presumed to be dangerous and possibly backed up by Russian muscle. Concentrating he realised that he might need to fire as necessary about the apartment from this vantage point if his shots brought out other unknown occupants from within, including any Russian trouble.

Westerman in one deft movement quickly brought the rifle up to firing position. The laser guideline danced for a second or two on the back of her skull. He gently the squeezed the trigger and fired three rounds in quick succession with the target falling straight down behind the sofa. Three fatal bulls-eyes in the back of her head; the small noise from the silenced rifle would not have disturbed any immediate neighbour. Then he immediately pulled away from his position and made his way back down the fire escape landing to link up with Cucksey. Mission accomplished. Now it was time for several satisfying pints of Moosehead beer and some relaxing female Canuck company.

# 17

Emma Darbyshire braced herself for the questions that would start to fly, and even though she had acquired a reasonable mastery of the politician's art of deft deflection when it came to difficult questions. She knew her assistant deserved better and also that Harriet would not let her off the hook so easily. Emma also realised that she didn't know how she could make it sound in the slightest sense a reasonable or justifiable course of action.

"I cannot, just cannot believe it. Right, Emma this has to be explanation time! Here and now. Spill those beans." Harriet rounded on Emma Darbyshire, when they stepped through the front door of Emma's house.

"I know. I don't really think I can explain," replied Emma as she fell back onto the welcome softness of the well-worn chintzy fabric of her sofa.

Harriet took a chair opposite and fixed her friend and employer with her trademark 'don't bull me look' and waited for some meaning, some plausible explanation in the beyond bizarre turn of events.

"I know it's out of character but I have good feeling about it. Heaven knows Harriet I am due my share of some good feelings. Don't I deserve that?"

"Emma, I am still trying to get my cranium round this one. For starters and in no particular order, what on earth do you think your constituents will think? And can you imagine the field day the papers will have over it. Apart from the Olympics, they are short of news. A gift for the silly season, but wait, hark I hear breaking news in the media famine for stories. The MP for Lincoln has come up with a fantastic free gift for news editors that will fill the column inches and airwaves."

"Well perhaps they won't find out for a while. I am not exactly planning a press launch. Perhaps I am not as newsworthy as you think, now I am merely a backbencher and out of the government."

"Good. Good. Your sense of humour is still intact. That's important, you must hold onto that Emma; although my sense of the ridiculous is being sorely stretched at the moment. For a while I was beginning to think you were well down the doolally road. Is this a new campaign to put Lincoln on the map? A crazy stunt? When the news breaks it will be over the internet like a viral marketing strategy."

"You how much I think of you and the work you do. I don't want you dragged into any embarrassing publicity. You must know that. I am sorry Harriet but I can't come up with any real reason for all of this. My heart just led me to accept and get on with it."

"Your heart led you, Emma that is absolutely nowhere near a good enough explanation. I need a satisfactory reason for all of this." Harriet's voice turned up a few notches on her well-practised incredulous tone.

She continued, "you have known him less time than it takes to get my hair done at Salon Marique. Emma, I didn't want to use the word, but I'm gonna have to. Rebound. Rebound. Reeebound! The divorce, then the sacking from the deputy leadership, hitting the old stressometer hard.

You've just jumped at the first thing. And I don't want to cruel. But who is he? A well-mannered homeless person, a drifter might be more charitable. Who has fallen in with the Nomad charity. He's disabled with his arm and who knows what other health problems."

Emma stared blankly towards the window.

"Actually he is also blind in one of his eyes."

"I didn't know that but look I am really sorry Emma I didn't mean to be hurtful about him and about what you have decided to do. Now I've a friend, Ann, who is a top-notch therapist," said Harriet.

"I'll bear the couch sessions in mind. Harriet, I know it looks strange and impossible to understand but I think I am beginning to love him and at this time I need and I want to be with to be with him. I know I'm not making an awful lot of sense. There's something else."

Harriet falls backwards playing at fainting onto the other sofa.

Her playacting brought a smile to Emma's face.

"We need to go to London there is something important about to happen. Please will you help me?"


Danny opened his eyes open at the sound of vehicle engines as the first of a number of large 4 x 4 vehicles with blacked-out windows began to draw up into the car park outside the small empty stadium. It was still early morning, just after seven am, and he began to watch the scene unfold from his eyrie in the church tower. A group of dark-suited and thick set men had emerged from the vehicles and had set about opening the main gates to allow vehicles to drive right through to the tiered wooden seating arranged in front of the stage. They moved in a co-ordinated fashion and Danny noted their organisational efficiency; by their polished actions they had the words top of the line security written all over them. As he surveyed the scene which was being acted out below him he was still unsure what would happen although his adrenaline began to flow as his late contact's information had not proved inaccurate. Romagne, a one croissant town, was bang on the nail.

Using his binoculars he turned slightly to see five or six dusty minibuses pull up and then after a brief chat with the advance crew, each drove through the open gates. All the vehicles windows was blacked out and Danny could see the lead guard of heavies start to fan out around inside the stadium and its entrance, and taking up what appeared to be a number of pre-programmed security positions. With this level of professional security it was clearly beyond the best in class French donkey competition final, Danny thought to himself.

Danny checked the control on his listening piece, nothing coming through apart from the ambient sounds of the stadium. No one had yet stood on the stage. Danny was beginning to think the device would prove to be a waste of time. He could now see a group of passengers emerging from the minibuses; well-dressed, suited, he noted. Each group was escorted by a couple of the security types who seemed to be taking their roles very, very seriously. With the powerful focus of his binoculars he could even see that the protection mob were all wearing earpieces and moved with a near-swaggering ease. Although to Danny, there appeared to be very little need for this level of security, as this place was virtually deserted. Someone had decided to take no chances.

His gaze was transferred to another the approach of another vehicle, pulling what looked like a horse trailer. It stopped outside the stadium and Danny watched as the driver led out a strong looking white horse from the rear of the trailer. The horse looked a magnificent beast and it made an imperious shake of its head, although Danny's equine interests had usually been restricted to those carrying his bet at Southwell or Haydock. It was already saddled and it had a handler holding the reins and gently stroking its head to keep it calm. The handler walked the white horse to the open gates of the stadium, stopped and waited there.

Danny turned his attention to the passengers discharged from the fleet of vehicles who were now taking seats in the small wooden tiered seating facing the stage. He could only see the back of their heads; Danny could only pick out two women in the group. As he fixed his binoculars on one of them, she turned to say something to the man sitting next to her. She turned fully round to her left, and her face then came into a clear view.

"Gerda Hoffmann, Gerda Hoffmann." Danny whispered incredulously to himself. He was taken aback that Gerda Hoffmann, the German leader, was here. Whatever was going on was political dynamite. He had backed the winning nag on this tip.

# 18

"Oh yes indeed. Lake Louise was stunning, truly stunning and then we went to Lake Moraine and rode the gondola up Sulphur Mountain. We can't wait to see all our video footage. And how was your holiday?"

Valerie Garfoot smiled good-naturedly as she made herself comfortable on the overnight flight from Calgary to Manchester. "I've just been visiting my niece who lives in Canmore. It's a wonderful area. I do so love the Rocky Mountains. Did you have a soak in the Banff hot springs? It is absolutely glorious," her gentle, but less than truthful, chat with her passenger neighbour on the Air Canada flight was not too onerous and later she was able to catch a few hours sleep, amid the meal trays, kids crying, and the general feeling of dehydration in the confined space of a Boeing 747 transatlantic jet. Valerie Garfoot was in for the ling haul in more ways than one.

She was now travelling under another false passport aided and abetted by a change of hairstyle and hair colour; and since she was no longer safe in Vancouver, she felt her only option was to fly back to where the next real decisive events would unfold. Several times her mind ran over and over the turn of events and she acknowledged she had, in one fell swoop, gone from predator to prey. She remembered a phrase her late father used to recite to her, 'dare to be a Daniel, dare to stand alone, dare to have a purpose firm, dare to make it known.' Perhaps her faith would now be sorely tested as she flew towards the lion's den of London. She needed her father's simple, but strong faith now. Faith, hope and love, abide these three. Tonight, she told herself it was hope, hope against the odds, she would cling to.

The holidaying couple next to her were so excited about their Canadian holiday adventure that they could never have comprehended in a million light years that they were sitting next to the former head of British Intelligence. Who at this very moment was being pursued by parties who she believed, against standard departmental policy, would be authorised to use lethal force to stop her. As the short social chitchat drew to a close and the flight purred on she wondered how long Canadian or British agents would take to find the mannequin propped on the sofa dressed in her clothes crowned with a not unflattering wig. She hoped in one sense that they would enjoy the humour of it; although she hadn't bargained on bullet holes piercing the plastic body shape and those bullets had been fired in the expectation that it had been her. In fact it was several hours later that the Canadian Police were breaking down the door of Apartment 634 to find the shattered plastic skull of a shop-window mannequin. The episode provided a rich seam of black humour to mine for the Canadian officers in the know. Valerie Garfoot closed her eyes and thought of her darling Leo and how she had to keep going for him. Would she ever be able to share the rest of her life with him? Perhaps this was a crossroads moment, leaving her with two distinct choices. First, reach Leo and run and hide to save my skin. Or take the harder road and try, even if it proves futile, to try and destabilise the attempt to snatch away British sovereignty. Leo's image faded in her mind as she thought of Danny and what, if indeed anything worth while, was happening over in France. It crossed her mind that her likeable junior colleague Danny may end up losing his life in this dangerous quicksand that they were both were being sucked down into. She thought the powers behind these events were probably too big to stop, at this stage and hopefully a more organised resistance will emerge later. What on earth was she kidding Danny about, by meeting in London, to do precisely what? She didn't know, and she knew that improvisation was not her greatest talent. A thick splinter of doubt entered her thoughts about whether Danny would take the easier road back to working for the department and thus seeking to help her apprehension. She felt a new sensation of complete and numbing impotence and Valerie Garfoot had known the, occasionally pleasurable, feel when you held and cracked the powerful state reins of power. Overcoming her tiredness, her medical needs, her fear for her own safety, her lack of power and dearth of deployable resources, she looked out into the black night, probably somewhere over the emptiness of Greenland; she felt a small voice of calm which told her to stand by her responsibility to the nation. It was a call of duty, which she had never felt so keenly, even when she had scaled the many hierarchies of the civil service. Her first priority at Manchester airport, after safely negotiating passport control, was a new supply of the medicine she desperately needed.

"Come in, it's good to see you both. Yes, Emma told me you wanted a chat. Please, please take a seat."

Ace and Tom both took a chair in the comfortable lounge at the Reverend Quiltfloe's manse.

"Tea, which I have on good authority, is on its way," said

Reverend Quiltfloe with a kindly smile.

"Now tell me how can I help?"

There was a short embarrassed silence as the Reverend Quiltfloe looked to Ace and Tom in succession to see who would speak.

Ace began," do you enjoy Shakespeare, Reverend?"

"Now that it what they call it today's parlance, a curveball of a question. Um yes, although I would not quite place myself in the scholar category. It was probably way back in my schooldays when I was forced to study his pieces. I suppose like most of us, I could probably stump up a few of the famous quotes. I've probably had most of my knowledge knocked out of me with all the rugger I've played."

Tom looked on and wondered where this was leading; it had the makings of a very long and slow evening. Why did Ace want to discuss literature? As it was Tom was still coming to terms with the whirlwind romance between his friend and the local MP.

Ace continued unabashed, "there is a piece from King John. I think it goes something like this. 'This England never did, nor never shall, lie at the proud foot of a conqueror. Come the three corners of the world in arms, and we shall shock them. Nought shall make us rue, if England to itself be true.'"

"Ah, very, very stirring. Do you want to discuss English literature? As I said I'm not really that conversant with the finer details," queried the Reverend.

He was glad at the moment for his wife, to break the slightly tense atmosphere, to set the tray of tea down for them.

"Now please help yourselves. Don't be too polite not to have a biscuit or two."

Ace returned to the Reverend's question, "no, not literature but perhaps more in the line of theology."

Tom helped himself to tea, and he couldn't resist a custard cream, and felt he should just let the talk go over his head and just enjoy the refreshments and the doze-inducing qualities of the comfy chair. Although he felt confidence in his friend and he would stand by him in most situations. Tom was still nonplussed by the strange turn of events where Ace was now apparently committed to Lincoln, after taking a wife. Who could have predicted that? A homeless man, with one arm and one reasonable eye, marries a Member of flaming Parliament. Tom reasoned if he hadn't been going through this sober patch he might have put it all down to an alcohol-fuelled dream.

"Theology ah well. The study of God, well I think I am a bit stronger in that area. My home ground as it were."

"Remember Reverend when our Lord said He was the Resurrection and the Life."

The Reverend nodded, but wondered where this was all leading, first Shakespeare then theology. It was not the normal fare of cosy manse chats with parishioners.

"And do you believe it is a sin to covet?"

Ace brushed with his left hand an imaginary speck of dust from his trousers.

Tom continued to gaze into space holding his cup of tea.

"Well Horace, it is one of the Ten Commandments. Do not covet, but perhaps today the word of jealously may be more a bit more understandable today. Yes, yes it is surely a sin."

"Then I confess Sir, for if it be a sin to covet glory, then I am the most offending soul alive."

"Most offending soul alive, well I'm sure that's a bit over the top. But Horace I am sure the Lord understands your heart and mind on this matter. Our Lord forgives those who come to him in repentance," replied the Reverend with a slightly quizzical look on his face, as he took a sip of tea, which he hoped would calm his distinct feeling of unease over the direction of the conversation.

"Thank you those words are a comfort. I know He calls on each of us to do good works but He appears to have chosen me to do works over an inordinate length of time; over many, many years. But I am merely an instrument in His hands. Kirby as a minister, do you believe in the resurrection?"

"Of course, of course the Christian faith would not exist without it. It is the fulcrum of history, the ultimate sacrifice and the resurrection of our Lord. His victory over sin and death."

Ace, ignoring the tea that had been provided, continued, "but do you believe, really believe, in the resurrection of believers?"

"Certainly. Each believer, following the sacrificial death of Christ, will be free from the sentence of sin. So yes, we all have a resurrection through Him."

"Could you imagine our Lord bringing back people from the other side to ensure evil doesn't triumph over good?"

The Reverend Quiltfloe grimaced, "bring back? Back from the dead? Well, I'm not sure on that one. He brought back Lazarus from death to demonstrate his divinity. Well Horace we seem to be exploring some very speculative areas of theological questions. I suppose ultimately, and pardon the cliché, but He does move in different ways for His plans to unfold. Our understanding of His plans is, I suppose like our own frail bodies, is very limited and inadequate. Through all my years as a minister I have come to a conclusion that you cannot second guess God, you can't just put Him in a box. In some ways history shows and it also chimes with some parts of my experience; that He seems to positively delight in using the very lowest and humblest to deliver His unfolding drama in this world of ours. Frankly, He can just use the oddest of people. Yes the very oddest."

The Reverend Quiltfloe could see that Tom was not paying the slightest attention and had switched off, probably had never even switched on to start with, to the ebb and flow of the conversation.

Ace responded, "that's very true Reverend, our Lord has cast many strange actors in this earthly play. Perhaps I hadn't mentioned it before but my late father was himself a minister and had a small rural parish in county of Norfolk"

At the mention of Norfolk Tom came back from his mental slumber, but he had to resist the temptation, that mischievously sprung up his mind, to utter the terrible cliché, 'more tea vicar?'

# 19

Danny took a fast swig of water from his plastic bottle as the tension of the scene had begun to dry his mouth. The temperature of the air was rising as the time headed towards mid morning. He watched with rapt concentration as two more vehicles, with similarly opaque windows, had pulled up next to the horse trailer and the majestically impressive white horse. Aware of some kind of movement in the stadium, he glanced back to the staged area and saw that they had managed to site two small public address speakers on the stage. Then as he focussed his sight through the binoculars he watched as, even at this distance, the obvious charms of an attractive dark haired young woman who was now standing in the centre of the stage; he could also make out that she was wearing a radio microphone. He hadn't seen her presence earlier. Danny maintained his gaze on her as he leant his body down towards the speaker to catch any of the announcements.

The young woman on the stage moved up and down the platform beaming a huge smile and holding both her hands outstretched towards the thirty or so people looking on from the tiered seating.

She began in French, then, repeated in English, German

and what Danny knew to be Mandarin Chinese.

"Most excellent distinguished guests, welcome. We are meeting today here in France to witness a momentous event. It is time for revelation, a time for hope personified, a time for action. Action rightly defeating and disposing of the dead hand of inertia. A time to pull back the curtains that have shrouded a great mystery. I mention that we are gathered here together in France, but what is France? France, yes it is a country of great culture and learning. But, is it no more than the footstool to raise up his glory so the four corners of the earth can see and benefit from the just and efficient rule to come? The achievements of what we now call France will be multiplied by legions. You here today represent some of the highest echelons of the civilised world. You have maintained government over the barbarians and the lawless who try to drag us back to the laws of the jungle and the dung heap. But now you as the custodians of power will rise and unite in a new world compact. Under the direction and rule of the strong one who will enable the world to harvest its true and vast potential. Our gift to the world will be more famous than the other French gift to the United States of the Statue of Liberty, but this living, breathing statue will be global, standing proud and unbowed in all the great cities of each continent. It will celebrate and remind people that the true line of authority has returned; the greatest yet humblest of public servants. It has been nearly two hundred years since the very embodiment of action walked amongst us."

Danny tried to keep the odd note in his pad as she went into the translations. What was she babbling on about, he thought, it was like a new age blather session for some mystical guru? Why didn't they use a proper auditorium, he could not fathom it one iota. But it was sure as oeufs are oeufs; something major was going on, why else would the German leader be here in the French rural outback listening to the woman babbling on about a new world compact, whatever that was. He strained at the English sections coming through his receiver, the words sometimes being lost in the breeze. She continued.

"As you all know when the possessor of the emperor gene, the most, great Napoleon defeated the Mamalukes at the battle of the Pyramids in 1798. He was then initiated by the keepers of the Egyptian sacred mysteries into the mystical powers of the Pharoahnic dynasty. During which time he had ecstatic carnal relations with a chosen slave virgin brought from the Far East. That communion was not in vain. This was the secret glittering zenith of Napoleon's life. History, as recorded in conventional wisdom, describes him as an eventual failure. He was consigned to Elba and St Helena. But the history as recorded has failed to see that the great one secured his greatest triumph, not on the battlefields of Europe or in the making of grand treaties and alliances. This was his real legacy, securing the line of heredity. The gene carrier returned to the east and in specially selected relationships has led to the return of the emperor to lead this world in a rule of great authority, which will sweep away feeble, frail and hollow democracies and dictatorships. In our age of great moral and political flaccidity, I give you the vigorous and vital, the audacious and authoritative, the wise and the warrior. I present to you the unifier, the power to fuse together the Occident and Orient, the magnificent Napoleon, the new Napoleon."

As she spoke several from the audience cheered and stepped forward and unfurled national flags which they placed on the ground in front of the stage, he could make out the French, German, Japanese, Russian flags along with the Stars and Stripes and the European Union flag. His view of the front of the stage was now partially restricted as the audience were now on their feet. The young woman looked to be beaming with joy at the procession of flags strewn on the ground.

Danny had been so engrossed in the strange spectacle in the small stadium that he had only just noticed that the white horse was now being led through the gate, and he could just see the back of the rider. His immediate impression was of a shortish-looking male with striking coal black hair. He wondered just what kind of Napoleonic historical re-enactment event he had under surveillance. The assembled body rose as one as the horse and rider, with an imperious strut, made its way around to the front of the stage. The rider held out his left hand to the cheerleader on the stage, whom proceeded to greedily kiss the outstretched hand. Danny could now see the rider as he moved round. It was a young man, possibly in his thirties, and to his surprise he appeared, like Danny himself, to be part Chinese or south-east Asian and part European. The silent rider's face was unsmiling, but even at this distance, Danny felt the steely determination exuding from the features of the centre of attention. Miss multi-lingual herself piped up again, as the audience returned to their seats.

"Thanks to your loyal support to our new world authority we will be able to move swiftly and decisively. The age of technology will ease our efforts and will enable us not to resort to crude and expensive warfare between nations. Now will be a time when all in our world will have basic access to food, water, shelter and education; it is his own personal desire to bring resources to each and all. The grateful citizens oppressed by dictators, greed, unjust trading and squabbling governments will rise in support for the Napoleonic line. Our priority is to take the reins of power without major bloodshed and ensuring that the days of order will be established at speed. Very soon the whole world will see the new Napoleon and with delicious irony the first to publicly bow the knee will be the British monarch and her pitiable leaders." Her voice rose with the last sentence, which seemed to inspire the loudest applause of the event.

She continued, "in just a mere two days time we will be at the famous Houses of Parliament in London and there the main powers of the European Union and the new emerging Chinese leadership group will announce to the world that the days of order have begun. At the head of the new order will be Napoleon, who will act as sole executive decision maker. Our friends in other strategic governments will deploy their resources as planned to maximise support for this change. Do not be surprised as a number of fast-moving coups occur around the globe, which may require some limited but absolutely necessary terminations of reactionary power holders. The United Nations will be reformed as the New World Directorate, which will implement all executive decisions."

Danny swallowed hard as he tried to take in the apparent lunatic outpourings of the woman on the stage, who appeared to be the voice of the silent and grimly fierce looking rider on the horse. He had always thought that the Napoleon complex was only applied half-humorously to aggressive short houses. Danny would have gladly dismissed the event as a gathering of power-seeking fantasists, save for the fact the information had come from his murdered contact and it was taking place in front of the political leader of the German nation.

The mistress of multi-lingual ceremonies raised her right hand in a Roman-style salute to the rider, who was the centre of attention as the descendant of Napoleon Bonaparte and was apparently on some far-fetched mission of global domination.

"At the start of the 2012 Olympics, the watching world will see and know, and then my friends, they will follow our leader into a glorious future."

The audience vigorously clapped. Danny, through his binoculars, focussed for a second on the white horse and rider and caught sight of the horse defecating and it was onto one of the flags strewn in front of the stage. To his mild annoyance it was the Union Jack. Danny had never been precious about such symbols of national pride. But then one of the audience, at the front noticed the same thing, jumped up and down cheering, waving his arms in exultation at the unintentional disrespect to Britain. The man then turned, with a beaming face to those on either side of him, as if to push the point home. Danny could now see his face. It was Alex Haye, the Prime Minister of Britain. The shock froze the blood in his veins, Danny's sighting was absolute positive and he knew he was not mistaken. The presence of the German leader now made some twisted sense as a confirmation. The bizarre scene had so caught him be surprise that Danny had straightened up from his crouching position for a brief moment.

The morning sun glinted off the edge of the old church catching his binoculars and one of the dark suited security goon's attention was drawn up to the church tower and he whispered into his communications device. Danny immediately saw that he had been spotted and was already vaulting down the stairs, bouncing off the walls; and in a matter of seconds had got his small Renault started and headed full steam out of Romagne. The adrenaline was pumping on turbo-chargers through his system as he swung out into the unfamiliar French country roads, with his accelerator foot to the floor. He had no need to return to his lodgings and decided to set off directly to Poitiers airport. Nervously flicking his eyes into the rear-view mirror, he was feverishly checking whether he had anyone in pursuit. The fear gripping him did not allow any other thoughts than to get a flight, just anywhere from this gathering.

As he turned a bend he caught sight of the front of a black vehicle following behind. Danny knew instantaneously, even with his foot full down to the floor, that he could not outrun whatever was chasing, so he decided to swing off through the small hedge and into a field of sunflowers. There was a dull thud as he went over the bank and through the hedge of the field. The Renault ploughed forward, pushing down the wall of flowers with their large yellow plate-like heads turned towards the sun. The farmer or anyone wanting to take a Monet- like picture of the harvest would not be pleased with the track he was now furrowing. Danny now felt his shirt darkening with sweat, and he wasn't entirely convinced that the cars suspension would last to getting out of the field and back onto the calming reassurance of tarmac. He was bouncing up and down in his seat as continued at full speed through the field. His hope that he had lost his pursuer was shattered along with his rear window and his rear- view mirror as shots were being fired at him. Danny felt his heart nearly leap out of his chest at the crack of the breaking glass around him. The fast dull thudding of the plants against the car's body kept a rhythmic chorus to the off-road diversion. He swung the car to the left and then the right to reduce himself as a target. The car continued to mow down the plants, buffeting him inside the small car as it surged over the field. If all else fails he decided to jump out the moving car and try and lose them on foot. He knew that if he could get any odds on that being a success was about as hopeful as the England soccer team winning another World Cup before the year 3000.

The flowers began to thin and he could see in front of him a short concrete platform in the midst of the sunflowers, and he was heading slap bang for it. He pulled the wheel to the left with all his strength missing the hazard by a hairsbreadth, with perhaps it just nicking the wing mirror and then he was straight through the hedgerow and back onto the road. Danny's feeling of relief pumped through his chest. As the sunflower heads and stalks still dropped from all parts of his car, he was grateful for the sheer guts the small car had shown on its off-road diversion. His pursuers had meanwhile gifted him an extra lead as their four-wheel drive had driven straight into the concrete pillar and had no doubt turned an expensive vehicle into an insurance write off. Although he had lost the facility of his rear view mirror, Danny's occasional glance back over his shoulder assured him he had at least snatched a fighting chance to make himself scarce; very, very scarce.

# 20

The Reverend Kirby Quiltfloe was rubbing his chronically sore hip, a painful reminder of his rugby playing years in the Scottish borders during his younger days. He was standing at the back of the church seating as he spoke to the congregation filing out from the end of the Sunday morning service.

"Ah Tom and Ace, I'm very glad you've made it again to the service. How are things?"

"Emma has helped me with the Council in getting me a one bedroom flat, while Ace is still in his honeymoon period," replied Tom buoyantly.

In fact, Mr Thomas Masterman Hardy appeared to be looking nearly ten or so years younger. His newly acquired abstinence from alcohol added to the intake of wholesome, nutrious food along with proper shelter, some furniture lifting for the Nomad centre and a reasonably decent set of clothes had worked a kind of redemptive magic. He could have been the star contestant on a personal makeover reality show. There was also in his eyes a distinct lack of the shiftiness that had been a result of his vagrant life, a nervousness which was not unlike the look on a dog's face who has suffered years of mistreatment. Tom's skin pallor had a healthy, ruddier glow, and it was coupled with a much needed improvement in his conversational skills.

"My dearest Reverend, you mentioned something to me of someone going to London to stand on parade for our sovereign," interjected Ace, whose visage had not been through the same rejuvenation of his companion. He still had a brooding greyness.

"Did I? Oh yes, I remember now. Our Treasurer Mr Rose's daughter Grace leads our local Sea Cadets. They have been invited down to a big event for the opening of the Olympics. They along with many others will be providing a guard of honour. I understand the world's VIP's are attending a reception with our monarch at the Parliament building. A good number are arriving by the Thames. It will be a real spectacle. There's Grace now, I'll introduce you."

The insistent ringing of Emma Darbyshire's mobile cut short her less than successful siesta. Whatever sleep benefits she had hoped for had just evaporated. She looked at the displayed incoming number and didn't recognise it. Her first instinct was to leave it and then inexplicably she answered it.

"Hello."

"Emma, it's Valerie."

"Oh how are you?" Emma Darbyshire's voice slightly quivered as she realised she was about to be dragged further and further into the unknown.

"Well, thank you. I am taking regular medication and I have just been able to get some more of my prescription. I will tell you about it sometime. Unfortunately, time is short. In fact I can tell you how short. Exactly two days left."

"Valerie, you know my life has taken some very sharp turns recently but I still believe in what you have been telling me and I am willing to help in whatever capacity." Emma surprised herself as she said these words, as the story that Valerie Garfoot had spun her was still shot through with her own personal doubt.

"I knew I could depend upon you. But don't think that you will needed to be used as an Al Qaeda type suicide bomber. Although what we are dealing with, will not in the first instance be resolved in a court of law. It will I am afraid to say be settled, one way or another in a bloody fight. I must tell you what we need to do. I have intercepted their latest bulletin and this gives us their next move."

"Bulletin?"

"Yes bulletin, they operate by issuing steps at a time so any leaks of information, does not disclose their main game plan. However, if we cannot disrupt them at this stage I am afraid we will have no other realistic opportunity in the short or even medium term. Now Emma listen very, very carefully."

Back at the offices of British Intelligence, Keith Bigham felt the remaining colour drain from his face as he read the email, which described the botched assassination of his erstwhile boss in a Vancouver apartment block. He felt his career dreams speedily dissipate into the ether, although part of him was secretly pleased that Valerie had not been killed. Three insistent questions swirled in his mind. Firstly, where exactly was his former manager Valerie Garfoot and what was she up to? Secondly, how was he going to break the news to the Prime Minister or his deputy Kevin Scotton? Finally, he was still wrestling with the moral dilemma of using lethal force on a British citizen, completely ignoring the justice system of this country and apparently being sanctioned at the highest political level. How could this action be right?

Bigham allowed himself a moment to dwell on his orders and the fact that he was complicit in the process. In his thoughts it required no great leap of imagination, to see himself in the dock and attempting to defend his role in trying to murder a British citizen by falling back on the Nazi defence at Nuremberg, 'I was only following orders.' The thought did not in anyway provide him with any level of comforting reassurance.

The panoramic view over the winding Thames coupled with the blue summer skies would normally have lifted Bigham's spirits. He often thought he was a sufferer from seasonal adjustment disorder and he always felt distinctly low during the seasons of the long nights and grey days; he attributed it to perhaps some distant Scandinavian ancestry. However the pressing dark mood that was on him, was in direct contrast to the weather being enjoyed by the Londoners below. It was an embarrassing failure that he would have to endure. Copybook well and truly blotted and spotted; compounded with the fact that Valerie Garfoot had literally slipped away from under his very nose, actually escaping from her own office. Bigham sensed that he would be prime candidate for the role of Mr Scapegoat in the coming days. In a corner of his mind he felt that it may be the falling on one's sword time in the very near future. He pushed his laptop to one side, breathed in and exhaled deeply and closed his eyes and began to wish he was doing any other job but this one. He stroked his left earlobe and then placed his chin into the palms of his hands.

A knock on his office brought the acting head of British intelligence back to alertness. The door partially opened.

One of his personal assistants stood in the doorway. Her dark purple scoop top betrayed just a hint of décolletage.

"There are two personal calls for you. Both callers won't speak to any one else. And they both reckon it's absolutely urgent that they speak with you and you alone."

"Just like buses. You wait and then two at once. Have they given their names?"

"One just says his name is Leo and the other has just said mention Charlton Athletic"

Keith Bigham's eyes widened, "ah I was told he was a big supporter. Put Mr Charlton Athletic through on the secure line and hold the mysterious Leo and I will talk to him straight after."

# 21

As the coach cruised smoothly southwards on the well worn tarmac of the A1 road, Tom looked out of the window on the flat fields of Lincolnshire and then Cambridgeshire. The road was already busy with traffic and a high density of articulated lorries with foreign plates heading back to the ports. He then turned his head slightly to the left to see his friend Ace fast asleep, which was quite a feat in itself with the lively chatter of the young uniformed Sea Scouts careening around the bus. The Sea Scouts were understandably excited and expectant about their duty on the Thames for the gathering of the world's leaders prior to the opening ceremonies for the London 2012 ceremony. Tom's mind began to run through the strange turns his life had taken since Ace had intervened in that West London alleyway when he was being confronted by a gang of thugs bent on mischief. It wasn't the wandering around the country; he had already done more than his own share of that. It was the fact that he had managed to pull himself together for the first time since he couldn't remember. Sobered up, improved his diet, his wardrobe, his whole life in a nutshell; at this rate, he concluded, he might be able in the near future to hold down a steady job and be a reasonably useful member of society. Tom didn't want to think any further than that aspiration. Strangely Ace insisted that Tom would continue to join him for Sunday services and he had fallen into line like it had been his usual Sunday morning past-time.

He also recalled a few things from the couple of sermons he and Ace had heard from the Reverend Quiltfloe. There was that word redemption. Redemption, it was word he didn't quite understand fully. He supposed it was like buying something back you had pawned at Cash Converters. However Tom felt that in some way he had been redeemed in some way by Ace's actions and was now happily being swept along on the unpredictable tide, which he was taking day by day because he realised that Ace could vanish as quick as he had appeared. If Ace did disappear then Tom reasoned that at least he had gotten a healthy degree of his own self respect back. Also Ace might not disappear he just might not want Tom hanging around any longer especially after he had ended up marrying the local MP, and that he knew would be perfectly understandable. He might be the reminder of a life that Ace wanted to forget, so it might be better for Tom to seek his luck elsewhere and let Ace and Emma have a bit of personal space, to work on their very new relationship. The shock of the news of the two of them getting hitched on a scale of one to ten, with ten being your hair turning white with fright was a good eight point five, and probably nearer nine. If that was a whirlwind romance, it was speedier than a feisty ferret strapped to a firework. The whirlwind courting that was so brief that Tom had not even noticed the romancing apart from one evening meal between the two of them at the Old Bakery restaurant. This episode was strange on at least three accounts he reasoned, firstly Tom would have bet the all the oil in the Middle East against the two of getting hitched in a matter of a few days after meeting; secondly, although this was a bit more believable, there was absolutely no publicity it appeared to be only known to a very small circle, of which he was one. Finally, she surely couldn't see Ace as a good catch? He thought there would have been a splash in the media at the very least with Emma being the local MP; now they were living together it would surely leak out in the next few months.

It also came back into Tom's mind, as he glanced at the sleeping figure next to him whose head was now resting on Tom's shoulder, about their visit to the historical society in London.


Over one hundred miles away in London the Eurostar service from Paris disgorged its teeming passengers onto the platform. Keeping within the centre of the bustling throng on the platform, Danny walked towards the exit all the time keeping his eyes alert for anyone who might be watching out for him. His alternative passport had successfully cleared controls and he had also employed a dark blue baseball cap so he could keep his face out of sight from the CCTV monitoring systems. He was not only needing to elude the new Napoleonic forces spiced up with some very strong Chinese flavouring, who were bent on seemingly ruling the whole planet, but he was also trying to elude his former employers in British security and no doubt every Police force in the country. He wondered perhaps if it really is safest in the eye of a storm. He kept his face blank with his eyes alert as he tried to stifle the doubts about why he had travelled back into the dangerous epicentre of this intrigue. An intrigue and conspiracy that may have profound consequences for Britain and all the other free democracies and also it may involve a great deal of spilled blood, and hopefully not his own. He used his old training which involved a few feints and changing direction at the last minute; Danny felt so far, so lucky. As he walked he asked himself once again, why, why me; why am I being the one who is being squeezed between both sides. Introducing Mr Danny Kebab.

Focussing on the task ahead and the parts of the plan that had been entrusted to him he knew he now needed to make a two or three phone calls and hope the luck somehow might begin to turn in his own favour. His favour, he knew, may not please everyone else involved; loyalties needed reviewing. He was determined that it was now time to lay off the risks he was taking and to buy his good self some copper-bottomed security. Breathing in deeply through his nostrils he knew the smell, he knew the grimy, mineral taste, the bouquet of metropolitan filth; this was London and for the moment he was going to park the danger in a corner of his mind, because this was London and he loved her choking atmosphere and feel to bits. Whatever was going to happen today Danny knew a full stomach might help, his blood sugar needed to be at a level to keep him fully alert; decided, breakfast it was then.

Back in Lincoln Emma Darbyshire nearly jumped into Harriet's car. Then they pulled out into the light traffic and made their way to the bypass, heading for the A46, which would then lead them onto the A1 South, the London road.

"Emma, do you think it is wise to ignore the instruction from the Parliamentary Office to go to the assembly point?"

"Maybe not," Emma replied with a fiery glint in her eyes. They both knew she was not a natural or instinctive rebel.

"Harriet did you manage to get through to your college friend?"

"I did. I haven't spoken to Prudence since our reunion

meet at Croyde Bay in Devon twelve months or so ago."

"I must try that surfing that you rave about. Do you think I am too old for a wetsuit?"

"Of course not," laughed Harriet, as she watched in her wing mirror a dark blue BMW pull past her at high speed.

"And your friend?"

"Well there are friends and there are friends. But Prudence is a real mate. She gave me her brother's number with no questions asked," Harriet face beamed with a triumphant smile, as she ran her left hand through her long straight chestnut hair.

"And? And? Harriet, now don't keep me in suspense."

"Yes I rang him. Brass neck or what! It was his personal mobile; only family and a close circle have this number. No doubt he would be pestered by the press otherwise," Harriet deliberately paused.

"Come on you tease!" Emma raised her voice good-humouredly.

"Firstly, he said he remembered me when I was at college with Prudence. Well who wouldn't! Umm, yes, the feminine charm certainly lubricated the process. Of course he was one hundred and fifty per cent focussed on his training. But as we women know all men can be unfocussed, if you know what I mean. But, now get this Ms D, he will be there at the place and time and will do whatever is necessary to help."

Both women let out a huge shout of YES, with Emma pumping her two fists in the air.

"I'm not entirely sure what we're rejoicing about, but who cares because I feel today something is going to happen. Perhaps it will make some sense of the madness of the last week."

"One thing Emma I'm glad you've kept your old surname. It will save us a lot of media hassle. What was your maiden name?"

"Hamilton. Emma Hamilton. It's a neither a here nor there name, I suppose. Even though my former husband has been a snake, I am happy to hang onto the name. And Horace did not want me to take his surname; in fact he does not like to bandy it about."

"What is it then?"

"Sorry, a promise is a promise."

"Well your maiden name puts you in with a Formula One driver and a notoriously corrupt Parliamentarian; no best stick with Darbyshire. By the way what's your new lovey dovey hubby doing today?"

"I am not to sure. I think he said he and Tom may have a day out with the Lincoln Sea Scouts. He's a real naval buff."

"Emma," shrieked her assistant. "I read in the Lincolnshire Echo that the Sea Scouts are part of the honour guard at the Olympics thingy. And that's just where we are headed."

"I hope he's not travelling with them. Let me get ringing round to find a mobile number for one of those Scouts. He only mentioned the other day that he felt something big was about to break and he idly wondered if he would get involved. I didn't let on we were going there or anything else for that matter."

"Yet again Emma, it makes absolute no sense. Well if nothing happens at this Olympic do, I am off shopping in Covent Garden. Have to get some benefit on this wild goose chase. Although I wouldn't mind catching the Stones playing at the O2 arena, they are doing five nights. I still enjoy a modern musical history lesson."

"There's something I should tell you. Something I haven't even told my husband yet. Harriet, I've missed my period."

The car moved at a brisk seventy miles per hour along the two lane bypass, which circled the west of Lincoln. Traffic was light as it was an hour or so before the commuters and school run had got underway, and the sun was making itself felt upon the car windows and it had all the makings of a beautiful English summer's day. They were about sixty miles behind the coach, which was ferrying Ace, Tom and the team of Sea Scouts; all of them heading for the capital of the nation, the sprawling majesty of London.

Earlier on that same morning simultaneous raids at three properties in the Home Counties by officers from MI5 had netted the heads of Britain's Army, Royal Navy and Royal Air Force. Each had been told they had been arrested on the direct orders of the Prime Minister following presentation of evidence that they were conspiring with the former head of British Intelligence to undertake a coup with a backing of a foreign power, namely Russia. They were to be held in secure conditions in indefinite detention until such time as the judicial system was in a position to proceed with a prosecution for this act of betrayal. The operation had gone smoothly and whilst each of them had separately expressed their absolute denial of the charges of treason, there had been no heroics and they had only to put their trust in what may be left of British justice. A comprehensive and leak-proof media embargo kept the lid on this near-surgical removal of Britain's military high command. It was an unparalleled and swiftly effective decapitation of the head of the British military organisation.

Their immediate deputies within the armed services were informed to report to the European Union military chiefs for all member nations. Overnight the European wing of NATO had been dissolved and replaced by the European Union military organisation. The President of The United States was currently being lobbied by high ranking members of Congress and the Senate to accept the new phoenix rising from the NATO ashes and to offer its full support to the aims and objectives of the new military power as a bulwark against the Russian threat. All the old cold war arguments and rhetoric were being dusted down and deployed through all the political channels, with selective speeches and articles being released to heighten the need for a strong front against the Russian menace. The increasingly nationalistic and resource-rich Russia with their continuing efforts to dominate the Near and Middle East needed to be counterbalanced by a strong combative Europe was the attractive core of their argument. Ears and minds in the US listened and soaked in the increasingly plausible rationale.

# 22

The procession of oily black government limousines smoothly pulled into the grounds of Buckingham Palace; the various knots of tourists in their shorts, summer tops and baseball caps were kept back from the entrance by a large, well-marshalled uniformed Police presence. Within the ornate gates the Busby-sporting Coldstream Guards carried out their ceremonial and watching brief. The public outside the Palace gates switched instinctively to advanced rubber-necking mode and began to use their array of digital wares to try and capture a shot of someone important or famous, which they might be able to bore their friends and relatives with when they returned home to Lake Forest, Illinois or wherever. A score of camera phones were held aloft in the ever-hopeful effort of catching some memorable image. With the right tele-photo lens they may have caught the backs of the Prime Minister and the Cabinet Secretary, plus the attractive long mane of dark hair of the young French secret service agent, who was now attached seemingly by an umbilical cord to Alex Haye, the United Kingdom's political numero uno. The Monarch of the realm was receiving an unexpected early visit from some big hitters.

While this scene was quickly unfolding a few miles away,

Danny was walking through the throngs of human flotsam flowing along Charing Cross Road, making his way towards his old stamping ground of that grand old thoroughfare known as the Tottenham Court Road. He knew these streets so well and every now then he walked into a shop and exited via a side door to shake off any would be stalkers. He reasoned confidently that he had been undetected on his return to Britain and after making his arrangements he would meet up with Valerie Garfoot's messenger and see if there was any hope in their plans to derail the new Napoleon and then play his own cards thereafter as he saw fit. Moving past the electrical shops, which heaved with cheaply assembled technology from the Far East, and the famous frontage of the Dominion Theatre; Danny felt the ambience tangibly lighten. He was now moving away from the relentless razzle dazzle of the retail bazaar of the souk-like West End, as he continued to briskly make his way towards the more refined air of Russell Square surrounded by offices for the better class of literary publishers. Unexpectedly his way was suddenly blocked by a man waving a magazine.

"Big Issue, Sir. Get your Big Issue."

Danny mumbled an apologetic no thanks and got back into his stride.

The bearded and unkempt magazine seller was wearing a worn-looking and crumpled navy fleece jacket and holding a wad of magazines in his other hand and a shoulder bag stuffed with more Big Issues, moved alongside him in a dance along the pavement. His official vendor badge was prominently to the fore.

"Come on Sir. Help the homeless. We're all brothers and sisters in God," he continued to follow and press Danny for a sale as they moved down the road.

"Look at the badge. I'm an official Big Issue vendor," said the seller as he kept up with Danny pace for pace.

Danny looked ahead and was surprised he didn't feel any irritation to the hard sell hassle on the street, he seemed to warm to the good natured vibes from the grinning man, and a Big Issue seller, who was apparently openly religious to boot. He quickly calculated that it might be easier to buy the magazine than to have him stick like a limpet and disrupt any potential meeting up ahead.

"Okay, okay friend, you win I'll take one." Danny fished in his pocket for some loose change, smiling as he did so.

"The Lord bless and keep you. You're a special man. Have a good day, a very good day," responded the seller with a grateful smile, pocketing the cash.

"Thanks," replied Danny taking the proffered magazine.

"Oh and take this," the Big Issue seller pulled out a copy of yesterdays Guardian put it into Danny's hand and then seemed to move like the wind and was soon gone out of view.

Danny hesitated for a moment at the speed of the surprise transaction. He looked at front page and saw that there was a message in felt tip pen in the margin" ring 07799 470 2927 and leave your number. If there is no reply within two hours assume we're relegated!" He understood the gallows humour from the message from Valerie Garfoot, as he looked around him and then rang the number.

The large ocean-going yacht with its resplendent gleaming white hull slowly made its way down the green and grey waters of the Thames and would shortly be moored adjacent to the Houses of Parliament. Tower Bridge was raised to allow the vessel to proceed. Clearly visible on board were a number of Chinese-looking sailors in all black uniforms, who were moving across the yacht with a military efficiency.

There were a number of Olympic flags with the interlocking rings and European Union on the yacht which were blowing in the breeze. At the top flew a larger flag, which appeared to a French tricolour with a red dragon which was holding a representation of the earth in its claws.

Outside the Palace of Westminster a massive security operation was in force with the public moved well back behind barriers. It was probably the largest sterile area that the Police had ever mounted around the Britain's altar of parliamentary democracy. The vehicle exclusion zone had been extended significantly further than the barriers originally installed to deter suicide bombers inflamed by radicalised Muslim militant extremists. The surrounding visible corset of ranks of uniformed police were stiffened by plain-clothes officers and strategically positioned small groups of army personnel carrying shoulder strapped weapons. They looked as if they were prepared for every security nightmare eventuality. Coaches had arrived at the perimeter of the security screen and passengers were funnelled through a checking procedure. The coach passengers were mainly Members of Parliament and Members of the Houses of Lords. They had previously been asked to assemble at the O2 Stadium, as there had been an unspecified security threat to the gathering for at the Houses of Parliament. The O2 Stadium was still in preparation for the start of a series of concerts by the Rolling Stones, those rockers who were marathon men in their own field of rhythm and blues and rock mythology. Clearly it was timed by the promoters as a marketing exercise to synchronise with the London Olympics. The event at the Parliament building had previously been diarised months before by Members as the launch of the 2012 London Olympics, but they had been advised at the time of the new security instructions that a major constitutional announcement would be made by the monarch to Members of both Houses, numerous European leaders and world statesmen. Other coaches were bringing in all manner of European leaders and global movers and shakers. There was a heady atmosphere that pervaded around all those moving towards the Parliament building. .

At one of the checkpoints an orderly queue was beginning to back up.

"I need your identification Sir, "queried the Policeman politely, bowing slightly to the smaller suited man with a shiny bald pate and who appeared to be in his late sixties.

"Look lad, I am the Member of Parliament for Barnsley. That's in South Yorkshire and I'll tell thee in Yorkshire we're great believers in straight talking. So move aside and let me get on with my job and you son, can get on with yours."

"I am very sorry Sir. But today we need written identification or you cannot proceed any further."

The MP sucked in the air around him, swelling his chest, "you obviously didn't hear me cock. I have been elected by the good folks of Barnsley. I do not need any flaming identification to attend the House of Commons. I'm known in there, just fetch out of the staff and they'll identify me."

He then pushed pass the Police constable.

As he did this he was immediately accosted by two other Policemen who frogmarched him towards some a group of Police vans. Those in the entrance queue could still hear the MP's shout of "police state" and "what about Oliver Cromwell!"

The queue's attention was soon distracted by the barriers being opened up to allow a large removals-size delivery van to back up to the entrance to the front of the Palace of Westminster. Several men in beige coloured overalls then began to disembark and they positioned a trolley at the rear of the van and began to carefully unload a large hard black plastic packing case.

As they slowly wheeled the trolley and package case towards the entrance they were met by further Police who were making a further check on all movements into the building. One of the four delivery men passed over the authorising delivery note and spoke up. He spoke in a flat, dry tone.

"It's the delivery from the British Museum, as ordered no doubt by someone high up in Whitehall."

The Policeman checked the yellow delivery note and responded, "it says here the Rosetta Stone. Why do they want that here, who knows? Anyway you're cleared to go and set it up. You should have been here an hour ago."

"Have you seen the traffic? And it looks like it's been raining Metropolitan Police officers for the past few hours. You've left the rest of capital free to the thieves and robbers. Wish we had your overtime squire!"

# 23

"He's not answering his mobile!"

Came the exasperated response from one of the MI5 officers standing up in the open plan office, as there was a call in for the acting head of British Intelligence to call the Prime Minister Alex Haye. You couldn't get a bigger protocol faux pas.

"Keith Bigham is going to get his arse kicked big time, if he doesn't get back to the PM. After Vancouver he can't afford another cock up."

The anxious looks of the various officers knew that this was rapidly becoming a major in-house embarrassment. Bigham was well aware that he had to be on standby in light of the major event at the Parliament buildings. What a choice time for Bigham to go AWOL. Although none of the officers were fully briefed on the event to take place, apart from the sketchiest details that it was being attended by a number of leaders and statesman, and was going to be a diplomatic starting gun for the 2012 London Olympics prior to the public jamboree. The Metropolitan Police were covering the main security details backed by a range of intelligence officers, the army and the personal bodyguards of the various worthies.

A freckle-faced female officer, cradling a phone between her ear and shoulder called out, "confirmed Westerman and Cucksey are in position at the site."

"Westerman and Cucksey? More like Laurel and Hardy after Vancouver!" came the cynical riposte from the office wag.

Inside the gilded splendours of Buckingham Palace the two male members of the royal staff stationed outside the closed door of the state room turned to each with a look of concern, both emphasised their concern with theatrical arched eyebrows. They continued to maintain their in-built royal servant's protocol of silence. Through years of training and experience they knew their role; the role of dignified discretion, absolute discretion. Their practised poise was the exact opposite of the situation, which was unfolding within the state room. Even the heavy, sound-dampening doors did little to mitigate the volume of the raised voices coming from the room. Indeed the two servants had never heard such a tirade of angry shouting from the Monarch before and it was being countered by an equally vigorous volume from what appeared to be the Prime Minister. It sounded like the queen mother of all rows. The Queen's husband could be heard using some of the salty language way back from his earlier career as a young man in the Royal Navy. There were also the unidentifiable sounds of others in the state room adding to the blow up. There was even the sound of some crockery being smashed. The servants were then taken by surprise as the door was suddenly opened with the monarch's private secretary coming out and requesting the royal transport be quickly prepared for a journey to the Parliament buildings. The Queen's husband was to remain confined to the Palace under semi-house arrest.

The coach chartered by the Lincoln Sea Scouts had nearly arrived at the drop off point for all those assisting in the guard of honour for the Olympic opening ceremony at the Houses of Parliament. The 45-seater luxury coach owned by P.C. Coaches of Lincoln, and fitted with all mod cons, slowly began to navigate and move along through the dense traffic of north London. The passengers although feeling travel weary paid attention to passing views of the city. Towards the back of the coach for the previous fifteen minutes the leader of the Sea Scouts Grace Rose had been in a deep and at times animated discussion with Ace, who had left his previous place next to Tom.

"I've got Emma Darbyshire on my phone for you."

Ace took Grace's phone.

"No, I'm going to the Parliament buildings. Emma I feel the call to action. I have nothing further to add... No, sorry, goodbye my love."

He passed the phone back without knowing how to switch it off.

"She is still on the phone to you."

"Grace, the conversation is over."

Grace carried on the call, "Mrs Darbyshire please can you tell me what is going on….."

A couple of minutes later Tom raised himself up from the coach seat and looked down towards the rear of the coach. He could see Ace speaking to the Scout leader in an unusually demonstrative manner, using his left hand to accentuate his points. Grace Rose was listening with a fierce intensity; Tom could see her cherubic face beginning to flush red. He looked up and down the coach there were about thirty Sea Scouts, all of them fresh-faced teenagers and looking proud and smart in their dark uniforms. Apart from the driver the only other adults were Tom and Ace. His mind struggled with the chain of events, as he had previously wondered with his time with Ace, just what was going on, apart from a free trip to London; perhaps he concluded that Ace was boring her with his knowledge of the British Navy under sail. Tom thought perhaps with now coming back to the capital could be as good as time as any, to say his farewells to Ace and to seek a new life elsewhere, especially as he felt fitter and more importantly, sober.

Grace Rose, with her bright eyes and round young face beaming with excitement, moved towards the front of the coach and stood facing her cohort of Sea Scouts. They all looked to her expectantly as their group leader. As the coach continued to move ever-slowly through the thickening traffic of the capital she spoke up.

"Attention, attention Scouts," she announced while holding on to the two seat backs to keep her balance.

"Yes Romarta, your attention now please! Thank you. As you know we have an important job today in being part of the guard of honour, along with a load of other uniformed organisations representing various parts of the country. Well there has been a slight addition to our duties."

There was a collective sigh from the Scouts.

"Get on with it," came up from one of the lads.

"Grace, I thought we could have some free time for ourselves after the guard duty,"

called out another of the crew.

"Caleb, I hope we can still have some time off too but this is really important. I've just been speaking to our MP Emma Darbyshire, who we all met at our last open day. I know it's a bit last minute but Ace who is with us today is her husband and she wants us to stick with him. I think he will give us some idea of what we need to do."

Another of the Scouts shouted out, "it's not doing any marching is it?"

Ace rose to his feet in the gangway as Grace slid down into the nearest spare coach seat. The Scouts looked at him slightly doubtfully.

Ace stood in the gangway and didn't use his left hand to steady himself, he seemed to flow with the swaying motion of the vehicle; he looked at the young faces and smiled and waited a few seconds before answering.

"No not exactly marching," as he spoke, the authoritative tone of his voice seemed to calm the doubts and dispel the dubious looks of the Scouts. They all became seriously attentive.

"As an old Naval officer I feel very proud to see young people like yourselves volunteering to learn the ways of the water and learning how to serve your country. This day, in the capital of our nation, you will need to play a small, but vital part in protecting the security of the realm. Forgive me for the short history lesson. I do not know if any of you have any knowledge of the British Navy in the age of sail. Suffice to say that this country's wealth and security came from the brave and resourceful sailors, who expertly navigated across many seas and oceans and met many challenges. 'Twas when Britannia ruled the waves. In those days the communication between ships heading for battle was by the flying of flags as signals. These flags would symbolise phrases, words or letters. There are two signals I want to tell you about before we arrive at our destination. The first one was for close action, a favourite of mine because that was how conflicts were settled on the high seas, by getting close to you enemy. The enemy, who on many an occasion had numerical advantage in ships and cannon. The second signal I want to talk about, which is fitting for today because it was used before a great battle. I had to change it for good practical reasons. I came upon my acting signals officer on the poop deck, his name was Lieutenant Pasco and I said that, prior to battle, I wanted to amuse the fleet with a signal 'England confides that every man will do his duty.' Pasco replied that if I would permit he would substitute the word 'expects' for 'confides', because the word 'expects' is in the signals vocabulary but 'confides' would have to be spelt, letter by letter. Time was short and the signal for close action would need to be flown very quickly afterwards. Yes, yes, England expects. England expects that every man will do his duty. And today England expects, yet again every man and woman, and yes indeed every young Sea Scout will do his or her duty. Now I will give you an idea how things might develop...."

# 24

Emma Darbyshire's mobile phone rang just as they had reached the outskirts of London, where they were taking a much needed toilet break at one of the identikit anonymous motorway services.

"Emma it's me, Valerie. Can you speak?"

"Yes. I am just at the services. Thank goodness. What is happening? Hopefully we are just about a good forty, fifty minutes or so from Parliament Square."

"Emma I am not sure whether our unofficial intervention to the proceedings will come off. Prepare for the worst and don't hesitate to make yourself very scarce if we fail. Don't put yourself in any unnecessary danger."

"I won't, rest assured. And I don't know either if we can disrupt this mad coup either. But I have never felt so strongly about something before. I don't want to think afterwards that I hadn't tried. Another thing, my husband has already gone on ahead."

"Emma!" her raised irritated reply resounded down the line, "we were trying to keep this information within as small a group as possible. But your marriage had already broken up?"

"Completely! Finito. Divorced, thank the Lord. This is

my new husband, Horace. I hope you can meet him, he's so … from a different age"

There was a short silence as Garfoot tried to assimilate the news that Emma Darbyshire's new spouse was already becoming part of the spanner that they were trying to throw into the works.

"Emma, just what does he think he can do?"

"I had only given him the sketchiest of details, which is frankly Valerie all I have. Anyway when I told him his eyes lit up and he said that this was probably what he had been waiting for and time was of the essence. I didn't think much of it because he is a bit prone to coming out with his rather dramatic utterances. Then he somehow, without informing me, inveigled himself onto the coach taking the local Sea Scouts to London, who are going to be part of the honour guard at Parliament."

"All I had asked was for you to be there and to be on hand to try and create a diversion at the right time," Valerie's Garfoot broke up slightly on the network and Emma walked to another spot on the car park to maintain the signal strength. She sensed Valerie Garfoot's tetchiness.

"Valerie, you still haven't yet told me everything you're planning to do. Before we get to Parliament and help you, I need to know what you hope to hope to achieve, after we play our small part. You're not going to try and kill this person with the Napoleon complex or assassinate the Prime Minister? I won't be involved in terrorism, whatever the so-called security need. If it is the case, you had better level with me. And level with me now."

"You can trust me Emma, although as events have rapidly demonstrated, it's hard to know who you can depend upon. One of my closest contacts is giving me cause for concern and I may have to assume he has switched sides. If you decide to contact the security services they will tell you I am public enemy number one and I must be apprehended at the earliest opportunity. Maybe not apprehended but fatally silenced. According to my contact in Vancouver I had only just avoided British state assassins in Canada. I am not set on murdering anyone and when I was still functioning head of British intelligence I would never have sanctioned, officially or unofficially, the pre-meditated killing of another. It's not like the films, James Bond licence to kill. No, the plan is simply to disrupt the event planned today where they hope to exploit the world's media and we need to try and interrupt it, whilst building up enough opposition to this betrayal of Britain and the subjugation of the free world. It feels like the whole democratic world is sleepwalking into a trap. Please carry out the tasks as we discussed before and hopefully I will be in touch. I do hope your husband does not put himself in danger. We are dealing with people who will kill without the slightest concern."

# 25

Oxford Street in central London was a humming buzz of shopping drones moving in and out of the retail honey pots, bristling with their brightly coloured bags festooned with logo after logo, and sales signs and the massive discounts offered to lure in the shoppers. The street with its world famous reputation could equally be one's version of heaven and another's version of hell on earth. Keith Bigham moved through the doors of the John Lewis Store and looked around. The acting head of British Intelligence, who was currently wanted urgently by the Prime Minister for reasons unknown, was apparently joining the rest of the predominantly middle-aged and middle classes in viewing the array of wares at the department store. Across the street Danny had watched his arrival through a first floor shop window across on the other side of the world famous shopping street. He surveyed the street like a hunted fox for any signs of a back-up team; there appeared to be none of the standard agents positioned closely to intervene if Bigham was to come under any threat.

Waiting another two minutes, he watched Bigham move around the entrance the store looking for his appointment, Bigham watched the shoppers looking all around him as the customers moved between the displays of merchandise.

Danny gave it another minute and then decided to make a move.

A few miles away across the city, the procession of limousine vehicles began to pull away from Buckingham Palace heading for the Houses of Parliament. The Monarch and her essential entourage were within the group of vehicles departing for the ceremony. It provided another chance for the visiting summer tourists to try and capture a shot as the small convoy of vehicles progressed through the gates. The tourists were certainly getting their Palace action quota today.

Outside the Houses of Parliament the visiting ship was now safely moored. There were no signs of movement on deck, with the Chinese crew visibly positioned around various parts of the vessel; they gave off an air of latent menace. Over half a mile away the group of Lincoln Sea Scouts had left their coach and were walking down along the side of the Thames, with Horace and Tom leading the way. Grace's mobile telephone rang, she concluded a short conversation.

She walked over to Ace, "it was Emma Darbyshire she said that she wanted us to make our way over to the entrance for MP's and she'll meet us there to discuss the next move. What is the next move?"

"Not exactly sure quite yet; but as I stated on the coach we are now a crew with a purpose. We all pull together. Thank you for the information from Emma, Grace, however I think we may need to chart a different course. Also I suggest you do not speak to her again on the phone until this business is concluded." As he spoke a Police officer, wearing a fluorescent yellow waistcoat, moved across the road towards them.

"Excuse me. Are you lot in the honour guard? Then you

need to make your way over that way."

Grace replied, "Thank you, we're just popping down to view the Thames and then we will be right there."

The Police officer moved off to some other priority directed from his earpiece, as the group briskly made the short distance to the edge of London's great river. For some of them it was their first visit to the nation's capital and they felt a little excited buzz at the sheer size and power of the great city. Here they were near the Houses of Parliament about to be a small part in the honour guard for the Monarch. However, this was now all up in the air as they had all as one put their lot in with their strange-looking but charismatic leader. Grace Rose's round and expectant face looked up to Ace who nodded back and they were all down at the edge of the Thames, with Tom being the last to get there. Just along in the distance they could see the splendid architecture of the Houses of Parliament jutting majestically on the horizon and standing tall like a historical beacon of British democracy. The Sea Scouts were gathered together looking towards Ace to see what they should do next; the short speech on board the coach had galvanised the group into following their new unofficial captain.

Ace reviewed the young, excited but nervous faces, "you remind me of some of the young boys who set sail with me to seek advancement from their lowly station, but also to find the respect of their comrades and find their own share of adventure. 'Tis a real novelty that I see the female Sea Scouts today; but they have my every confidence that they will do as England expects. A word of warning though, this I fear is the moment of danger. I do not want any young martyrs created here today. If there is any fear of serious injury I want you to seek shelter. I, and perhaps Tom, will go further in the dragon's den to face any infernal fireworks. Right now to it ye young tars!"

Within the Houses of Parliament the delivery men from the British Museum had now erected the Rosetta Stone in front of The Speaker's chair in the Commons. Several flags were displayed either side of the Stone, there was a Union Jack, a European Union one and several with a French tricolour with the addition of a red dragon in the middle. The table which usually stood between the facing benches of the government and the opposition had been removed. A number of microphones were also in front for the spectacle with a small group of technicians preparing their television cameras to record the event. A select group of journalists were being briefed in a committee room about the event to take place. The journalists were beginning to get both excited and boisterous as the briefing indicated that there was to be a major constitutional announcement from the British Monarch and the Prime Minister, in relation to a new global alliance based on the European Union and their wider partners. The cynical old hacks were completely nonplussed by this development and could not believe that this Olympics political opening jamboree was now being transformed to an event of profound political importance. The generous lashings of alcohol made available to the journalists began to dull their inquisitive urges about the upcoming announcement.

# 26

Valerie Garfoot just felt a double spasm of biliousness as she made her way on foot towards the Parliament buildings. She knew that the stress of the extraordinary events, which were compounded with her existing condition were putting her small middle-aged frame under extreme stress. Her role had changed from the hunter general to virtually powerless prey, from being the hammer to being prostrate upon an anvil. Time was now short before Britain, so far as she could understand the machinations of the conspiracy; it was about to be handed over in a glorious sleight of hand to an alien power. Swallowing hard, she struggled to get some oxygen into her lungs, it was if she drowning on dry land. She felt impotent in the heart of the great city, where her position and authority had been swept away in one frightening and totally unexpected move. She pushed the fears for her own safety as far as was possible to the back of her mind. Her adrenaline was fighting a losing battle with her weakening body and the clammy tightening of her airways betrayed the impulses of panic and fear. She realised that she needed to remain calm if she was going to be any further use in this situation. Fumbling for her phone she pressed the first name on her contact list, and was relieved that it was answered quickly

"Emma, where are you?"

"Hello. Well we're here at Parliament Square. I've missed the registration at the O2 stadium and I'm ready to cause a rumpus at the entrance. I've got a lot of female anger to vent."

"Yes, but don't get yourself hurt. I have two tricks up still my sleeve which will hopefully be more than a fly in their ointment. I suspect their leader is already at the House waiting for our heads of government to pledge allegiance before the world's press and this will be the signal for all their other orchestrated chess moves around the world. My lookout has told me that the Queen left the palace a few minutes ago. I hope to be meeting one of my agents shortly. That is if he is still onside, but I have to take the risk," informed Valerie Garfoot slightly breathlessly as she quickened her pace.

"Valerie, I've also organised something that might cause an upset. It has an Olympic theme."

Inside the House of Commons the technicians for the cameras had been asked to wait outside leaving only armed soldiers and a group of hawk-like Chinese in black paramilitary outfits that guarded each of the entrances. From behind the speaker's chair entered the two Chinese, who had been the principal negotiators with the late entrepreneur Jeremy Wheater. The smooth English speaker and the thick set one, who had an unsmiling frown of a face and was undoubtedly the link to their faction within the Peoples Liberation Army. They both surveyed the cradle of British democracy and took a moment to regard the new stage centrepiece of the Rosetta Stone. Seconds later entered the prime mover. He was flanked on either side by two Chinese guards holding automatic weapons. For the occasion he was dressed in a sober dark business suit with a collar and tie; his face looked more European in contrast to the two natural Chinese. The two Xanti men stood to one side and waited respectfully for the new Napoleon to speak.

"Friends, very shortly," he declared, "the arrogant and perfidious rulers of this accursed damp little island will be bowing and scraping before the new and vital order. Today we light a fire that will burn with a fury that no authority will be able to put it out, it will be inextinguishable. Together we have combined the transcendent powers of the Occident and the Orient. The greatest power of the west has come from the great minds that generated the age of reason and the French republic, enabling a way forward to extirpate the dissolute royal and political class degenerates and enabled Napoleon to show the way forward for the human race."

"Extirpate?" queried the English fluent Chinese.

"Extirpate? Ah yes, it means to pull out by the roots. Your Chairman Mao knew a thing or to of such things. He knew how to uproot the diseased roots of society. I know your English is excellent but how is your grasp French. La France compte que chacun fera son devoir."

The one who understood French smiled in return.

The new Napoleon moved away with a flamboyant flourish of his hand, "anyway I now need to make the final touches to my speech before the audience is assembled. We are about to shake the world on its very axis."

Westerman and Cucksey moved through the crowd behind the barriers outside Parliament, their faces etched with a resolute grimness, like a pair of intrepid hunting dogs who had scented their piece of the action. They were still on their mission unaccomplished. Both of them were wearing small earpieces, which would provide them with any information about the sighting of Valerie Garfoot. The pair were part of a larger network undercover team of up to thirty agents who were combing various strategic parts of London, where they believed the target may decide to re-appear. There was a view from within intelligence headquarters that she would return to this country and in some way cause some mischief for the government; the possibility of running to the land of her Russian sponsor had been at this stage ruled out. However, if Garfoot entered Russian territory or one of its satellites, there was every confidence that the Russian agents currently on the secret UK payroll would despatch her within seventy two hours of her making contact with the Russian authorities. British intelligence were confident that she would find no resting place, Russian safe house or any position from which to interfere in the matters of state.

Westerman held his hand over his earpiece and suddenly looked over to his colleague, who was about ten feet away. They both smirked and gave each other the thumbs up sign; possible jackpot and literally within striding distance.

The message through their earpiece had told them that someone resembling the target had been picked up on CCTV and was heading for the Houses of Parliament, and therefore moving towards the waiting net.

# 27

"We need to hire your vessel," the operator of the pleasure boat, which served the mainly foreign tourists wanting a sight-seeing cruise on the Thames, squinted at Tom.

The skipper stopped rolling his cigarette.

"Hang on mate it's not for hire to joe public, the rate for a trip is a fiver a head. You get a commentary as well, all the sights from the Thames," responded the operator, looking at the group of Sea Scouts and at the same time rapidly calculating a fast and handsome profit.

Tom continued. "No, we just want to sail down to the Houses of Parliament and maybe stay a while."

"How long, a couple of minutes for some snaps?"

"Well I'm not entirely sure how long," he replied truthfully.

"Unless you've got a couple of grand in readies you can forget it about private charter. Look pal, the usual trip starts in ten minutes." It was his usual 'take it or leave it' tactic; one that paid off more often than not.

The operator, who didn't have any other punters in the fray, was just about to move back to the cabin of the boat when Ace walked forward.

For a nearly thirty seconds Ace stood wordlessly in

front of the pleasure craft captain. Ace looked into the skipper's eyes and appeared to be searching into the man's soul.

"Good sir, your country has an urgent need of your craft, and for your services take this medal for your costs," he said continuing to look him straight in the eye.

The bemused operator stroked the two days growth on his chin, decided against smoking his cigarette and then looked at the medal he had just taken. He flipped it over to look at both sides of the medal and then nodded affirmatively. He slipped the medal into his pocket.

"Okay mate, you're the skipper for the day."

It reminded Tom of the effect Ace had made on the Notting Hill antique dealer.

"Good," said Ace waving all the Sea Scouts on board. "This is my latest command. Dear sir cast off and head straight towards yonder buildings at full speed. Further instructions will follow."

As they loosed their moorings, Grace Rose came up to Ace.

"Ace, I'm not answering the phone as you asked but I keep getting these text messages for you from Emma Darbyshire."

"Text messages?"

Ace looked at her slightly uncomprehendingly and then asked her to show them to him. Grace passed the mobile phone to him. Holding it outwards he covered his good eye and held the phone one way up then the other, and then announced he could see no messages and then he passed the phone back. He then went to stand next to the operator at the wheel of the craft. Ace's face was lit up with anticipation. The Sea Scouts chattered with excitement as the vessel slowly moved under diesel-power into the flow of the Thames and now the skipper seemed to have had an immediate personality by-pass, as he now looked for all intents and purposes to be all action and keen to please.

The amiable hubbub of the media hacks troughing at the buffet was shattered as one journalist suddenly climbed on the table and threw a stack of printed sheets into the air. All the embarrassed eyes in the room turned to look.

"It's an outrage. They're trying…"

His words were abruptly curtailed as he was dragged off down from the table by two security guards who quickly bundled the journalist out of the room, while other officials scooped up the scattered sheets. They even removed them from some of those present who had managed to pick up a copy out of professional curiosity.

"Sincere apologies for that exhibitionist, he was probably from the Daily Sport ha, ha, ha. The excitement or the buffet must be too much for him," laughed the public relations officer in charge of marshalling the media.

He continued. "Just ten minutes to wait and you will all be getting a ringside view of history in the making; quite honestly it's a media chance in a lifetime. Until then we will keep the beer and wine flowing, staff will be bringing through some more food. After the announcements we have some detailed press packs, which will provide full details of what you have just witnessed to enable you to report this event successfully."

The fleet of limousines carrying the Prime Minister's and the Monarch's parties were just moving through to enter the cordoned off zone around Parliament Square. The crowds which had been building throughout the day crowded the nearby streets and lined the temporary barriers, which had been installed to enable the smooth and uninterrupted flow of the official, high profile traffic to Parliament.

Suddenly the lead car of the fleet slammed on his brakes as a man dressed in a full lion costume had vaulted the barrier and stood in the road blocking the convoy. Police officers quickly moved to apprehend the lion man. A few laughs and ironic cheers came from the bystanders who were enjoying a bit of slapstick as the lion man sprinted away from his more conventionally uniformed pursuers. One of the Policemen slipped over trying to catch the lion man who was proving to be very nippy, twisting this way and that ensuring the cars were temporarily stopped. Some of the crowd and no doubt the authorities thought it was another Fathers for Justice stunt. However the fleet couldn't start up as the lion man easily sprinted around the four Policemen who were now trying to lay the long arm of the law on his leonine shoulders. The nearby crowd were warming to the slapstick pantomime being performed in front of them.

At last two of them caught hold of him, allowing the other two Police to ensure he would be removed from the vehicle pathway. The furry costumed individual then pulled off his lion head and tossed it onto the black shiny polished to perfection bonnet of the first of the limousines. A loud gasp went up from the crowd near to the incident which was matched by a stunned look from his apprehenders.

One of the Policemen spoke, "are you impersonating Oliver Metcalfe as well?"

"No officer, I am Oliver Metcalfe, the very self." With those words he shook free of the Police and jumped up onto the bonnet of the lead car and then onto the roof, leaving a nicely creased shiny limousine bonnet in his wake.

The nearby crowd were reacting as if an A-list pop star

celebrity had appeared before them and cheered, shrieked and screamed at the unmasked lion man, who had now been unmasked as Britain's great Olympic running hope. A wave of mobile phone cameras sprouted like fast growing fungal spores from the crush of people who had moved down to witness the extraordinary incident.

Oliver Metcalfe outstretched his arms in and managed to shout, "keep our Britain free from takeover! Keep this country free!"

One of the officers had managed to get onto the bent bonnet of the lead car and pull Metcalfe down into the hands of the waiting Police. Booing immediately started from the nearby crowd which had swelled as the scene had unfolded. Within minutes television and radio news were commenting on the bizarre incident and were urgently trying to verify through official channels whether it was indeed the international runner Oliver Metcalfe who had disrupted the official party wearing a lion costume. As he was led away, one of the Policemen seethed under his breath that you just couldn't make this stuff up.

# 28

Inside the stationary third car in the line of vehicles sat a pale, waxwork-like and glassy eyed Prime Minister. Haye looked like a Madam Tussauds dummy having a ride out to see the sights. Alex Haye stayed completely silent as the entourage was blocked by the costumed antics ahead. His constant companion of the last few days Mademoiselle Rives looked urgently out of the window and asked the driver why was their a delay. The less than satisfactory answer spurred her to her phone.

"Hallo. Yes, it's me. There is some kind of demonstration; it has slowed us down. Are you ready?"

Her features betrayed a tiger-like fierceness beneath her undoubted feminine attractiveness.

A mere two streets away Valerie Garfoot stopped to catch her breath, over the noise of the traffic she had heard the excited crowd sounds from the athlete cum lion demonstration. Already tired from the jet lag, her medical condition, trying to keep one step ahead of her pursuers and still attempting to upset the Napoleon-Chinese applecart, she felt the little remaining energy she had was now virtually extinguished. She knew she was running on empty. Garfoot walked a few steps towards a street bench and sat down; the former intelligence chief felt her eyes bulge slightly from her raised blood pressure and she managed to hold back a trickle of tears. The rest was a blessed relief. She hoped her journalist friend had managed to do inflict some damage in the press briefing. Her mind began to torment her that she had only probably achieved a very minor irritation, a mere pin prick on the conspiracy juggernaut, in between the days unfolding dramas? Today was she realised the probably last throw of the dice before the humiliation of the British government. Leaving the pinnacle of the country's leadership, namely the Prime Minister and Monarch, both about to submit before an alleged ancestor of Napoleon, who is carrying out his forefather's ancient mandate. Payback from two hundred years; she mulled over the ironic shame of this turn of events. Gathering herself, she rubbed her eyes and took her phone. She was still nursing concern that maybe Danny had not rung the phone number which had given him the message of where to meet her. He was late; he may have to be written off. She determined to give him two minutes and then go to the Parliament buildings to see if any of their sabotage efforts had made a dent into the forces working against them and to make contact with her trusted Police Commander contact, who would hopefully implement another small skirmish against the enemy. Garfoot realised her war chest of weapons was very much less than she had hoped for before she had left Vancouver. At least three of her contacts had refused to play ball, and they had probably warned the secret services that she was bent on disrupting the day's events; she wondered if she was just spitting into the wind that was blowing in hard like a hurricane from the Far East and re-enacted Napoleonic France. Valerie Garfoot wiped away a few beads of perspiration on her forehead, and she reasoned that if the enemy pulled off their outrageous sleight of hand it was time for her, and if Danny reappeared, to melt away and find a safe refuge. Then re-group and prepare, if at all possible, the lines of resistance, in Britain and across the world.

One hundred yards away on the same street two running male figures stopped and seemed to focus on Valerie Garfoot as she sat alone on the bench. They began to run towards her and both men knew it was their golden and timely opportunity to redeem their Vancouver shambles.

Her nostrils caught the scent of her own perspiration. As she was slightly bent forward with both hands on her phone she heard a voice to her right hand side.

"Valerie, are you okay?"

She slowly looked up as in a dream, "oh Danny I'm so glad to see you. I feel so drained; I don't think I have anything left to give today. But I'm sorry to have doubted you."

Garfoot blinked and felt her speech and movements all seem to go dissolve into a dreadful slow motion.

Cucksey and Westerman were now closing in like heat seeking missiles locking on and now they were within thirty yards and moving at a pace. Each was now holding a firearm with a silencer pressed against their respective right thighs. Garfoot glanced across from Danny and down the street as she heard the sounds of the padding steps of the two MI6 officers closing in on their target. A shiver of cold fear ran through her and she instinctively knew that she was seconds away from her end. In the split second she felt an overwhelming peace wash over her as if to prepare her for her fate. She knew she had done her best, yes, to the bitter end she had gone beyond her call of duty. The thought of losing Leo her love, bitterly stung her senses. She felt every part of her was attached with industrial-strength Velcro to the bench of as she tried to pull herself up and turn towards Danny.

"Danny, save your self," she just managed to squeeze out to the impassive Danny

Another hand firmly held her left shoulder. She turned in surprise.

"Valerie, no tricks required."

She looked into the resolute and unblinking gaze of Keith Bigham, her former number two and now the chief of spy-catchers.

# 29

"Harriet you'd better go and see your friend Oliver and see if he is alright. Brave, brave man. I hope they haven't hurt him in anyway. Whenever you can get to see him, please thank him. I know he has put his reputation on the line and just before his shot at glory. I'm not sure how we can repay him."

"I'm convinced he'll be alright. They're not likely to damage our best hope in the Olympics. I think they'll cover up the whole business as a bit of a practical joke or PGT, pre games tension."

They had reached the Police control point for the access to those who cleared to enter the Houses of Parliament for the event.

"Go now. I'll try to get in and see what I can do. I'm worried about my Ace; he's not getting back to me on the phone. If you see him, tell keep safe and I'll be back in Lincoln in the next day or so. I'm going in now. I'll ring when I can. What's that noise?"

A muffled chanting was heard in the distance.

As she approached the control point Emma Darbyshire was pleased to see that one of the Policemen who was well known to her from his duties guarding Number Ten Downing

Street. He happily waved her through.

In one of the ante rooms off the main chamber, the new Napoleon was admiring his uniformed self in a full length antique mirror. It was a dark navy coloured uniform with a number of silk-ribboned honours of both sides of his chest. He was accompanied by a security group of Chinese guards. Each had a menacing short machine gun-like firearm slung over their shoulder.

There was a short knock on the door and entering the room, another one of the Chinese security guards came in to brief him on the delay of the convoy.

His eyes and nose flared at the news and then he appeared to contain himself and spoke calmly.

"Request support from the army reserves held nearby. I do not want any further delays. Also make it clear to all members of our armed guard that I do not want any shooting today unless I give the specific order. Absolutely no shooting; this handover of power must be achieved, and seen to be achieved, with an imperial dignity. Not only with dignity, but with a certain élan, that only those of us with French heritage can display. This is a turning point in history, right here today. Now go."

The guard did not reply but swiftly moved as ordered.

Napoleon with one more admiring glance, was now satisfied with his groomed appearance and he then began to crow to the small group around him.

"Yes, according to their tradition, the British Monarch cannot enter the Houses of Commons. Ah if only this island had a leader now with the balls of Cromwell. Then perhaps we would have had a more worthy challenge, than these miserable and gullible rodents. In a few minutes the Monarch will be bowing at the knee and acknowledging that at last there is hope. There is leadership for this world. Ah yes, she will be crossing the line and she will now be a commoner too.

Ha, the haughty crown of Albion brought very low, to its proper resting place. It couldn't be a much more of a plainer picture to the watching world. My forefather said let us be masters of the Channel for six hours, and we are masters of the world! What would he say if he could see this scene today? He mocked this grey, sodden and morose island-race as a nation of shop keepers, well today they are no longer open for business. A withered, sterile, empty testicle of an empire, which was still clinging on through its American friends and Commonwealth, and its mendacious manoeuvrings in the European Union club for failed politicians. Britain hanging on by its poodle paws to a place in the United Nations Security Council. We now have control of the military and security forces, plus the fool of a Prime Minister in his our palm and we will use the corrupt shell of the European Union charade to link with the renewing life force from the east."

He then held both hands aloft slowly turned around the room and shouted, "I am ready."

# 30

The ageing white and red painted pleasure barge flecked with spots of red rust slowly chugged its way up the Thames towards the Houses of Parliament, whose profile stood out dramatically on the river shoreline. The darkening clouds and tangible change in air pressure suggested rainfall was imminent. Seconds later the drops began to fall, although not enough to dampen any of the lively young spirits aboard.

Tom left the group of Scouts and made his way down to rear of the vessel where Ace and the skipper were by the vessel's wheel, which steered them slowly forward through the tides of the Thames. The rainfall was unexpectedly heavy and the Sea Scouts had wisely sought cover in the middle section with its canopy used to protect passengers from the vagaries of the British weather. The rain was working with the breeze to whip in hard and it stung Tom's face. He reached Ace and Steve the skipper, who seemed to be both smiling and enjoying the rain on their faces; with the look they had, it was if they were sailing a transatlantic luxury liner.

"Ah Tom, we have chosen well. My new friend Steve will sail us right up to our destination in no time," announced Ace upon Tom's appearance.

Tom could see that his usually quiet and thoughtful friend

had become decidedly animated now he was on the water and heading into a situation which Tom still couldn't quite fathom. It was as if this had been the moment that Ace had been biding his time for; a time he wished to relish involving action on the water. Although Tom thought this near decrepit pleasure barge hardly matched up to the warships of old that so fascinated his friend; well let him fulfil his fantasy he told himself. Get it out of his system.

"You're both going to be soaked at this rate," Tom wasted his words into the wind and rain towards the pair, who seemed perfectly oblivious to the downpour.

"Tom, my friend I cannot command winds and weather."

Ace turned to the grinning unshaven face of the skipper, "time is everything; five minutes make the difference between victory and defeat. Our country will, I believe, sooner forgive an officer for attacking an enemy than for letting it alone."

Tom shook his head again this time in bemusement and turned away to get out of the wind and rain. Even at this distance he could hear crowd noises from somewhere nearby the Parliament area.

Inside the polished dark wooden panels of the House of Commons the selected Members of Parliament, representatives of European and other governments, plus other assorted characters of the world's governing hierarchy class were seated and expectant. A section to one side had been reserved for the well-lunched media pack and all the television camera crews were in position. They all looked towards to the front where normally the Speaker sat in his chair regulating the parliamentary debates. This was now a focal point for the presentation; the Rosetta Stone seemed to draw the eyes of all in the crowd. There was the odd shuffle in the seats and sounds of throat clearing, but all seemed to be keeping quiet as they sensed the importance of the occasion. The silence was now being disrupted by the sound of what appeared to be organised chanting from somewhere outside the building. Concerned officials moved to close any exterior windows and switched on some light classical music to try and maintain the correct dignified atmosphere. Someone was despatched to find out the source of the external aural irritation.

The rain and breeze began to ease and the sun forced itself back onto the grateful London skyline.

The door that Black Rod would hammer on to summon the Parliamentarians to hear the Queen in the House of Lords now opened. Triumphal music signified the delayed entrance of the Queen and her party. Her head was bowed and she appeared to those within close viewing distance that she had a face like the blackest thunder. Officials stewarding the event kept the party positioned just through the doorway, whilst the rest of the party stood, a chair was thoughtfully provided for the Monarch to sit on. Behind the group around the Queen was another group. This included Alex Haye and his now permanent companion the French Intelligence Officer Mademoiselle Rives, Sir Peter with a small number of assistants and close support plain clothes police bodyguards. The lights were now dimmed around the seated areas and bright banks of spotlights picked out the front of the hall where the draped flags and the Rosetta Stone were displayed. The classical piano music was now replaced by a brooding electronic sound, featuring deep resonant notes from some recorded banks of synthesisers. The change in music seemed to put the audience on notice of something important. To the surprise of most of the onlookers a large cinema screen was unveiled from the ceiling of the hall.

The blank screen was slowly filled from left to right with the coloured circles of the Olympic symbol. These were then followed underneath by the words London 2012. Then strangely for a few seconds the figures 20 before the date switched to 18, and then back again to 20. A few of the audience narrowed their eyes as it moved between 2012 and 1812 and put it down to the liquid entertainment at lunch. The image stayed for a minute, before the figures faded back to a blank canvas.

Emma Darbyshire was seated very close to the main doorway and was only a few feet away from her former partner at the head of the British government, Alex Haye. Pretending she needed to make an urgent visit to the toilet she made her way, apologising as she went, moving down the row. She reached the end of the aisle as the screen was portraying a collection of Olympic records being broken, showing runners, jumpers, swimmers and so on. Emma Darbyshire was now merely a couple of yards away from the Prime Minister's group who were behind the Royal party. She edged towards him.

"Alex, I need a word."

The Prime Minister turned his head towards her and looked straight through her with absolutely no sign of recognition. His eyes were wide open but without a spark of his essence, the pallor of his face was, even taking into account the hall lighting, a sickly grey. She shivered at the sight of him and didn't know what to do next, apart from repeating her request.

"Alex, please may I have a word."

Sir Peter standing next to the PM caught sight of her and quickly motioned for security to remove her at once. As she was still staring at the Prime Minister she saw his constant companion Mademoiselle Rives peer across at her and then, as a crude insult Rives flicked her tongue in lascivious fashion. Before Emma Darbyshire could respond to the situation, she felt two men take hold of both her arms and very quickly moved to eject her out and then through the main hall doors.

"Let go of me now! I am a Member of Parliament. You're bruising my arm."

The two attendants were totally unresponsive to her pleas and her struggle. They easily held onto her and minimised any disturbance by deftly and at speed removing her to outside of the Parliament building.

Back inside the screen had now changed to, what appeared to be a slickly produced documentary, describing all the ills affecting the planet. The commentary briefly emphasised the dramatic pictures which covered issues of climate change, hunger, poverty, war, injustice, and environmental degradation, unsustainable levels of debt, political and business corruption, crime and racial and religious tensions. The commentator began to build a case for change and suggested that the world was crying out for a fundamental remedy and an alteration of course. A time for the world to set free its own champions that have the capacity and vision to initiate and implement real, tangible change for the good of the planet and its long suffering people. The film then moved through a passing collage of great national leaders and also the huge changes wrought in China and India in the last thirty years.

The film then unexpectedly showed a short clip of the Egyptian golden statue of Anubis on a barge floating up the Thames during 2007. The very size of the statue had Tower Bridge opening to let it sail through. Its arrival was for the Tutankhamen exhibition at the O2 arena. The audience continued to view the film with rapt attention. The film then showed shots of the pyramids of Egypt and their historical significance intertwining with the military exploits of Napoleon in that country. It made great play of the major intellectual advances and knowledge gained by the 'savants,' who had accompanied the Napoleonic French army. Finally, it then briefly covered the discovery of the Rosetta Stone and its key role in the eventual interpretation of the ancient language of the Pharaohs. The Hollywood-standard propaganda sell of the film had begun to win over any newcomers to the conspiratorial cause. The smoothly persuasive and inspirational events on the film did not appear to smoke out any audience members of the dissident tendency. Even if doubters remained, the supporters of the new Napoleon were strategically placed throughout all the sections of the hall to stage manage a positive response to the event.

# 31

Napoleon took one final admiring glance in the mirror, and touching his dark fringe into place; he then flicked his hand nonchalantly to signal to his bodyguards that he wished to be accompanied out and into the main hall. The time of his unofficial coronation and unveiling to the world had arrived. This event would be the starting gun for a number of synchronised coups all around the world, moving like the power of a jet. With Britain being the first to publicly bow the knee and the empty shell of the European Union falling into his palm, it only relied on his partners in the People's Liberation Army to wrest the levers of power in China and then Napoleon and his key supporters knew they had real critical mass. A leverage of critical mass that would allow themselves sufficient momentum and significant room to manoeuvre themselves into all the slots of power that mattered and then to move at high speed smashing through any areas of organised resistance that emerged. The torpid and soporific mass of the world's educated population would be oblivious to the implications of the impending events due to its speed of implementation and people were generally more focussed on mundane things and distracted by the increasing price of daily living, the recession and the latest celebrity news.

On stage the film had finished and two suited men approached the microphones. Every single person in the hall recognised them. One of these was the previous Secretary General of the United Nations and the other was the former two-term President of the United States, who was still respected as a world statesman even after being beset by several salacious scandals. They both shook hands warmly and confidently surveyed the esteemed audience.

The former Secretary General of the United Nations spoke first, "Ladies and Gentleman. Welcome, welcome to this special event to, on one hand celebrate the start of the 2012 London Olympics and on the other to be part of history in the making. The Olympics show the best spirits of the world's athletes straining to improve and perfect their performance across a whole range of competitions. And it is most appropriate that we are here today in the world famous British Houses of Parliament. Arguably it is the birthplace and best continuing exponent of representative democracy. However as the challenging film has just showed us, what now confronts each one of us as citizens of planet earth cannot be combated by either standing apart, or atrophying through inertia, or by not allowing true human talent to act decisively for the best interests of every nation under the sun. I now will handover the proceedings to the former President of the United States, who I know needs no introduction. It's all yours, President."

The former US President, who himself knew what it felt like to be the most powerful man in the world, stepped forward to the microphone, whilst displaying his charming southern smile to score maximum effect for the audience and the cameras. He still possessed reserves of animal charm to incite the desires of most of the females in the hall; an ex-politician as surrogate rock star.

"Your Majesty and esteemed friends, before we enjoy the spectacle of the Olympics in the wonderful city of London, England, I have a confession to make. Please forgive me, but you know I'll be rooting for all those fine athletes from the States. Oh yes indeedy. Well I am so proud to be involved in today's event. I know a goodly number of you already know about, how should I put it? Yes you know about the way forward and how we will meet the considerable challenges that we face. Well it is mighty well time that the whole world got introduced to the man who will lead us all to a better place. Thinking back to my presidential terms, I would have loved to have the freedom to move and change things across this world of ours for the better. But getting back to point, well hand on my heart, I trust him. Remember if we ain't got trust between us what have we got! And I have been networking through all my considerable range of contacts to help ensure that we can all benefit from the many mighty dividends that he will most surely deliver. Oh yes he surely will."

The President wiped a bead of glistening sweat caused by the heat from the television arc lights. He paused as he milked his preachy delivery, and put both hands on the clear Perspex lectern. "Before we introduce Napoleon. Well he's Mr N to me. A couple of things, yes Napoleon that's his real name and he just likes to be called by the one name. But, and this is not unimportant my friends, he is descended directly from the great French leader Napoleon Bonaparte. The fella sure has one gold-plated ancestry, as you will also soon see he also has some heavy duty far Eastern pedigree. Now people he is the one who is going to bind together the east and west. I'm talking about international unity, a real international community and a dynamic direction of purpose. Too much has been wasted on cold and hot wars. Well that's probably enough from me for the moment. What we are going to see today is a real turbo-charged kick-start. Also I believe that working together with Napoleon will ensure future peace between the American eagle and the Chinese dragon; we don't want anymore superpowers confronting each other, we want to work together. Now as a US citizen I love our special relationship with Britain so I am so pleased to be here, perhaps a midwife to great things, to see the beautiful UK take a lead and fall four square behind Mr N. Now I am about to be joined here at the front with her most regal Majesty the Queen of Great Britain and the Commonwealth, alongside the British Prime Minister as well as the esteemed President of the European Union."

Triumphal orchestral music began to come out of the speakers.

Outside the Houses of Parliament the rain had stopped and the sun had appeared raising the ambient temperature, the air pressure however was pressing down and leaving the atmosphere decidedly muggy. Emma Darbyshire was already hot from embarrassment and she felt a red-faced, throbbing fury at being frog-marched out of the House, a place she had an absolute right to be as the elected Member for the constituency of Lincoln.

"Unhand me now!" She growled to completely nil effect.

"Right let's get her into that van over there," grunted one of the six-footers to the other security officer as they kept a tight grip on each of her upper arms.

Emma Darbyshire, even in her predicament, was surprised at the activity outside as Police officers and security personnel appeared to be running about forming some defensive lines in front of the Parliament gates against a large crowd pushing towards the building. The noise coming from the crowd was like a football match, with organised chants. She could hear the clear strains of 'England, England,' being belted out by what must have been a huge mob of men now laying siege to the Parliament buildings.

The Police officer in charge of the van saw them approaching and opened the rear doors. One of the security men pressed his hand on the back of head to ensure she wouldn't hit the top of the van doorway.

"I'll take over now," interjected a loud male voice from behind them.

Cucksey and Westerman stood either side and flashed their ID cards at the security men. They released their grip on Emma Darbyshire who rubbed her hands over her arms where she was expecting a matching rash of bruises. She looked at the two casually dressed newcomers, who projected a definitely heavier and scarier front than the uniformed security that had ejected her.

From behind Cucksey another man she didn't recognise stepped forward.

"Hello, Keith Bigham. Emma Darbyshire I believe. I'm head of Intelligence and my, my how the tide is turning. You're coming with us, now."

# 32

The slow moving sixty foot pleasure barge bumped hard into the vessel moored next to the Parliament buildings. The moored vessel itself was empty, as all its personnel had been summoned to support the emergency defence against the unexpected crowds, which were seemingly bent on pushing there way into the buildings.

"Get it nearer that side," shouted Ace to the skipper, who were still both drenched from the heavy shower.

Tom and Grace moved back towards Ace at the wheel.

"We are now close by the enemy and at first sight it does not look like we have any opposition on this craft. Grace, listen carefully I want you and your Scouts to get aboard and find out what this thing is steered by and find any ways you can to put it out of action. Then get back on here with Steve, who will take you back to a safe spot."

"Understood," she replied.

"And understand this if there is any danger whatsoever, and I mean any danger. I want you to remove yourselves if it can be done safely or if not then give yourselves up peaceably."

"As I said, understood," she was smiling as she went away to pass on the instructions.

Tom had a worried look on his face, "Ace, I'm not certain what we're trying to do. It seems like we're going to get arrested. Inciting youngsters to damage this yacht; this is criminal stuff."

Ace let out a hearty laugh, which made Tom worry about his mental state again.

"Inciting youngsters! I could not tread these perilous paths in safety, if I did not keep a saving sense of humour. No they are doing an act in the service of the country. This Tom I believe is part of the enemy's fleet."

He looked at the disbelieving face of Tom his friend and then at the seemingly convinced face of Steve the skipper, who was nodding in agreement.

Ace continued to direct activities and had no qualms about his friend's concerns.

"There, there Steve that's it. Right hold it steady, Grace, get someone onto the yacht and throw down a rope." He then looked at Tom, who had closed his eyes and was shaking his head in frustration.

Ace put his left hand on Tom's right shoulder.

"It will be no disgrace if you do not want to go any further. Stay here with Steve. But Tom, I would welcome your support and to come with me into whatever awaits us. As I intend to confront the head of this beast and do whatever is within my power to stop it in its tracks," Ace looked away from Tom as one of the Scouts had climbed aboard the yacht and had thrown down a rope to help everyone else up.

"Capital," shouted Ace, with a dancing gleam in his eyes.

Tom shuffled away on his own, back to one of the seats at the front of the craft.

The roads and pavements around Parliament Square were now jammed with crowds of men. The previous groups of sightseers had moved away probably driven away by the now threatening ambience enveloping the area. There was a thick soupy atmosphere that can only be achieved by the presence of a large aggressive mob. The rhythmic chanting continued unabated as they pressed up against the shut gates of the Parliament building. Some of the chanting was coming from different groups and they were singing football songs about their respective beloved London football clubs, it was if they were trying to get into a cup final at Wembley. The Police on the fence, directly facing the mob, were concerned that this unexpected gathering might soon erupt into them fighting amongst themselves and then they'd have a major riot on their hands. The Army reserve units were still blocked in and without using heavy handed force, they couldn't break through to support the police and security personnel now seemingly penned in at the Parliament buildings. The Chinese security detachment from the yacht looked out at the sea of faces; they then demanded an explanation from the Police, who were supposedly in charge of security. They had no explanation as to why the crowd had changed its composition but they agreed to maintain the standoff without enflaming the mob and causing any unnecessary casualties by trying to clear the area by force. The Chinese stressed that the orders from above were clear and peace must be maintained, nothing should be allowed to besmirch the day. They did not want another Tiananmen Square on their hands.

There was at this stage no signs of any animosity between the various members of the noisy and boisterous crowd, who must have represented every football team from London, there were fans from Tottenham, Crystal Palace, Orient, West Ham, Charlton, Crystal Palace, Chelsea, Arsenal, QPR, Brentford, Dagenham and Millwall. Some of the Police who had dealt with football matches over the years were nervously getting ready for the first spark to kick off the mother of all mass brawls; they had never seen such a gathering of known football faces. The Police commander was on the radio urgently calling for more resources with which to deal with the unprecedented situation.

Back in the hall the Queen followed by the Prime Minister and the President of the European Union were slowly advancing up the main aisle. All eyes in the hall followed their progress towards the front stage in the shadow of the Rosetta Stone. The Queen's countenance was entirely grim, whilst her eyes were burning with a fierce and flaming anger, some of those close by could see a small trail of tears began to cut into the thick powder on her cheeks. The Prime Minister appeared utterly vacant as he loped behind and, just to his side the Spanish President of the EU confidently strode along and was beaming a smile that could have lit up the centre of Brussels in a power cut. As they moved within about fifteen feet of the main stage the music changed to a slow triumphal hue and the volume had switched up several notches.

The lighting in the hall was now noticeably dimmed, with the stage area being the focus of an increased level of light. One spotlight picked out the Queen, the PM and the EU President. To the right of the two presenters another light focussed on the stage directly in front of the Rosetta Stone. Suddenly striding into this space the new Napoleon stood and with a strong, unwavering gaze surveyed the hall like a master showman. He slowly rocked on the balls of his feet and clasped his hands together behind his back. The projector showed a full-colour close up of his face; his mixed European and Chinese ancestry could be clearly seen in his features. The two presenters seemed to lose all their usual gravitas and behaved like two fawning courtiers with their bowing and scraping, they both stepped across to shake his hand and then drew away again to the side of the stage, so as not to hog any of the new leader's limelight. From the floor the Queen looked up at the man who now held the centre stage with the full undivided attention of the audience and the array of media cameras, she fixed him with a laser like stare of complete contempt and then without warning, she suddenly stopped in her tracks and turned and started to go back towards the exit.

Napoleon looked down from the stage and his lip slightly curled in a disparaging sneer. The Prime Minister and EU President then took the Queen on both sides and gently ushered her forward again. Napoleon then slowly swaggered forward to speak into the microphone.

# 33

The white foam spray from the fire extinguisher jetted against the back of the Napoleon's head, the surprise and force of which made him stumble away from the microphone. White foam was dripping off the stage. A collective gasp of shock rose up from the hall. Staggering to one side he flapped at the torrent of foam directed onto his head. His head and shoulders were now a white foamy mess. The hall was filled with shouts of uproar, security attendants rushed towards the stage area. All the recording cameras were instantly stopped from filming, and all the journalists were being quickly escorted out and taken away by security to a closed room.

People were standing in their places looking around to try and see what was happening. Security staff moved quickly directing and cajoling the audience to move towards the exits. The air was filled with a hubbub of voices filling the chamber of the hall. Some rows were jammed, as some older members of the audience had stumbled in the crush trying to leave. One group were frantically signalling for first aid as one man had collapsed unconscious onto the floor.

Napoleon had turned to see from where the attack came from, his shoulders heaving with fury as he unsuccessfully attempted to wipe away the foam. Moving past him, two armed Chinese guards rushed around the rear of the stage area. They then pulled a struggling Ace from out of the wings and the two Chinese guards, on either side, rapidly forced him down onto his knees with Ace's only good arm violently twisted up behind his back.

Napoleon stormed over towards him, still flicking the dripping mess of foam from his hair. The guards forced Ace's face up by pulling his hair violently back.

"You piece of excrement! You have only delayed the inevitable. We will just have to set the stage again. It won't change a thing." He then spat venomously into Ace's solemn, acquiescent face. "Who do you work for?"

Ace did not reply.

"Who do you work for?" His continuing silence was rewarded with Napoleon kicking him hard in the side of his face. Ace's head dropped from the force of the blow.

He then managed to raise his head, "thank God I have done my duty," Ace said looking directly into his assailant's eyes.

"God ha! Well let him protect you now. Take him away and find out who his paymaster is and then kill him. Let him meet his god."

As he finished speaking there was a slight creak and then Napoleon turned and screamed as the Rosetta Stone fell forward onto him and pinned part of his lower body to the stage floor. He screamed obscenities. The guards immediately left Ace and strained to free Napoleon's leg and hip from the weight of the masonry. The still kneeling Ace felt a strong pull on his collar that pulled him to his feet.

"Move, get out of here."

Ace could now see that Tom had not let him down.

From below the stage Mademoiselle Rives, opened her bag and took out a handgun and set off towards Ace and Tom. As she ran past the Queen, Rives tripped and flew head first and crumpled into the aisle. The gun spun out of her hand. The Queen indulged herself a small wry smile and pulled in her foot which had tripped the unfortunate French secret service officer. Sir Peter intervened left the inert figure of the Prime Minister and picked up the gun for Mademoiselle Rives, who had quickly recovered. She now moved panther-like and was now in hot pursuit of the two impromptu party poopers. The Rosetta Stone had now been heaved up and it allowed a shaken and a badly bruised Napoleon to stand.

Napoleon rapidly surveyed the debacle of his inauguration; he looked out at the group including the Queen and the PM and President, and then he could see at the Hall entrance the final members of the departing audience being replaced by others coming in. There were uniformed Police mixed with other men, including some wearing brightly coloured scarves, seemingly all intent on heading to the stage area.

Napoleon, sensing something amiss ordered his guards to gather and form a defensive line to safeguard his retreat to the yacht so he could check what was happening and how soon he could set up the handover again for the cameras. He also asked his bodyguard to ensure the British Army reserves on standby now cleared the area using whatever force was necessary. He now realised that thanks to some pathetic juvenile pranks with a fire extinguisher, that it was now time to take the imperial gloves off.

The first group of the incoming mob then reached the group at the foot of the stage and then waited looking up at the new Great Wall of China. On the stage a group of the Chinese security attachment were fanned across in a line. All were armed with short stock machine guns. They looked impenetrable.

"Bigham, it's about time, where have you been? There has been a serious incident." Sir Peter was animatedly waving his arm in uncharacteristic fashion. The Prime Minister still silent, looked like he hadn't troubled the land of Nod for three or four days.

Completely ignoring Sir Peter, Keith Bigham signalled across to the Police and others who were facing the stage, to halt.

"Everyone hold the line and don't approach the stage until I give the order," he warily looked at the line of eight armed Chinese guards on the stage.

"First thing is we need to get Her Majesty to safety." Two uniformed officers offered their hand to the smiling Monarch and courteously helped her towards the exit.

"Bigham, the Queen will be needed again shortly when this mess is cleared up," interjected Sir Peter.

"Second thing," Bigham's answer was cut off by one of the Chinese firing several shots into the ceiling. Everybody in the hall ducked. A few pieces of plaster and clouds of dust descended from the ceiling. Bigham waved frantically at the uniformed officers to pull back two of the scarf wearers who had continued moving towards the stage. The firing of the shots had already done the trick with every one in the hall now wisely retreating backwards.

"Second thing," he continued, "is we don't want a fire fight in here. And as it happens, Sir Peter I am placing you under arrest."

Cucksey and Westerman stepped across and held Sir Peter tightly by each arm.

"Bigham, what are you doing? Have you gone stark raving mad? I must protest," he started, only to be interrupted by Alex Haye collapsing unconscious onto him and then sliding off and gashing his head bloodily on the end of one of the wooden bench ends.

# 34

"You're bleeding," Tom tried to stem the gently seeping cut in the side of his friends face. "And we've got to get out of here, they've got guns."

The pair of them stumbled back through a maze of empty corridors and side rooms leading to who knows where, Tom frenziedly looking for an exit. Ace moved alongside him, but he still seemed dazed from his beating. He then abruptly stopped Tom from moving forward.

"Come on," seethed Tom.

"No, leave me here.  Tom I must get back to the fray. Leave now and please make sure that all the Scouts are safe and then get clear your self."

"I am not leaving you, you stubborn old fool, we've got to run for it," said Tom still dabbing at Ace's head as they stood in a long corridor.

Ace moved in front of Tom and put his left hand on his shoulder, "Hardy, that is an order. I repeat an order, shipmate."

Tom shook his head with a mixture of sadness and anger and then left Ace standing in the corridor and without looking back, sprinted towards a far door that offered him the best way out.

Ace slipped through the door of an adjacent office to wait.

Outside the first armoured vehicles of the British Army reserves were nosing forward towards the Parliament buildings. The snaking line of olive green army vehicles came to a halt. Their progress was stymied by a sea of people who had spread out across all the approach roads to the Parliament buildings The vehicle drivers were checking with their commanding officers what to do next as the crowd was not parting; it was an unyielding solid mass and seemingly operating like one giant living organism. The orders were re-iterated, that they must break through to the Parliament buildings, and it was now irrespective of any casualties. A wave of sound welled up from the crowd, increasing in volume as the thousands joined in.

"Like a tree standing by the waterside, we shall not be moved."

An army officer climbed on top of the leading vehicle and raised a megaphone to his lips.

"Attention. You must immediately disperse from this area. You are putting the security of this country at risk. We will use force if you do not disperse. This is your last warning. I repeat your last warning. Clear the area."

The officer then paused and scanned the sea of heads facing him and the army convoy. The short silence was then broken.

"We shall not, we shall not be moved," along with cries of "Rule Britannia, Britannia rules the waves."

The army officer looked on with visible grim frustration, gritted his teeth and began to climb back into his vehicle to order the vehicles to drive forward into the crowd. He stopped just before he got back in as the crowd directly to his left were shouting and waving to him to look at something. He clambered back on top of armoured vehicle, still holding the megaphone, and amidst the group he could see it parting with a wedge of uniform Police officers moving through the previously dense crush of young men. The crowd seemed to melt away to allow the police a way forward, the army officer could see that the Police had their batons drawn to force their way through.

The group of uniformed officers was now within fifteen feet of the leading army vehicle. The last of the protesters stepped back from the wedge of Police who had forced their way through. The army officer looked down and hoped that a way could now be punched through with the minimum of casualties. Now only ten feet away the Police allowed someone from within their group in plain clothes to move up towards the front. He then called out to the army officer.

"I'm Keith Bigham; I'm the head of British intelligence. Now I'd stop there if I were you."

# 35

Oblivious to the unfolding and chaotic events in the noise and the unprecedented mayhem that was outside in Parliament Square, Tom's mind was completely taken up with the task of escaping from the immediate danger of men with guns. The choking level of fear was constricting his throat as he tried to suck air hard into his lungs. His shirt was getting damp with perspiration as he desperately looked for a way out, seeking a haven from the threat around him. Momentarily, he now felt in luck as he ran towards the lime green lit fire exit sign, which was like a flotation aid to a drowning man. With a quick flash of a glance behind him, he pushed through the door and was outside. The cooler air of outside washed his face. While his chest vibrated like it was in the front row of a concert where Motorhead were ploughing in yeoman-like fashion through the Ace of Spades, he could see over to his left the gleaming and imposing white yacht with some more black uniformed guards milling around on it. Unintelligible shouts were floating in the air from over towards the yacht area. Tom ducked down and moved away to his right keeping low like a rodent. From his position he quickly realised there was no quick way out and back to the streets of London town. Employing his previous vagrant skills that were useful for making himself scarce, he wedged himself out of view behind some wheeled rubbish bins. Crouching down he could see in the distance the pleasure boat that they had come in on had nearly sailed back to its starting point; and he was partially consoled that at least the Scouts are safe.

A perceptible droning buzz was slowly getting louder in the background. Tom now saw one of the guards run down from the yacht to confer with the uniformed Napoleon figure, who also had just arrived outside the Parliament building; they were about thirty yards away. It was the man whose show Ace seemed intent, even to the point of risking his own neck, on stopping. Well, thought Tom irreverently, at least Ace had magnificently foamed all over his grand parade. From his vantage point he could then see a dark haired young woman run up to the man that Ace had attacked. Tom could see clearly even at this distance that she was holding a gun in her right hand. Still keeping himself crouched down and as out of view as possible, he looked across and he now felt all his alarm bells ring as he saw the pleasure barge carrying the Scouts, circling back in the Thames water. They were seemingly chugging straight back to the yacht and therefore back into the danger zone. What did they hope to achieve by such a move? He ground his teeth as he fretted. Tom felt the heavy sheet anchor of fear keep him rooted in this safe spot; he did not want to put himself any further into the firing line.

With an increasing hum from its rotor blades a large black military-looking helicopter now dominated the skyline at the rear of the Parliament buildings. Tom shielded his ears with both hands. Napoleon and the female moved back to escape the down thrust from the blades, as the pilot expertly parked the helicopter into the space between the yacht and Parliament. On landing, with the slowing blades allowing the noise levels to fall, it opened its doors and Napoleon signalled for two of the guards to board with the armed female. A loud resonating crunch made them all turn to the yacht, as out of their sight line, the pleasure craft had rammed the yacht leaving an expensive and unseaworthy gash in its side.

"Napoleon, you must leave. Your security is paramount," shouted the female.

"They have ruined my inauguration."

"But it is only a delay. We must ensure that the enemies who have shown their face do not get a chance to harm you. I will make my own way back."

"Yes, yes, okay then. But when I get my hands on those responsible, I will slowly teach them what it means to suffer. They will pay."

She nodded and looked around protectively and then to the guards, "now stop anyone who is following from the building. I will attend to whoever seeks to meddle with the yacht."

They set off at a pace back into the Parliament building.

She pointed him towards the open doors of the helicopter. Napoleon watched just to see the female agent sprint down towards the yacht, calling at the same time for assistance from the remaining guard on board. As she reached the boarding gangway one of them signalled to her with upside down thumb gestures that the yacht was in someway kaput and hors de combat.

"Remove any sensitive equipment and get the speed boat ready. Then we will deal with the intruders."

She turned sharply at the shouts from behind her.

The helicopter had started its rotors, but Napoleon was on the ground and being held in a tight choking neck lock.

Tom was now watching the scene open mouthed; and thought *Ace you mad, mad fool you're going to get killed at this rate.*

The other member of the helicopter crew was trying to level a machine gun but could not aim it for fear of hitting their leader. The helicopter slowly began to rise and Ace and his target ducking their heads, retreated from the powerful draft from the blades. A rope ladder descended.

"Let me go and you will live," gasped Napoleon through what remained of his airways.

Ace said nothing but continued to edge his quarry away from the nearby rising helicopter. He continued to clasp the Napoleonic pretender firmly and appeared to be trying to move him back towards the Parliament building.

To his horror, Tom now spotted the female agent running towards the turned back of Ace, aiming her pistol. He swallowed hard and instinctively throwing caution to the wind, ran full pelt towards her as she halted to take practiced aim. Tom had no thought but only to knock into her before she could shoot. The collision of their bodies coincided with the gun going off. They both crashed heavily onto the unforgiving concrete. Tom, winded, gasped and felt the handle of the revolver smash brutally into his face. Without a moment's delay she had risen and, like a possessed wildcat, she sprinted over towards her Napoleon. He had already boarded the rising helicopter and was at the hatch opening with a member of the crew, both shouting and desperately gesturing for her to climb. The helicopter was now fifteen feet above the ground and the end of the rope ladder end was no longer touching the ground. Without so much as a glance at the prostrate body of the man whom she had shot, she grabbed both sides of the ladder and begin to climb in. The helicopter pilot now swung up and out over the wide berth of the Thames.

A part of the side of the helicopter fuselage suddenly burst into a shower of white and blue sparks. The shock of the impact made the female agent lose her grip on the ladder and she plunged over a hundred feet into the waiting waters below. The pilot managed to keep control of the helicopter as it shook from the assault and then it continued to swoop away from the scene without a moments delay.

Tom lifted his head, which was shot through with pain, and noticed some of the Scouts on the yacht and they were waving what appeared to be a ship's distress flare gun. He then propped himself on his elbows and slowly turned to look where the helicopter had been and felt a deadening shock through his chest at the sight of Ace's body lying motionless. Tom forced himself to his feet and he limped his way across to his friend. As he got closer, he could see the flow of blood from the gunshot wound flowing from the bullet's point of entry in his shoulder and down onto the ground. Immediately he realised that Ace's injury was life-threatening.

"Ace, Ace," Tom gently cradled his friend's flopping head.

Ace then slowly opened his eyes, and Tom looked into his face, which had now turned into a porcelain smooth death mask.

"Tom, my friend, stay with me a while. My time is short." His breath sounded weak and laboured.

"No, don't worry, I'll get help. Don't strain yourself." Tom tried to sound reassuring and worriedly looked around but there was no one but the two of them.

"You know I am gone. Thank God that I have once again done my duty. You must go and ensure the Scouts are not in any danger. Remember me to my Emma; tell her that I will always, always love her"

Tom looked anxiously at the pool of blood; he took his jacket off and tried in vain to staunch the flow of rich crimson blood.

"Tom, I know I am dying."

"I'll get an ambulance."

"Thanks for all your help over the last few months. Now look after the Scouts, it's an order shipmate," he managed to emphasise the last few words.

Ace then slowly closed his eyes.

Tom instinctively kissed his friend's forehead.

"Now come on mate. You're not going to die. Hang in there. Once I've checked the Scouts, I'll be back with help. Now hold on Ace, you're going to make it," in his heart Tom knew the words sounded empty and hollow, as he feared Ace's life force was seeping away right in front of him.

He gently laid Ace's head to one side and then ran the short distance to the yacht, just in time to see a departing speedboat cut the Thames into foaming waves. Pulsing with anxiety he then immediately turned back to search for medical help for his friend.

# 36

The bright October morning was fresh and clear as the first-time guests began arriving at the royal estate of Balmorals up in the land of tartan and heather. On arrival each of the guests was welcomed by the Monarch's private secretary. They were all assembled in a large drawing room giving each guest time to freshen up from the journey north. The secretary then announced the day's running order; they would be spending the whole afternoon and evening in the royal family's presence. A bed and breakfast experience par excellence, that was not available or ever would be available via lastminute.com. They were informed that the Queen had wished it to be known that it would be a relaxed, informal, and the usual strict royal protocols of greeting and conversation would not be enforced. The purpose of the occasion was to allow the Queen to personally thank each guest for their efforts and for her to hear first hand the sequence of events. The royal secretary made it known that the Queen felt there were some pieces missing to the story, and she wanted to finally put the pieces personally altogether, like one of her beloved giant jigsaws.

Each guest was eventually then taken through into the ante room awaited the arrival of her Majesty. The

Queen then came in and thanked them as a group and, sensing some guest's unease at the surroundings, gave them a reminder that she wanted all to relax and enjoy their time at Balmoral. She added that throughout the afternoon and evening she would be taking every opportunity to talk about each of their individual role in the defence of the realm. The first of the guests were now led through into a large and beautifully decorated drawing room and were directed to begin eating the superlative buffet, including wild smoked salmon, the finest of Scottish meats and cheeses. The Royal household servants were on hand to pour whatever drinks were required. At this moment they were joined by other senior members of the Royal family, who were there in a grateful, back patting mode.

After everyone had served themselves and were as ready and as much at ease as they ever would be, the Queen started her first round of conversations. She was first introduced to Danny by Keith Bigham. Danny, overcoming an unusual bout of nerves regarding his first Royal one to one, managed to relate his role in the proceedings.

"I am a serving member of the intelligence service and basically I had an informal network with its former head Valerie Garfoot, through which I was keeping her abreast of certain Chinese intentions connected to the UK. In fact I had cultivated an excellent source at their embassy who was unfortunately murdered by the conspirators. However his vital information led me to the next stage. I only shared this information with Valerie who thought that our service had been penetrated and they already had their own agents working covertly within our own intelligence community."

The Queen began to frown in a concerned fashion.

"I'm afraid that part it is only too true. But don't worry Ma'am we are hopeful that we will shortly be able to pluck out the remnants of their people. Rest assured, we will leave absolutely no stone unturned. We shall not waver in this action," interjected Keith Bigham, trying valiantly to allay her Majesty's fears.

Bigham cleared his throat and continued, "Your Majesty, Danny is an exceptional intelligence officer and he proved his mettle, by having to the swim against the tide of the UK security services. He was acting on his own instinct, putting himself very close to the coup leaders and risking his life for Britain, and many other countries. I suppose, your Majesty, we can also claim some credit from this unfortunate episode for his top-rate training so that Danny could succeed in his exploits and stay in one piece."

The Queen smiled and shook his hand, "you have my most sincere thanks, although our gratitude will not be shown publicly as you understand the country must never realise how close we were to disaster. I commend you personally and behalf of the people of this nation."

Danny's face split with the biggest grin since he backed an outsider to win the Cheltenham Gold Cup.

"Now do tell me about how you organised those rather noisy crowds outside Parliament, who managed to delay their fiendish plan."

"Well I have a lot of connections in the football fan world. I asked through my contacts that all the London clubs send some of their lads down to blockade the Parliament building. I suppose to stand for Queen and country."

"You don't mean those horrible hooligan types?"

"Well yes, I am afraid so. The fan leaders from each clubs said they would be on their best behaviour and not start fighting amongst themselves and generally be a nuisance. And they did keep their word. It seems that they might grow up a bit and give the aggro the boot. Make football matches peaceful again."

"Aggro? What is this aggro?" queried the Queen.

"Ah Ma'am it is short for aggravation I believe. Delinquent aggression might be a good description for it," interjected Bigham, and at the same time raising his eyebrow at Danny and his injudicious use of the vernacular.

"Well I hope they will. Nothing like our wonderful Sea Scouts, I wonder how they're getting on. My grandsons were keen to take them sailing somewhere special rather than feel they have to sit with all us oldies. They will certainly have built a good appetite for tonight's meal. Also I have decided to invite them to the Palace next month and I will be personally awarding them all with a special medal. I would like to spoil those young people a little bit. Now please excuse me I must circulate. We will talk again."

Amid the sound of people conversing and the gentle click of Wedgewood crockery, the various guests were brought around to converse with their Monarch, who was seated on one of the luxurious sofas

"Oh young man I recognise your face."

Oliver Metcalfe smiled and basked in the recognition.

"You Majesty, I brought the gold and silver medals to show you," as he fished the medals out of his jacket pocket.

"I hope your Majesty wasn't too disappointed about the silver?"

"Disappointed? Absolutely not! The whole country was thrilled by your races. I must tell you I clapped with joy when you won the 1500 metres."

"I am honoured indeed."

"Now do tell me what part you played in the events at Parliament."

"Well an extremely minor role. I was persuaded by my friend Harriet over there that I must try and delay the progress of the limousines heading to Parliament," explained the Olympic athlete quite bashfully.

"Well young man I was in one of the cars and you did

the right thing."

"I made a bit of a fool of myself and dressed up in a lion costume but so I understand from all the high ups here, I did my bit to help the country. But I hear by all accounts that you managed some nifty footwork in the Parliament building."

The Queen laughed. "Yes, I'm not just a constitutional head you know! I do occasionally like to intervene in political matters. But you did do your bit for our country and you put your Olympic dreams at risk. I will enjoy talking with you at length later. Now I would like a word with your young companion, Harriet."

As she got up from the settee to head over to where Harriet was in deep discussion with Danny, she was gently intercepted by Keith Bigham, who guided her to a couple on the other side of the room.

"May I take the opportunity to introduce you to the former and much missed head of British Intelligence, Valerie Garfoot and her new husband Leo."

As the two guests gently acknowledged the presence of the Monarch, her smile helped put Leo particularly at ease.

"Valerie, I know we've met before. Now this is your new husband, so congratulations are in order."

"Thank you. Yes Leo is also retired from the intelligence services. That is the Russian security service. Unfortunately our relationship would not have been tenable in my previous position and as you know the coup forces had tried to smear me with working for Russia," explained Garfoot.

Leo, dark haired with some distinguishing grey, nodded respectfully.

"Don't worry Ma'am his loyalty is first and foremost to me now."

"Absolutely my dear," added a smiling Leo.

"But Valerie at one point we had British agents trying to assassinate you. To my mind it was a very shameful episode in the history of our country."

"Well I'm glad that Sir Peter is now having plenty of enforced reading time at your Majesty's pleasure. I am also glad that Keith Bigham has been selected to take over my post. He is a good man to have at the helm and he wasn't afraid to take the right course of action and, like me I suppose, to dramatically change tack."

"Please don't mention that snivelling swine, Sir Peter. I know my ancestors would probably have Sir Peter's miserable head on a pikestaff near the Tower. I suppose he is only poor Peter now as I had the exquisite pleasure of stripping the knighthood from him. Anyway, I understand you have been unwell, Valerie?"

"Yes, unfortunately my late husband brought back hepatitis from one of his business trips. My medication keeps me reasonably well but the best medicine I have is Leo. I am so glad your Majesty that this outrageous attempt was thwarted, threatening the sovereignty of our country and very nearly the end of the free world, as we know it."

"And it was thanks to your help that..."

The Queen was interrupted by one of her staff announcing at the doorway that the arrival of the Prime Minister. The announcement turned the heads of all the guests in the room.

"Ah so glad he could make our day," said the Monarch, as she continued her chatting to the former head of British Intelligence.

The Prime Minister confidently entered the room and proceeded to walk over to the staff member providing the refreshments and took a cup of tea. He then scanned the group as if to decide who he should speak to first and after a sip of tea he moved across the room.

He bowed his head slightly and his voice was a little husky as he spoke, "it's good to see you Emma. I know I should have contacted you earlier but things, as you know, have been very, very messy."

"Alex you know I'm not the sort of person to harbour a grudge..... I know you've taken back the reins of power at least a month ago, but it wouldn't have taken a couple of minutes to give me a ring," her eyes bored into him.

He cleared his throat, "I know, I know. I can only ask for you to forgive me. I'm sorry...... I haven't really got an adequate excuse. I hoped you would be here today with all the others who helped make a stand. They have all been absolutely terrific. Emma can we try and move forward?"

Emma Darbyshire raised herself from her seat and put her left palm on his right cheek and then kissed his other cheek. The Prime Minister then put both his arms around her in a short embrace. Alex Haye looked down at Emma's new shape.

"Well congratulations appear to be in order. I didn't know that you were expecting."

"No, it has been a lovely surprise and so far it has made me feel very, very happy."

"I would like to meet the lucky fellow sometime."

"There is something…"

Her conversation was interrupted by Harriet coming up to them. Her face and eyes gleamed with a steely determination.

Emma spoke first to try and prevent any fireworks, "now, now Harriet, Alex and I have literally kissed and made up, so please do not give our Prime Minister one of your inimitable verbal blasts."

"Harriet, pleased to meet you again," offered Alex Haye with a cheery but hopeful smile, hoping he wasn't about to endure a sharp angry outburst.

"Mr Haye."

"Alex, please," he replied.

"Okay Alex then. Now I have been informed, as far as I

am allowed to know, about what went off in this conspiracy thing. I've even had to sign the Official Secrets Act to boot. Now I do understand that you weren't exactly in control of your own faculties. So I feel can cross you off my most wanted list of grudges. However, and there is always a however, since all the craziness you have not contacted Emma, who has been loyally carrying out her work as a backbench MP. Don't you know she has been continuing to work hard for her constituents? So why didn't you get in touch?"

"You're right, I am at fault. I need and intend to spend a good deal of time with Emma over the next few weeks. As you know the gist of the terrible events, Sir Peter as a member of the coup had me drugged up and basically in thrall to a rogue female French agent. I frankly admit that I do not come out of my relationship with her with a single shred of credit. Although Sir Peter and the French woman had disabled me to a certain extent by pharmaceutical means, I still feel thoroughly ashamed of falling for that seduction ploy. Thankfully the doctors have now given me the all clear to get back to work. But I can't help thinking that this country and the western world's security and freedom were hanging by a proverbial thread. It was thanks to the people gathered here that the plot was well and truly scuppered. Well I might as well come out and say just what that part of that conversation with you Emma will be all about. Quite honestly Emma, you can have your pick of any of the cabinet positions, and I already have the support of the whole cabinet on this. And Emma that means any post, including mine as the Prime Minister. I am absolutely serious about this offer."

At the unexpected announcement, Emma's eyes widened in tandem with Harriet's slight jaw drop.

"Alex, now that is a very generous proposal. It's a bit out

of the blue so I need to give it some serious thought. You know that I have not particularly lusted after the positions of power. Now I do promise that I will think seriously about the offer of a cabinet post. I do still feel, more than ever, that you are and should remain our PM. But my first request Alex is for maternity leave."

"Granted! And you can come back when you're good and ready."

Harriet then interjected, "and what happened to the French femme fatale?"

"Ah, yes, her, no it's a good question and one I hoped Bigham and our intelligence services could have answered. Apparently by all accounts she fell from the escaping helicopter into the Thames. Following extensive searches no body was found. We can only presume she drowned and her remains have yet to surface in the water or be discovered somewhere later. Although I suppose we cannot discount the unhappy possibility that she has made good her escape."

"And the plot leader?" asked Emma.

"Ah him yes, the self-styled new Napoleon, well for one thing you cannot say he lacked vision. I'm afraid it's another unfortunate situation; he has disappeared, although every friendly agency is hunting for him. There is as yet no sign of the devil. He does not seem the type of character who can lie low for too long and when he pops up, hopefully he can face justice. We're also not sure how much of his global network is still in place. Of course we got a few of the obvious ones in this country like our former cabinet secretary, but you can probably count our successes on two hands. Early days I suppose and Bigham is on the case."

"Well Alex you know I had never liked Peter, but to think he was a traitor... Someone in his position and with his background,"

"Quite honestly when I regained my faculties and was

given the whole sorry tale I was as astounded as you. But what on earth was he promised? And don't we all feel frustrated at times with how things in the world today seem to drag downwards. Sir Peter, I mean Peter, I keep forgetting, well he obviously bought into the grand plan. Anyway he will have plenty of time to rue his luck in his confined and hopefully bleak quarters in Belmarsh."

One of the royal staff came over and hand signalled to Harriet, nodding towards the door.

"Ah excuse me I've got to go, it's a little surprise I've organised," announced Harriet with an attractive glint in her eyes.

Meanwhile The Queen had managed to corner Tom who had sheepishly been keeping his distance at the back, trying to be invisible.

"Er yes, yes your Majesty, "Tom felt his voice waver and crack and he felt his face redden with embarrassment.

"You know Mr Hardy that we are all very proud of what you did. I also understand that after all the excitement that Emma Darbyshire has managed to find you a job in Lincoln."

"Yes, Emma helped me apply for a job with the Council as a car park attendant. It's steady work, helping people. "

"Enjoy it?"

"So far, so good. It feels good to have steady work again your Majesty."

"Now Mr Hardy can you answer me something that puzzles me deeply. Your friend, who is I believe called Ace or Horace, and who rather dramatically and bravely disrupted their little party in parliament, he was shot wasn't he?"

Tom nodded in assent, his mind awhirl at being in the presence of the Queen and receiving her rapt attention.

"And you went to get help, but when you came back he had gone. Was he dying when you last saw him?"

"I'm not sure. Well yes, I suppose he was. It looked bad, serious like."

"Well the security services have told me that he either fell to his death in the Thames or managed to slip away. But if he had managed to somehow slip away he would have needed urgent medical treatment and so the authorities could have traced him. Why would he want to slip away, it's a trifle odd? Your friend appears to be a real man of mystery and he has some left questions unanswered. Oh I wish I could've met him to thank him. Is there anything more you can tell me about him?"

"I've unfortunately come to the sad conclusion that I won't see him again. You want to know something about him? Well I don't know too much about him myself. He met me when I was sleeping rough and saved my bacon so to speak. We wandered the streets together for a few weeks; he was an old Navy man. Lost his right arm to some injury, at some time when he was in the Naval service, perhaps an accident, I don't know. Expert he was on the age of sail, cannon and broadsides and all that history. A real lovely bloke, but he didn't seem from this time at all."

The Queen now fixed Tom with an inquisitive eye, "now Mr Hardy I need to know something else about Ace our missing hero, surely you know something else to satisfy my curiosity. Perhaps you didn't know that I love thrillers and mysteries and it seems Mr Hardy we have just lived through one. If through the day you remember something, some titbit about him, please seek me out, and I will ask you again after the dinner this evening."

Tom, rubbing his hands together, looked across to where the Prime Minister was standing, "well your Majesty perhaps I shouldn't say or maybe you already know but my friend Ace is married to Emma Darbyshire the MP over there and she is expecting his child."

The Queen clapped her hands together. "Mr Hardy, excellent quite excellent, you're information has delighted me. Now you must excuse me, as I must have a word or two with her. Absolutely fascinating, and I wonder why I had not been informed earlier of this news."

As the Queen moved towards the subject of her last conversation, Harriet came up alongside Tom.

"Enjoying the high life Tom?"

"I've just met the Queen. Harriet now pinch me hard here on my hand. I'm just making sure I don't embarrass myself or any of you lot who I now count as my friends. I don't want to say the wrong thing or break anything."

"Embarrassment? You're not embarrassing me. You should be feeling pride at you have done; the government, including all the Windsor's here are proud as punch for the bit you played in stopping the takeover of our land. Tom, think about it, you're with a small band of British heroes. It seems we all had little parts to play and it all worked for the good. I don't think I did much at all apart from supporting Emma and arranging Oliver Metcalfe's lion antics. Now Tom, I want to show you something in the other drawing room through there. Come on and I will show you, it's got something you'll be very interested in."

"What is it?"

"Can't spoil a secret."

Harriet then led the still self-conscious Tom out of the room. He pulled at the edge of his collar to try release some nervous tension and decided that he would take the tie off at the earliest opportunity. Looking at the walls he felt as if he were strolling through the National Gallery as they passed glorious artwork after even more glorious artwork. The brand new charcoal-coloured suit he had acquired for the occasion was helping him to feel even less comfortable in his movements; and the last time he wore a suit and tie, was many, many years previous. At the end of the corridor she stopped and had a word with one of the Royal servants who were standing outside a door on the corridor. Turning around Harriet silently beckoned Tom forward.

"Tom I have got some interesting people for you to meet."

"Alright, okay."

He followed her through the doorway and saw in the room, sitting on two sofas facing him, a middle-aged woman and a male and female teenager. They were all dressed up in their Sunday best. There was an awkward silence as Harriet pulled Tom, who had seemed to freeze, through the doorway and into the room. As she entered the room the three people stood up smiling when they walked in.

"I don't think introductions are necessary," said Harriet nodding towards the family group. She looked back at Tom as she left the room and could see tears beginning a slow trail down his cheeks.

Back in the main room, the Queen had made her way over to Emma and shook her hand.

"My dear you've been through so much. You have my deepest commiserations. But on a happier note, I believe congratulations are in order. Now, can I ask, is it your first child?"

"Yes, it's my first and it makes me feel so special. It has helped to soothe some of the pain. I know that my husband's body has not been found but I can only assume the very worst. Perhaps the pain of separation will lessen when my hands are full with the baby. There will be probably be little time left for my own tears."

The Queen putting a comforting arm around her, "there are no words, or anything I can say to help your grief, apart from, I'm terribly, terribly sorry. And to lose him so soon after you were married. But by all accounts he was a fearless fellow, you've no doubt heard of his acts of daring that tipped the balance in our favour. His inspired actions with the fire extinguisher; and now looking back from our safe vantage point I suppose it was quite a hilarious scene. He was a true British hero; we Britons have never been short of bravery when the challenge arises. I do sincerely hope this baby that you're expecting will be a beautiful reminder of him. Do you favour a boy or a girl?"

"Just a healthy baby and a reminder of my husband is all I want."

"Any plans for the future, will you return to the cabinet?"

"I'm not sure on that one, your Majesty. The baby comes first, but I think probably yes. I feel I have got something more to give on the political front."

"Good for you. It'll do those other politicians good to have a mother around with a young one in tow. It will remind them all about what is important in life. We will talk more during the day. And my dear I want you to keep my secretary up to date with the progress of your pregnancy and I will want to see you and baby when it is practically convenient. I can remember all those years ago when I was expecting I had a strange craving for mint sauce, just think mint sauce of all things. Have you had any strange desires?"

"No. Well I suppose I have. When I was back home in Lincoln I had a powerful urge to get on the train down to London, which I did, staying for a week or so and then going back to Lincoln, with the same thing happening all over again."

"That's all? Just a feeling you had to come to London?" enquired the Queen.

"Not completely I suppose. As everyday I spent in London I was drawn or felt more like driven, by who knows what, to spend a couple of hours sitting in Trafalgar Square looking up at one of the great monuments. In fact the tallest one and then I felt a lovely warm glow in here," she patted the front of her dress and the baby to be.

# POSTSCRIPT

It was a chilly unforgiving March wind that blew through the main city centre streets and walkways of Lincoln. At this part of the morning the pedestrian numbers were relatively light and the shoppers had not yet gathered in any great numbers. Emma Darbyshire proudly pushed her navy blue pram into the wind and coming off the High Street, opposite the entrance to Ruddocks, and into Park Street. She smiled down at the little face that was enjoying the warm and cosy confines of the pram. Heading past the Bead Gallery and the Salamander clothes shop, she was making her way through to the Healthy Hub for an appointed tea and chat with her assistant, Harriet.

She was stopped en route.

"Hello, Emma."

"Beverley, how are you?"

"Well, but a bit tired after a last night's late marathon Council meeting at the Guildhall. I thought it would never end. Now let's see your little darling. Oh, Emma she's perfect, absolutely bonny." Councillor Beverley Lamont was bending down and peering at the bright eyes that more than met her inquisitive gaze.

"Thank you, yes, I know she is; although the little tinker

knows how to keep me up at all hours. My whole world now revolves around her orbit."

Councillor Lamont straightened up, "What do you think to the news?"

"News, what news?"

"Yes I just caught it on the television screen in the City Hall reception. There has been a major terrorist incident in Tunisia; Alex Haye was over there meeting the Tunisian president. They hope to give a further update within the next hour."

As she finished speaking, the baby suddenly gave out a long, piercing and eerie cry.